"What
mess

"You know what [...] That character in th[...] ke a tornado and che[...] erything in its path."

"That's not fair! I'm not like that."

"Yeah, you are. Ever since you whirled into town, you've done everything in your power to make me miserable. Do you think I don't know you've been running around all day, asking questions about me and my brother, bothering my friends—"

"Your friends? I've got news for you, Hayes. You're grossly lacking in the friends department. I couldn't find ten people in this town who could even recall *talking* to you, much less counting you as a friend." Kate poked him in the chest. "And it's pretty obvious why. You've got a personality problem only electric shock could fix."

Bret gave her an incredulous look. "You think I've got a personality problem? Well, lady, let me tell you something. You're the most irritating person I've ever had the misfortune to meet. You're annoying. You're devious. Your mouth stays open so much I'm surprised something hasn't nested in it by now. You've trespassed on my property, ruined my breakfast, followed me around with no purpose but to harass me. And I've had enough!"

Dear Reader,

In *Coming Home to You*, the worst nightmare of horsebreeder Bret Hayes has rolled into Lochefuscha, Alabama. She is Kate Morgan: beautiful, intelligent but also very dangerous. Her unauthorized biography of his late brother, James, will cause more pain for his family. And she could uncover their complicity in the death of the once-famous musician.

Bret is determined to do whatever it takes to get rid of the "ratchet-jawed" Kate. If he can guide her away from the truth—and tape her mouth shut—everything could work out. Or maybe not. He's fallen in love, and she's the one woman in the world with the power to destroy him.

I thought it would be interesting to pair a journalist with a man who has dark secrets and to explore the issue of personal rights versus the public's right to know the truth. But the heart of this story is a wonderful romance between two people who are perfect for each other. It simply takes them a bit of time to figure that out.

I loved writing this story. I hope you enjoy reading it.

Sincerely,

Fay Robinson

Coming Home to You
Fay Robinson

HARLEQUIN®

TORONTO • NEW YORK • LONDON
AMSTERDAM • PARIS • SYDNEY • HAMBURG
STOCKHOLM • ATHENS • TOKYO • MILAN • MADRID
PRAGUE • WARSAW • BUDAPEST • AUCKLAND

ISBN 0-373-70961-7

COMING HOME TO YOU

Visit us at www.eHarlequin.com

Printed in U.S.A.

ABOUT THE AUTHOR

Fay Robinson believes in love at first sight and happily ever after—beliefs based on experience. Some years ago, she wrote a story on a firefighter for her local newspaper and that night she told her best friend, "Today I met the man I'm going to marry." She and her firefighter recently celebrated their twenty-fifth anniversary.

Fay lives in Alabama within one mile of the place where her paternal ancestors settled in the early 1800s. She spends her spare time canning vegetables from her husband's garden and researching her family history. You can write Fay at P.O. Box 240, Waverly, AL 36879-0240. And she invites you to visit her Web site at http://www.fayrobinson.com. You can also check out the Friends and Links section at http://www.eHarlequin.com.

Praise for *Coming Home to You*

"Fay Robinson is a writer with a great feel for human emotion. *Coming Home to You* is a wonderfully moving story of a family's loss and a man's guilt over his brother's death. It's a lesson in learning to trust and love, and I absolutely couldn't put it down."
—Sharon Sala, author of *Butterfly*, MIRA BOOKS

"*Coming Home to You* is top-notch.
A compelling, delightful blend of the tense and tender.
Ms. Robinson has outdone herself."
—Vicki Hinze, author of *All Due Respect*

"*Coming Home to You* is unforgettable. Fay Robinson made me laugh and made me cry. A wonderful love story of great breadth and depth. I wish it hadn't ended."
—Lindsay McKenna, author of
Morgan's Mercenaries: Heart of Stone

For my mother, who was fearless.

And for Jan Nowasky, the sister of my heart,
for cutting the path and leaving the light on
for me to follow.

Acknowledgment

My deepest appreciation to Mayo Lancaster
for his help with the research on horsebreeding.
And to Auburn, Alabama, Police Chief Ed Downing
for answering my questions and letting me cool my
heels temporarily in a jail cell. You're right, Ed.
It sucks. Any errors in this material are mine and not
theirs. Thanks also to my husband, Jackie,
whose gentleness and love of horses inspired
the hero of this book.

CHAPTER ONE

THE GROWL STARTED low, deep in the dog's throat, then exploded into an earsplitting yodel. Kate froze with her hand outstretched toward its misshapen head and her body bent at an uncomfortable angle. The ugly mutt couldn't weigh more than twenty pounds, but most of that was teeth. Long sharp-looking teeth. And they were inches from her fingertips.

"Sweet little dog," she cooed, trying to calm it.

Her words had the opposite effect. A ridge of fur shot up on the dog's neck. Another yodel burst from its throat, then settled into a long menacing growl. Its one erect ear flattened against its skull.

Oh, great. Now what?

She considered jumping up on one of the porch chairs, but discarded the idea. None were tall enough. The pickup truck she'd noticed parked at the side of the farmhouse wasn't an option, either. Too far away. Getting inside the house seemed her best chance for escape.

Two feet to her left, the front door stood open behind a rusting screen. Moments ago she had knocked, then cupped her hands and peeked in, admiring the hardwood floor and the old washstand covered with family photographs.

Something else had caught her attention as she

snooped, something that only now penetrated the conscious part of her brain. The hook on the screen door was in the eyebolt. The door was locked.

Wonderful.

The dog inched closer.

She remained rigid, poised for flight. Sweat poured from her hairline down her face, but she dared not wipe it away. The dog returned her stare. Sporadic fits of a loud throaty bark punctuated its growl.

Twenty seconds.

Thirty seconds.

Her arm quivered from the strain of holding it out.

Forty seconds.

Her watch unexpectedly chimed the hour—six o'clock—with a soft *beep beep* that seemed ten times louder than normal. She jerked. The dog lunged. Moving faster than she ever had in her life, Kate cleared the porch and ran, the angry mass of fur nipping at her heels.

At the edge of the yard, shrubs of some kind formed a low hedge. Beyond it she'd parked the white Ford she'd rented at the airport in Birmingham. Her vivid imagination created a picture of what would happen if the dog overtook her before she made it to the car. Blood. Gallons of blood. Great chunks of flesh ripped from her legs. She'd die in a tiny redneck town in Alabama and never see her father or brothers again.

The thought made her move faster. She plowed through the hedge rather than trying to jump over it, remembering the name of the plant when the prickly leaves hit her skin. Holly.

"Aaaawww!"

Now she was decorated *and* about to be mauled. Leaves hung from her skirt and stockings, the needle-like points stabbing her with every movement.

The dog almost had her. In desperation, she made a flying leap for the limb of a nearby pine tree, losing her shoes on the way up. She wrapped her legs around the branch and dangled precariously from its underside while the dog jumped and snapped, twice catching her clothing and nearly jerking her back to the ground.

Using all her strength, she hauled herself upright. After a few calming breaths, she took inventory: only minor scrapes on her arms and legs from the tree's scaly bark, but her clothes were ruined. Her skirt and blouse, a lovely bone color that morning, were streaked with the red dust that always seemed to hang in the air. The torn lining of her jacket drooped below the hem, resembling paper after it's been put through a shredder. She felt her hair. Even the clip that kept the unruly tendrils out of her face was gone.

But she wasn't seriously hurt. And as long as she didn't fall off the limb, the beast below couldn't do further damage.

"Bad dog!" she yelled down, then groaned as it went for her new shoes.

EVEN BEFORE HE SAW the animal, Bret knew Sallie had treed something dangerous in the yard. The dog had a unique voice for each type of prey. A series of short yips meant she was chasing a rat or a chipmunk. A yodel was for something larger, like a rabbit or one of the bobcats that lived in the swampy area at the far end of the pasture, near the creek.

Sallie only barked in answer to the late-night calls of dogs on neighboring farms. Growls she reserved for Willie and Aubrey, the men who helped him with his horse-breeding business.

This wasn't a rat or even a bobcat. The way Sallie was carrying on, it had to be bigger. And meaner.

With only a rope halter to control the stallion, Bret raced from the barn to the house. The powerful bay moved under him like an extension of his body, reacting instinctively to the pressure of his legs and his booted heels against its sides.

His concern for Sallie turned to annoyance when he saw the unfamiliar car. Not a bear in the yard, as he'd thought. A human. A trespasser.

He slowed the horse to a gentle lope. Sallie had stopped her wailing and stood at the base of the big pine tree near the drive. She had something in her mouth, angrily shaking it from side to side. At first Bret didn't see the driver of the car. Then he spotted two shapely legs hanging from the tree.

"Stop that!" a feminine voice yelled as a stick came sailing down, clearly intended for Sallie, but missing her by at least three feet. "Leave those alone!" Another stick and a barrage of pinecones showered the ground.

Bret nudged the horse closer to get a better view of Sallie's catch. It was female all right; she straddled the lowest branch. Her skirt was hiked to the middle of her thighs, showing holes and runs in her stockings.

She'd twisted off another small branch and was getting ready to pitch it at Sallie when she noticed him.

"Oh, thank God, you've come! That ugly thing almost got me."

He gave her the hardest most unfriendly look he could muster, but it wasn't easy. She was the prettiest thing Sallie had ever treed. She definitely had the best set of legs.

"Ma'am, you're trespassing. The Keep Out sign on the gate is plain enough for any idiot to read."

The woman raised her eyebrows in a gesture that made him feel as if *he* was the one who'd done something wrong, then amusement lit her green eyes. "An idiot? Really?"

Bret took off his baseball cap. Sweat beaded his brow and he wiped it away with the back of a gloved hand. He slapped the cap against his leg, not so much to dislodge the dust that covered the brim, but to give himself time to ease his irritation. It didn't work.

The gate and the fences leading to the house were plastered with warnings. No way could she have missed them.

"This is private property. You'll have to leave," he said, putting the cap back on.

"Just like that? You're not going to ask me why I'm here?"

He already had a good idea. She wasn't local; her clothes and jewelry were too fancy. She wasn't a client, because he only worked with a select number, all personally known to him. That meant she was probably a reporter. A couple of the more determined ones had tracked him down over the years. He'd thrown them out, just as he was about to throw this one out.

"Ma'am, I'm not interested in why you're here,

only in seeing you leave. Now please climb down and get in your car.''

''Okay, but you'll have to help me. I'm stuck.''

The muscles in his face tightened even more. ''What do you mean you're stuck?''

''Stuck as in…can't move. The lining of my skirt is caught on something back here and I can't pull it loose.''

She twisted and tugged at her skirt, trying to free it, but the movement only made it ride higher on her thighs.

Bret shifted with uneasiness as a long expanse of leg became visible and he caught a glimpse of ivory lace. ''Lean forward,'' he snapped. He nudged the horse up to the branch where he could investigate the problem. Damn fool woman. She had no business climbing trees if she couldn't get down.

He took off his gloves and hurriedly tried to work the fabric loose, but her sweet scent filled his head and made it hard to concentrate. He had the disturbing sensation that he knew her from somewhere. Those big green eyes. That slightly crooked mouth….

Glancing up, he found her watching him. She tucked a strand of long hair behind her ear, hair that was chestnut-colored and looked as soft as the coat of a newborn foal.

''Are you really throwing me off your property?'' she asked.

He yanked harder at the tangle of threads. The sooner she was on her way, the better. Strangers, even pretty ones, could be trouble.

''I guess so,'' she answered for him. ''And here I

thought Southerners were famous for their hospitality.''

He reached in the pocket of his jeans for his knife. When he had cut away that part of the trapped material, she eased forward on the limb and pulled her skirt free.

''Climb down,'' he told her.

''I will, but—'' she pointed at Sallie ''—can you get rid of that first, please?''

''Sallie, go to the house.'' The dog ran to the porch and curled up in front of the screen door.

Bret slid from his horse, scooped up the woman's shoes and remounted. ''Here.'' He thrust them at her. They were covered in dog slobber and puckered with holes.

She held them up and sighed. ''Great. The next time I need to strain vegetables, I'll know what to use.'' She steadied herself on the branch with one hand and used her other to slip on a shoe, making a sound of disgust. ''They're wet.''

''Climb down,'' Bret ordered again.

''You know,'' she said, easing into the other shoe, a pained expression on her face, ''you didn't even ask if your dog bit me. I felt her mouth on my ankle, and I think I should go in the house and put antiseptic on it.''

''She didn't bite you.''

''I believe she did.''

''No, she didn't.''

''How can you say that when you haven't looked?''

''Lady, the dog didn't bite you. Stop stalling and get down.''

"I'm not stalling."

"If Sallie had bitten you, we wouldn't be arguing about it. She'd still be hanging on."

The woman shuddered. "You're kidding. Does she often *hang on* to people?"

"Always."

"You mean she clamps down and won't turn you loose?" When he nodded, she asked, "Did you train her to do that?"

"Of course not. She just does it. Now, I'm tired of telling you. Get in your car."

She stared off into space, apparently deep in thought, then glanced at his horse. "I guess things like that are bred into dogs, like racing and working are bred into horses. That's what they call a quarter horse, isn't it? I don't think I've ever seen an animal so beautiful. Is he your only stallion?"

"No, I have three."

"Three? Gosh. And I bet they're all that healthy-looking. And how many mares do you have?"

"Sixteen."

"So how many of those would you normally breed in a year's time, and how many babies would you get?"

"Usually I'd breed all of them if they're—"

He swore, realizing she had somehow dragged him into conversation. Did she know he bred horses for a living or had she made an educated guess?

"You're doing this on purpose, aren't you?" he asked.

"Doing what?"

"Chattering. Trying to make me forget you're not supposed to be here. Confusing me."

"No, I wasn't. Are you easily confused? You know that can be one of the first signs of a serious illness. A brain tumor. Alzheimer's. Dementia. Although I would think you're too young to have Alzheimer's. This confusion you have, is it like short-term memory loss or more cognitive?"

He groaned loudly. "You're the most exasperating woman I ever tried to talk to."

"Do you have trouble talking to women?" She clucked as if she felt sorry for him. "No need to feel embarrassed. An estimated two million men in the United States have the same problem. There's even a name for it. It's called Fe—"

"Stop!" he yelled, holding up a hand.

She casually plucked a pine needle from her skirt. "Are you confused again?"

He eyed her with suspicion. "Are you purposely trying to drive me crazy?"

"Why, heavens, no. Are you paranoid, as well as confused?"

He raised his arms and grabbed her before she understood his intent, lifting her from the branch and setting her sideways on the horse in front of him.

"You're leaving," he said gruffly, kicking the horse into a trot. His arm came around her waist to hold her. She clung to it in panic.

Bret pulled her closer, his anger fizzling the moment he felt her fear. He stiffened as he got a stronger whiff of her perfume. The fragrance was exotic, like some delicate flower. He'd forgotten how good a woman could smell, how soft she could feel.

They reached her car, but he didn't immediately dismount or set her on the ground. She gave him a questioning look. His gaze settled on her mouth, an unusual mouth that curved upward only on the right side when she smiled. When she wasn't smiling, like now, it dipped only on that side and made her seem younger, even vulnerable.

He knew that mouth from somewhere, and having it inches from his own was making him want to do something crazy.

"Who are you?" he asked, curiosity overpowering his impatience.

"Ah, there *is* a normal human being beneath that grumpy exterior. I was beginning to wonder."

"Are you a reporter?"

She hesitated, then shook her head. "No, Mr. Hayes, I'm not a reporter. At least not now. But I *have* come a long way to talk to you, so I would appreciate a few minutes of your time. I promise I'll be brief."

Her use of his name made his eyebrows knit together under the brim of his cap. "Do I know you?"

"No, we've, um, never really met in person." She looked away and fanned her face with her hand. "Could we go into your house where it's cooler and maybe have a glass of iced tea? Whew, it's so humid out here. Is it always this hot in August? How many days has it been since you had rain?"

"You're doing it again."

She turned to face him. "Doing what?"

"Chattering."

"Oh, sorry. It's not intentional. I promise." She shot him a big lopsided smile in apology. Desire came out of nowhere and slammed him in the gut.

The reaction was understandable, he told himself.

He hadn't had a woman in…hell, too long, and this one was particularly pleasing to look at with her long flowing hair and small well-curved body. She couldn't be more than five feet tall, but every inch of it appeared soft and feminine.

If he could tape her mouth shut, she'd be perfect!

"Who *are* you?"

"I think, considering the way things are going, we might get along better if I didn't tell you that yet."

"Are you under the impression we're getting along at all?"

"Well, no, but it's my nature to be optimistic."

"That's too bad. You've got five seconds to tell me who you are or I'm putting you on the ground and calling Sallie."

"Wait, please, that's not—"

"Two seconds."

"Oh, no, don't!"

He loosened his hold on her waist, pushed her forward and acted as though he was going to drop her to the ground.

"All right, all right," she said quickly. "I'm—" she cringed when she said the name "—Kathryn Morgan."

"Damn!" She hit the ground, landing on her rear an instant after his expletive rent the air. "Sallie!"

The woman scrambled into her car. She slammed the door before Sallie could grab her.

"You didn't have to sic that vicious animal on me," she said through the open window. "All I want to do is talk to you."

He dismounted. "My attorney has made it clear *several times* that I'm not interested in talking to you,

Ms. Morgan. I don't want to be interviewed for your book, and I don't appreciate your sneaking onto my property and interrupting my work.''

''I'm only asking for a few minutes of your time to outline my project.''

''You can't have it.''

''But by cooperating on the story of your late brother, you'll have the opportunity to influence what material on James is used. This shouldn't be an unauthorized biography, Mr. Hayes. Help me. Don't force me to print his story without your involvement, please.''

''Leave. Now!''

''Won't you reconsider? The previous books about James and his band, Mystic Waters, have only skimmed the surface of his life. They've concentrated on the drinking, the suspected drug use, the women. None have fully explored his music or his gift for composing.''

''He's been dead six years. Let him rest in peace.''

''But the timing of this biography is critical. The twentieth anniversary of his first album is next year. People will want to know more about him.''

''You're as bad as those tabloid people, always wanting dirt about people's personal lives.''

She shook her head. ''No, I don't print innuendo or gossip. I spent years as a journalist. I respect the truth and I always present it fairly.''

He braced his hands on the window frame and leaned down. His anger made his voice shake. ''Ma'am, I'm familiar with your reputation, but it doesn't change the fact that anything you write, no matter how fair or accurate, no matter how well-intentioned, will make my family have to live through the pain of my brother's death all over again. They've suffered enough, and I won't help you hurt them just so you can make a few bucks or win another damn Pulitzer."

"I'm not writing this book for the money or for any award," she said shortly, her composure slipping.

"Why, then?"

"Because it's a compelling and interesting story. James wasn't simply a music idol. He represented the emotions and conscience of an entire generation. I want to write his story. I *have* to write it."

He straightened and put his hands on his hips in what he hoped was an imposing stance that conveyed his irritation with her answer.

"Everything comes down to what *you* want, doesn't it? Well, let me tell you what *I* want. No contact from you again. *Ever.* Leave this property and go home where you belong. Don't harass my mother or my sister with any more phone calls. Don't write my attorney." He narrowed his eyes, his expression as menacing as he could make it. "And if you're crazy enough to come out here again, I'll feed you to Sallie. I think she'd enjoy that almost as much as I would."

She reddened. For a moment he thought she might lose the self-control she was obviously struggling to maintain, but she only shrugged.

"I imagine I'd be a pretty tough chew, Mr. Hayes, even for Sallie." Starting the engine, she put the car in gear. "But I'd really rather not find out."

CHAPTER TWO

LOCHEFUSCHA, ALABAMA. The name of the town was on a sign along the main road. Population: 13,402.

"What's the origin of that word?" Kate asked the desk clerk at her motel. "Is it Indian?"

"Yeah, the Creek tribe," the woman answered. "Means eternal sleep."

"Death?"

"Uh-huh."

That figured.

Her room was a green-and-blue nightmare of floral prints and cheap furniture, but the air conditioner sent out a stream of air colder than she'd ever felt. She turned it up as high as it would go and hung over the vent until her overheated body returned to normal.

She peeled off her clothes and tossed her shoes and stockings in the trash. After that, she took a long bath to soak her aching muscles. Thirty-three was too old to be climbing trees. Her legs and back were killing her, and her tailbone felt bruised where Bret Hayes had dumped her on the ground.

She was loath to admit it, but her pride was bruised, as well. Her credentials were among the best in the business, her last two books international bestsellers. She'd been so sure that if she located Hayes and spoke to him in person, she could convince him to cooperate. Being turned down, particularly in such a humiliating way, hadn't occurred to her for an instant.

She rubbed her sore backside. Well, whining about today's fiasco wouldn't help. She'd simply have to come up with a better approach. He had to leave that farm sometime.

At eight o'clock she stuck her notebook in her purse and set out on foot in search of food and information. The sun was a ball of fire against the descending curtain of twilight, and a solitary star announced the coming darkness.

She walked from her motel through the center of town, an uneventful trip of no more than ten minutes that did nothing to improve her first impression of the place. Grim. Small. The narrow buildings were mostly two stories and leaned against each other like weary soldiers after a battle.

As far as she could tell, the only choices for dinner were the Burger Barn down from the motel and the Old Hickory Grill on the courthouse square. She found an empty booth at the grill and ordered the All-You-Can-Eat Pork-Rib Special. Her plate came with a quart jar of iced tea and a roll of paper towels for cleaning her hands.

The waitress was a weathered blonde named Marleen whose plump body was threatening the seams of her uniform. "Hon, need anything else?" Marleen asked when Kate had finished her second plate of ribs.

She wiped her mouth. "I'd like information about someone, but I don't want him to know I'm asking." She gave the waitress a wink. "You know how men are when they think a woman's interested in them."

"Oh, I gotcha," Marleen said, winking back, a

willing conspirator. She slipped into the seat across the table. "Hey, Tammy," she called to the other waitress, "I'm takin' a break." Then to Kate, "Okay, who's the guy?"

"His name's Bret Hayes. He's a horse-breeder. Owns a place out on Highway 54 west of here. Do you know him?"

"Big good-lookin' fella, but unfriendly as all get-out?"

Kate chuckled. "That sounds like him. His late brother was a famous singer and musician."

"Oh, I didn't know that. The guy I'm thinkin' of has these killer blue eyes."

"That's Hayes. What do you know about him?"

Marleen didn't know much. He kept to himself, she said. He came to town every Saturday morning at eight, sat in the same booth and ate a breakfast of bacon, eggs, grits and biscuits. He always ordered a second meal to go.

"And he has this major thing for peach cobbler," Marleen added. "Comes in a couple times a month and buys a whole one to take home."

"What about close friends or girlfriends?" Kate asked. "Ever see Hayes with anyone?"

"No, no one except that Logan woman from Pine Acres."

"Pine Acres? What's that?"

"A place they send kids who don't have anyplace to go."

"You mean a children's shelter?"

"Well, sort of, but it's a ranch. The kids live there until they find homes for 'em or they're old enough to get their own place and stuff. Kind of like an orphanage, only real nice, and they've got adults who live with them and watch over everything.''

''Is he dating this woman from the orphanage?''

''Don't think so.''

''But you said you saw him with some woman named Logan who works there.''

''Jane Logan. She runs the place, but I don't know if he's dating her. I saw them at the movies once, but they had a bunch of the kids from the ranch, so I figured he was helping.''

''A chaperon?''

''Yeah, I reckon he does that, since he built the place.''

Kate felt the familiar surge of adrenaline that came when she had a good lead. ''Bret Hayes built this children's ranch?''

''Yeah. Didn't I tell you? He bought the land and donated the money to get it goin'.''

PINE ACRES. Back in her motel room Kate set up her laptop computer and inserted the name into her files. She wouldn't have difficulty getting information. Most of what she needed would likely be at the county probate office or the library. She flipped open the telephone book and copied the addresses.

Her next step was to call Marcus at home. The phone rang three times before the answering machine came on. Kate waited through the brief message. ''Marcus, if you're there, pick up.''

Instantly he was on the line. ''Kate, where are you? I've been worried to death.''

She smiled, amused at his overprotectiveness. Marcus was two years younger, but of all her brothers he watched out for her the most. He was also the best researcher around and had worked with her for the past four years.

"I'm in Lochefuscha, Alabama." She spelled it for him from the name on the complimentary notepad by the telephone. "I'm at an exquisite little place called the Highway Hideaway, decorated in Early American Garage Sale. A trucker's paradise, according to the sign out front."

"What's going on?"

"I got a lead on Bret Hayes, so I thought I'd fly down and see if it panned out. I struck pay dirt, Marcus. He's living here."

"No wonder he was so hard to find. What's he doing in Alabama?"

"Breeding horses, apparently."

"You're kidding. Are you sure you've got the right guy?"

"Positive. And he didn't deny it."

"You saw him already? How'd it go?"

She sighed. "Horrible. He wouldn't even think about helping."

"Sorry, sis."

"Me, too, but I'm not giving up. I've still got four months until deadline, and I'll spend every minute of it, if I have to, trying to get Hayes's cooperation."

"But what about the book on Marshall? You said you wanted to get started on that right away."

The late Thurgood Marshall was the subject of her next biography, but she was having difficulty calling the James Hayes book complete. The research on James was solid. The writing was the best she'd ever done. But the story had gaps, unanswered questions about his life that only someone very close to him could answer.

And that was the problem. James, the band, their manager, Malcolm Elliot, the equipment handlers—all had been on the plane the night it left Rome, Georgia, on its way to Chattanooga, Tennessee. It had crashed in a thunderstorm in the north Georgia mountains, killing everyone on board.

Only Lenny Dean, the bass guitarist, was alive. If you could call it living. A drug addict, he had tripped out one too many times on PCP, and his mind was gone. He hadn't been on the plane the night it went down. He'd been wasting away in a mental hospital for the past nine years.

James's mother, Marianne Hayes Conner, had refused to cooperate on the book. So had his stepfather, George Conner, and his sister, Ellen Hayes. Bret, his younger brother, represented not only Kate's best chance to get what she needed on James, but her only chance. She *had* to get his cooperation, and get it quickly. Otherwise, this biography would never be what she'd envisioned.

"Pull off the Marshall research for a couple of days," she told Marcus. "I'd like you to follow up on what I found out here. Maybe we can come up with something that'll help me when I approach Bret Hayes again."

"What do you need me to do?"

"Find out what you can about a place called Pine Acres. It's an orphanage or foster-care facility. And do some more digging into Hayes's finances. I want to know why someone who inherited millions of dollars is living like a country bumpkin."

"Bad investments? Gambling? Drugs?"

"Maybe, but his criminal record is pretty clean. A few misdemeanor convictions for brawling but nothing major. He's supposed to have put money into this orphanage, but I don't think that would account for all of it. And this sudden streak of generosity bothers me, anyway. From what I've pieced together about him, he doesn't strike me as the type to give money away once he gets his hands on it. Lose it doing something stupid, maybe, but not give it away. Oh, that reminds me. Find out what you can about the cost of breeding quarter horses. And check with the Secretary of State's office for public records on his business. Let's try to estimate how much he's invested in it and what he's worth."

"Why the interest in his financial situation? What difference does it make how well-off the brother is?"

"Probably none, but I sure would like to know what I'm dealing with here. If he squandered the fortune his brother left him, it would be some story for the book, don't you think?"

"Is that what you believe happened?"

"I'm not sure. I don't want to make any assumptions before I get the facts, but my gut tells me something isn't right about this guy. Most of his life he walked in the shadow of an older brother who had everything—looks, money, talent, fame, some say even the woman he loved—but when he inherits money and gets his chance to live the good life he's always wanted, what does he do? He buys a horse farm in an out-of-the-way place and spends part of the money building an orphanage. No way does that add up."

"I see your point. I'll get right on it. But hey, you watch yourself. He won't like it when he finds out we're digging around in his finances and his business records. You be careful."

"I will."

When Kate hung up, she went back to her computer. Tomorrow she'd spend the day asking questions, but tonight she needed to look through what she had on Bret and refresh her memory. She'd downloaded the files with his name on them into her laptop before she left, the information gleaned from interviews with childhood friends of the brothers and their high-school classmates.

She skimmed it. The stuff was pretty routine, although she'd found it useful while writing the early chapters about James's life. Bret was five years younger than James. He'd spent less than a year at the University of Tennessee, then gone through one dead-end job after another. More than once his brother had bailed him out of trouble and supported him financially.

She got her pad and made a note to ask Marcus to call some of Hayes's former employers. Why was he living in Alabama? Why not live in Tennessee where he could be close to his mother and sister? Because of creditors? To get away from the media? The man carried his desire for privacy to extremes, that was for sure. All those signs... That horrible little dog...

Whatever the reason, she was too tired to chase after it tonight. Tomorrow was soon enough. When she had more information from Marcus, she could start to piece things together.

She closed the file and went to bed, but she

couldn't sleep. For a long time she lay staring into the dark. She tried to close down her mind, as well, but it ran too fast, presenting her with too many questions and not enough answers.

Hayes would be attractive to the ladies, no question there. That handsome face and dark hair probably sent female hearts fluttering with little effort; that big muscular body no doubt made hormones race out of control.

Restless, she rolled over and punched up her pillow.

He had the same chin as James, slightly dimpled in the center as though someone had stuck a finger there and left a soft impression. And like James, Bret had also inherited his mother's deep-blue eyes.

But that was where the similarity between the brothers ended. James had been tall, handsome, but thin as straw. Bret was tall and most definitely handsome, but his muscular arms and chest strained against the fabric of his shirt. When he'd dragged her down onto his horse today, his body had felt rock-hard.

An image of his quaint house and vegetable garden off to the side popped into her mind. The garden had a scarecrow dressed in sun-whitened overalls and a plastic Halloween pumpkin for a head. Flowers filled the yard. A nice little farm, but nothing elaborate. His truck was old, and his house was in need of painting and repair. The dirt driveway had potholes.

She'd expected a different lifestyle. Where were the expensive cars? The big house? He'd inherited thirty-six million dollars when his brother died. What had he done with all that money?

HE COULD SHOE a horse, dig fifty fence-post holes by hand in a single afternoon and grow a pretty fair tomato, but he was the worst cook east of the Mississippi. He knew it. Sallie knew it. Even she wouldn't eat anything he fixed.

So once a week, when his stomach rebelled at the thought of eating another bite of his own cooking, Bret drove to town and ordered breakfast. His mouth started watering when he pulled out of the driveway, and by the time he parked the truck in front of the Old Hickory, he'd worked up a powerful hunger.

Man, oh, man, real coffee, instead of that instant stuff! And gravy that tasted like gravy, instead of lighter fluid! He could already taste it.

He sat down in his favorite booth in the back corner, the one people rarely used because one of the seats was ripped and had been mended with silver tape. He liked the corner because it was far from the jukebox and out of the stream of traffic from the kitchen. He could eat in peace. He didn't have to nod or say, "Hey, how ya doin'?" to people who passed by his table.

He even liked the smell of this place in the morning, with bacon browning on the grill and coffee perking in aluminum coffeepots, instead of those drip machines.

He ordered his usual, opened his newspaper to the sports section and folded it so he could read and eat at the same time. When his order came and he bit into those perfectly prepared eggs, a bulldozer couldn't have moved him out of that seat.

He hadn't counted on a 110-pound bulldozer with a smart mouth.

She sneaked in while he was reading about the Braves, and he didn't notice her until some guy let out a long low whistle. He looked up to see her threading her way through the tables toward him. She moved with the confidence of a woman who knows she's beautiful and doesn't try to pretend otherwise.

The moss-green dress was the same color as her eyes. The skirt stopped at midthigh and swished enticingly around her slender legs when she walked.

She slid into his booth with a cheery "Good morning," as if they were old friends meeting for a pleasant breakfast. He could feel the envy of every man in the place.

He threw down his fork and it clattered on the plate. He gave her a look that said she was about as welcome as tight boots on a blood blister, but she just grinned at him and stole a piece of his bacon with her fingers.

"What are you doing?" he asked, annoyed at having the best hour of his week ruined by Kathryn Morgan.

"Eating breakfast." She turned around and signaled to the waitress.

"Not with me." When she reached over to get more bacon, he covered it with his hand. "And stop eating my bacon."

She laughed at him then. Laughed at him! As if she found him amusing!

"Okay, stingy, I'll get some of my own." She turned to the waitress who had appeared with a menu and coffee. "Hi, Marleen. I'll have the same thing he's having, and bring us an extra order of bacon."

"No," Bret said.

"No, you don't want extra bacon?"

"No, I don't want to have breakfast with you."

"Oh, don't be such a grump. Eating with me won't kill you."

"Ms. Morgan, why are you bothering me again? I told you I wasn't going to talk to you. Now leave, or I will."

"If you want to leave, go ahead, but I'm planning to enjoy my breakfast. I'm absolutely starved."

She poured cream in her coffee and casually stirred it with her spoon. She had the look of someone who was settling in.

Marleen waited for him to make up his mind. She glared at him, which made him feel like a first-class jerk.

"Bring her the stupid food," he said with a growl, snatching up his folded newspaper. "And go ahead and start cooking my extra order."

He'd ignore the pushy ratchet-jawed woman. That was what he'd do. Just pretend she wasn't there, finish his breakfast and do his errands in town. Maybe she'd get the message and leave if he acted like she didn't exist.

But that wasn't easy to do. She had started watching him—no, *studying* him. She'd propped her elbows on the table and her chin rested on top of her clasped hands. He could almost feel her gaze touch his hair, his chin, his chest, and he didn't like what it was doing to him.

That he found her physically attractive only increased his irritation with her. That he wondered if she found *him* attractive made him angry at himself.

He was glad he'd just shaved, had on a pair of his

newer jeans and one of his good shirts. And yet he hated being glad. He hated that he could see, even without looking at her, the soft curve of her lips and how her eyes sparkled when she was amused—like now.

The harder he tried not to look at her, the harder it became. When he took a sip of coffee, he stole a glance over the top of the newspaper, and she smiled at him.

"You clean up real nice," she said as if she'd read his thoughts. "But you need to learn not to grind your teeth when you're irritated. You'll give yourself a headache."

He slammed down the newspaper and gave up all pretense of ignoring her. "You know, for somebody trying to get my help, you sure are going about it the wrong way."

"Am I?" She cocked her head. "So what would work? I've tried asking and pleading."

"And now you're up to badgering and aggravating."

"I'm sorry if you feel badgered. I honestly didn't come here to be a pest. If I could get the information I need any other way, I'd pack up, leave and never bother you again."

"So do it."

She shook her head. "I can't. I have to finish this book. The good things James did in his life are in danger of being lost. Instead of honoring him as the genius he was, most people remember him only as a drugged-out rock star killed in a plane crash."

"And you think *you* can single-handedly change how people remember him?"

"I'm sure going to try. No man's life should be defined solely by his death, particularly a man like James. Don't you want to help me preserve his legacy?"

He didn't answer. He picked up his newspaper and tossed a five-dollar tip on the table. He paid his bill, grabbed his second order from the cashier and went out the door, letting it slam noisily behind him.

He'd parked his truck across the street. He walked to it and opened the passenger door. As he did every Saturday morning, he unwrapped the extra bacon and eggs and spread them on the paper sack for Sallie. He didn't have to look back to know the annoying woman was watching him out the front window of the grill.

Help her preserve the legacy of James Hayes? Now, that was a laugh. He didn't want to preserve that legacy. He'd spent the past six years trying to destroy it.

CHAPTER THREE

Chattanooga, Tennessee

"THAT NOSY WOMAN'S going to ruin everything."

George Conner stopped his frantic pacing to look for the cigarettes he'd carried for fifty of his seventy-three years, desperate for something to calm his nerves. The phone call from his stepson had rattled him. Kathryn Morgan. In Alabama. Asking questions. Heaven help them!

He patted his shirt pocket. Belatedly he realized he didn't have any cigarettes. Marianne had forced him to give them up last year, along with everything else that made life worthwhile. Cigarettes. Booze. Red meat. She even regulated their lovemaking, if you could call what they did lovemaking.

He'd probably live longer, but what for? When a man gave up his pleasures, he might as well be dead. And if that Morgan woman uncovered his lies and he was headed for prison, he preferred to go with a cigarette in his mouth, his pants down and a shot of Jack Daniel's in his glass.

He flipped open the wooden box on the bar, taking out one of the hand-rolled cigars he kept for friends whose wives weren't as dictatorial as his own. He held the cigar under his nose and savored the smell. Marianne watched him without comment until he put it in his mouth, then said in that maddening voice she used when she wanted to scold but didn't want to sound like she was scolding, "I know you're not seriously considering lighting that."

He hesitated, knowing he shouldn't smoke cigars yet barely able to resist now that he'd gotten a taste for them. But then Marianne raised one eyebrow and that small gesture decided the issue. Mumbling a curse under his breath, George tossed the cigar on the bar, not as fearful of having another heart attack as being on the receiving end of Marianne's wrath for the rest of the day.

He walked to the table where she sat, where she always sat, by the wall of windows that offered a spectacular view of the city far below. This room was her sanctuary in a dark monstrosity of stone, parapets and turrets that jutted obscenely above the trees at the top of Lookout Mountain and had earned the ire of the good citizens of Chattanooga. The Castle, most people called the house, although there'd been other less-flattering names over the years. The Dungeon. Hayes's Folly.

Marianne hated it as much as everyone else. She had hated it every day of the nearly twenty years they had lived here, but no one other than George would ever know that. James had built the house for her as an expression of love. So she'd never move. That was an issue they had argued and settled a long time ago.

"Darling, sit down and I'll have Agnes bring you some freshly squeezed juice," she told him, taking a sip from her own glass. But he was too nervous to sit. He stood gazing out the window with his hands deep in the pockets of his polyester slacks, absent-mindedly rattling his keys—and apparently Marianne's patience—until she'd finally had enough.

"George, please," she said shortly, drawing his attention. "He said he could handle her and he will. Now come sit down and relax."

Relax? Not likely. She, on the other hand, looked as if she didn't have a care. The undisputed favorite in her menagerie of animals had jumped into her lap, and she sat rubbing the old cat with unhurried strokes, pausing to scratch under its neck and feed it a treat from the bowl on the table. They were a matched pair, with their silver-white hair and startling blue eyes. They even had the same expression of cool disinterest.

"That woman is probably worming her way into your son's house right now, and you're entertaining the cat," he told her.

Marianne put the animal on the floor and casually brushed the hairs from her lap. "What do you propose I do?"

"Go down there."

"That's unnecessary, I think. She's probably already gone."

"And if she's not? If, in her snooping, she somehow uncovers what I did…"

"She won't."

"But he might tell her. Have you considered that?"

Anger flashed in her eyes. "Don't be ridiculous. He'd never do anything to hurt his family."

"Not consciously but—"

"Not ever! He'd never betray us, so stop this nonsense and get hold of yourself."

George blew out a breath in exasperation. Arguing with her wouldn't do any good. Marianne had always been blind when it came to the children. Bret's jealousy of his brother was nothing more than sibling rivalry in her eyes. And James had been unhappy for months before Marianne could admit he'd become disenchanted with the success he had worked so hard to achieve.

Even Ellen, the child they shared, was perfect. Marianne refused to see that their daughter's repeated relationships with men who abused her were a form of self-imposed punishment.

"Fine, M. You sit here with your head in the sand and wait for everything to fall apart," he said, walking to the door and jerking it open, "but don't ask me to."

"Where are you going?"

"The country club."

"But Agnes will have lunch ready in a few minutes."

"I plan to drink my lunch."

"George Conner, don't you dare," she called after him, but George had already decided he damn well *did* dare and kept walking, not bothering to respond.

WHEN THE ELECTRIC GATE at the end of the yard clanged shut and she could no longer hear her husband's car winding down the narrow mountain road, Marianne allowed herself to give in to the fear she'd hidden from him.

She'd fought numerous threats from unscrupulous

writers over the years, writers whose half-truths and lies about James has caused more pain than any family should have to endure. But this biographer, Kathryn Morgan, had a reputation for honesty and integrity, for uncovering the truth. And that made her more dangerous than all the others combined.

If this woman looked deeply into their finances, saw how they'd used the money from James's estate and the several million in royalties his music continued to produce each year, she could become suspicious. But was she smart enough to figure out what they'd done? And why?

Unsure, Marianne went to her desk in the study, unlocked the bottom drawer and removed the thick file she'd commissioned more than a year ago on Kathryn Morgan. The folder's front cover had a photograph attached, but she only glanced at it. What interested Marianne were the newspaper clippings, the stories the woman had written as an investigative reporter for the *Chicago Sun-Times*.

Reading everything took nearly an hour. Finishing the last article, she closed the file with a trembling hand and sat back in her chair to consider what she must do. She'd gotten them into this mess. The responsibility fell on her shoulders to get them out of it. But how?

She had hoped strongly worded letters from her attorney and the refusal of requests for interviews would discourage the biographer from writing this book, or at least from digging deep enough into their past to reveal their complicity.

But no, this woman was not so easily dissuaded. She had been a gifted child, and gifted children became gifted adults. By forgetting that, Marianne had committed a grievous error and put everyone in jeopardy.

A memory from long ago came to her: the old house on Tennessee Avenue and the secondhand piano with its yellowing keys that had occupied a corner of the den. In the memory, Jamie was only three or four and sat on the stool at the piano, his legs still too short to reach the pedals.

He couldn't yet read, but he was already composing. He played for hours every day, determined that the music coming from the keys would match the music he heard in his head. That intensity, that obsessive need to perform perfectly, had been difficult for her and David to watch in their young son.

As Jamie grew older, his obsession for music and his need to perfect it hadn't lessened. He'd quickly mastered several instruments and by the time he turned fifteen was composing music that would make him famous.

This writer was equally talented, and although it was with words and not music, she possessed a similar intensity and obsessive need to finish what she started. She wouldn't quit like the others.

Marianne returned the file to the drawer and took out the small black-and-white snapshot she also kept there. The photograph was creased, slightly out of focus and more than twenty-five years old, but she treasured it for the bittersweet feeling it always gave her when she looked at it.

"Say, 'Weasels want weenies on Wednesday,'" David had told the boys just before she'd snapped their picture, sending them into a fit of giggles. At the time, she hadn't known it would be the last photograph of the three of them together.

Less than two weeks later a car had struck and killed David as he crossed the street in front of the foundry where he worked. Jamie had been ten and Bret five. She'd struggled financially and emotionally to raise them alone until George Conner had given her a job as a receptionist in his dental office and married her a few months later.

Loud knocking on the door of the study and their housekeeper's voice jolted Marianne out of the past and into the present. "Mrs. Conner, lunch is ready, ma'am."

"Thank you, Agnes. I'll be there in a minute."

She put the photograph back and started to close the drawer, but David's face drew her gaze again. Dear sweet David who had thought her flawless and had vowed to love her always. He'd never have believed her capable of such deceit.

"What would you think of me now," she whispered to his image, "if you knew I sacrificed one of our sons to save the other?"

CHAPTER FOUR

THE SMELL WAS the first thing Kate noticed—manure and urine, mixed with other odors of the animals penned in the large metal building. She'd never been to a horse sale before, had never touched a horse until yesterday, when Hayes had jerked her rudely down from the limb of that tree and onto the back of one.

This place was full of horses, and they could be looked at, stroked, even ridden if she cared to do so. She didn't. She wasn't that brave. Or crazy. But before she left tonight, she intended to at least rub one to see what it felt like. *That* she was brave enough to do.

Glancing around, she suspected right away that she'd chosen the wrong thing to wear. The pristine white slacks and top were cool but impractical for the dirty barn. They made her stand out like a beacon in a sea of denim, boots and western shirts.

She had taken extra care with her makeup and pulled her hair into a practical yet flattering French braid, but here, cowboy hats seemed mandatory, even for the women, and the most popular hairstyle was no style at all. She hadn't felt this out of place in years.

She shrugged off her self-consciousness, having learned a long time ago that worrying about being different was even worse than being different. *People can't hurt you unless you give them the power to hurt you.* Wise words from a wise man. She had listened and remembered.

She sidestepped a pile of manure covered with thousands of tiny flies and wished she hadn't worn open-toed shoes. Wood shavings inadequately covered the dirt floor, which was littered with empty popcorn boxes, cigarette butts and peanut hulls. More than once she'd watched someone spit tobacco juice.

The place was awful. Why would anyone willingly come here? But they did. Hundreds of them. The crowd was so large near the main entrance Kate could barely move. And then she saw what had attracted everyone: along one wall were tables where vendors sold hand-tooled belts, buckles, hats and clothing.

Twenty minutes remained until the horse sale began, so she eased through the crowd and walked up and down the aisles admiring the horses, separated from them by the flimsiest of metal fencing. Their bodies glistened with sweat from the heat, which large exhaust fans at each end of the building couldn't remove. The air hung hot and heavy with moisture, and the rumble of thunder could be heard over the country songs playing over the public-address system.

She spotted her quarry the same moment he spotted her. Bret Hayes stood at one of the pens talking with two men. His expression instantly turned hard. He said something to the men and stalked toward her.

"Come with me," he said, roughly grabbing her elbow.

"I don't think I want to."

"Too bad."

She struggled, but it didn't do any good. He outweighed her by at least seventy-five pounds and had arms of steel. As he dragged her from the building into the dark night, her brother's warning to be careful echoed in her head. For once she wished she'd listened to him.

"WERE YOU PUT on this earth to drive me insane?"

In the quiet of the parking lot Bret's voice came out at a deafening level. He couldn't believe this annoying woman had tracked him down again. The Saturday night horse sale was one of the few pleasures he had in his life, and he wasn't about to allow Kathryn Morgan to ruin it like she'd ruined his breakfast.

She stood at the side of his truck and horse trailer. Bret paced the dirt in front of her, afraid that if he stopped moving he might be tempted to put his hands around that pretty throat and squeeze.

How had this one tiny woman been able to plunge him into a living hell in less than forty-eight hours? She'd shot holes in what he'd come to think of as a comfortable, if not perfect, life. Like grit, her abrasive personality rubbed him raw.

He'd bitten back what he wanted to say until he got her away from the crowded barn. But now, at the far end of the dirt lot where the curious couldn't hear them, Bret released his pent-up anger. He stopped abruptly in front of her and leaned down until their faces were inches apart.

"What did you think you were doing, following me here? Don't you have any respect for a person's privacy? I've told you over and over again to leave me alone and you don't listen."

"I wanted to see what a horse sale was like."

"The hell you did."

"I did!"

"You expect me to believe you had no idea I was going to be here?"

"Well…"

"I thought so."

A zigzag of lightning pierced the dark sky, and thunder lumbered across the hills. A few large drops of rain peppered the vehicles and the ground. When the rising wind threatened to whisk away his cowboy hat, Bret reached up with one hand and held it in place.

"What gives you the right to mess with my life? Do you know what you remind me of? That character in the cartoon that whirls around like a tornado and chews up everything in its path. You eat people alive before they even know what hit them."

"That's not fair! I'm not like that."

"Yeah, you are. Ever since you whirled into town, you've done everything in your power to make me miserable. Do you think I don't know you've been running around all day asking questions about me, bothering my friends and trying to trick them into telling you something juicy you could use in your book?"

"Your friends? I've got news for you, Hayes. You're grossly lacking in the friends department. I couldn't find ten people in this town who could even recall *talking* to you, much less counting you as a friend." She poked him in the chest. "And it's pretty obvious why. You've got a personality problem only electric shock could fix."

Bret gave her an incredulous look. "You think *I've*

got a personality problem? Well, lady, let me tell you something. You're the most irritating unlikable person I've ever had the misfortune to meet. You're annoying. You're devious. Your mouth stays open so much I'm surprised something hasn't nested in it by now. You've trespassed on my property, ruined my breakfast, followed me around with no purpose but to harass me. You've turned my life into a nightmare. And I've had enough!''

Thunder cracked loudly overhead and the rain that had threatened for days finally began to fall in earnest; it came down in torrents to soak the thirsty ground and sent steam rising with a hiss from the hot metal of the trucks and trailers. The dirt parking lot became a swamp in a matter of seconds.

The woman lifted her hands in a gesture of frustration. ''Why am I standing here listening to this?''

She stomped off muttering loudly to herself, but she hadn't gone more than a few yards before she slipped and went down in a puddle. The sight of her sprawled on the ground in those white clothes did a great deal to improve Bret's bad mood. He laughed.

She crawled back up, flinging mud from both hands, cursing because she'd also broken the heel of her shoe. His amusement deepened her anger, and she turned and threw the shoe at him, missing. She took off the other shoe and threw that, but it missed, as well, making him laugh harder.

''You have lousy aim, Morgan.''

She whirled and squished off in the mud. He watched with a satisfied smile as she climbed into her car, cranked it and tried to move, burying her wheels in the slush. The lot was for pickups and trailers with heavy tires, not fancy rental cars.

Bret grabbed his slicker from the truck and exchanged his hat for a baseball cap that the rain couldn't ruin. He leaned against the door, folded his arms over his chest and waited for her to ask for help. He was going to enjoy telling her no. She could get a ride from someone else. *He* wasn't giving her one.

When she didn't get out, he went over and tapped on the window. She opened it slightly and he leaned down and looked in. For once he had the upper hand with this woman, and he intended to take full advantage of it.

"Ah, Morgan…" She glared at him, and that made him chuckle. "Morgan, you should've known better than to park this car down here. I guess common sense isn't one of your strengths."

"Go away."

"Better plan on sleeping here, because there's no way you're getting out of here tonight, even with a tow truck. Yep, it's gonna be at least morning before this car's going anywhere."

"Leave me alone!"

He grinned. "You might find a ride, but that's pretty dangerous, asking some stranger to take you home. And irritating as you are, you're likely to get yourself murdered between here and the motel. Now that would be a real shame."

His words had the desired effect. She rolled up the window, flung open the door and pushed him out of the way. She stomped to his truck, searched until she found her shoes and put them on. He thought she'd head for the barn, but she limped toward the highway.

Apparently the woman wasn't only stupid, she was crazy. Did she plan to walk? The town's one half-decent motel was three or four miles down the road, but she'd never make it in the dark, in the rain, without good shoes.

He watched as she passed beneath the last light and the darkness swallowed her. Well, it wasn't his problem. Maybe after this experience she'd go back home.

KATE HADN'T GONE far when a dark-colored truck rolled up beside her. *No. Not him. Please, not him.* She kept walking.

The passenger window slid down. "Get in, Morgan, and I'll take you back to the motel."

"I'd rather walk."

"Don't be stupid. Get in before you fall and break your neck or get hit."

"And deprive you of the pleasure of knowing something bad happened to me?"

A car came up behind them, swerving to the other lane at the last second. A horn blast conveyed the driver's anger. Hayes cursed. "Will you get in the truck before we're both killed?"

Deciding it was ridiculous to let her anger overrule her good sense, Kate relented and got in the truck. He produced an old flannel shirt with ripped seams.

"Here, this is headed for the garbage, anyway. You can use it to get some of the mud off you."

Kate used the shirt to dry herself as best she could. She undid her braid, bent her head and rubbed the shirt vigorously over her hair. When she lifted her head, she found him watching her. He quickly shifted his gaze back to the road.

"What did you hope to accomplish by following me tonight?" he asked.

"To talk to you, for once, without us arguing."

"You make it impossible for me to keep my temper."

"I seem to have that effect on you."

"Because you enjoy creating chaos everywhere you go!"

"Are you going to start yelling at me again? Because if you are, you can stop this truck right now and let me out. I'm wet. I'm covered with mud. I'm cold. I'm not going to sit here in misery while you tell me again how horrible I am when I'm simply trying to do my job. And for your information, nothing has *ever* tried to nest in my mouth."

He reached down and turned on the heater. Warmth poured into the cab, pushing back the slight chill she felt from being in wet clothes.

"Thank you," she said begrudgingly.

"You're welcome," he answered curtly.

They continued in silence until Kate couldn't stand it anymore. "Look, I'm really not trying to turn your life into a nightmare. I'm only trying to get information that's very important to my book. The people at the feed store and the hardware store agreed the best places to catch you were here or at Pine Acres, so I tried here first. I thought it would be less intrusive than my showing up unannounced at the children's ranch, and I really did want to see what a horse sale was like."

"You've been even busier than I thought. Did you interview everyone in town?"

"No, just the ones I could trick into telling me

something juicy about you," she quipped, repeating the accusation he had made against her earlier.

A fleeting grin crossed his face but was quickly replaced with his usual sour expression. "I don't doubt that."

"Do you want to know what I found out about you?"

"That I'm a candidate for electric shock?"

Kate forced herself not to smile. Well, well, the man had a sense of humor. "Besides that."

"Why don't you enlighten me?"

"That you're either a saint or a pretty good actor."

"Oh, why's that?"

She turned in the seat so she could better talk to him. "Your old high-school classmates remember you as a guy only interested in making a fast buck. Yet the few friends you've made here, like Emma Lang at the library and Mr. Harper at the feed store, talk about you with great affection. Miss Emma said you donated a hundred thousand dollars to renovate the children's area, and I went by and took a look at the new playgrounds you had built at the elementary and middle schools. Apparently you've also set up some kind of free dental program for low-income children." She shook her head. "I don't get it. Did James's death really change you that much? What happened to that guy who used to think only of himself?"

"Why is this any of your business?"

"Agh!" she said, frustrated. "Where did you learn to be so stubborn?"

She thought he actually smiled then. "The same place you learned to be so relentless."

"Hayes, even relentless and stubborn people know when to compromise. Can't I talk you into letting me interview you?"

"No. I don't even like you."

"You don't have to like me. The book is for James's benefit, not mine."

"Go home, Morgan. You're wasting your time here."

They reached the motel and he parked his pickup with its long trailer at the side of the building. He started to get out, but she leaned over and grabbed his arm.

"Don't you even care what I write about *you* in this book, what people think about Bret Hayes?"

He hesitated, but then said, "No. I don't care."

"People believe you resented James's success and coveted what he had."

"Do they really think that?"

"Yes, they do. Is it true?"

"No, Morgan, I never resented him or his success."

"You didn't want to *be* him?"

Pain flashed across his face. "Yes," he said, his voice thick with emotion. "In the six years since he died, I've wished a thousand times I could change places with him."

THE RAIN STOPPED and the dark clouds that obscured the moon thinned until only a few raced across its silver surface. The neon sign above the motel office buzzed like a giant insect, its bright colors reflecting on the wet pavement, creating a surreal atmosphere.

The parking lot was empty but for a single car.

Raucous laughter and music coming from the tavern across the road explained why the rooms were all dark and the motel seemed deserted.

Hayes had been silent since his revelation, afraid perhaps of having said too much. And his words *had* been revealing, telling Kate two things she hadn't known before: He'd loved his brother. And he still suffercd from his death.

She took out her room key and opened the door. When she turned to look up at him, she felt uncharacteristically tongue-tied and strangely sad. She wished she could think of something profound to say, but the only thing that came out was, "Well…thanks for the ride."

He nodded.

She started to offer him her hand, decided it was a foolish gesture and withdrew it. "See you around, Hayes."

"Not if I can help it, Morgan," he countered, making her chuckle.

He crossed the parking lot, hands pushed deep in the front pockets of his jeans. Kate watched him go with an unexplainable sense of loss. When he had almost reached the corner of the building, she called out, "I met Jamie once, you know."

He stopped and turned. "What?"

She walked from under the shadow of the overhanging metal canopy out into the moonlight where he could see her and she wouldn't have to shout.

"I said, I met your brother once. It was years ago, and although I only got to spend a few hours with him, I've never forgotten it. I was a scared kid trying to survive in a tough college program with people who were a lot older than me and resented my being there. Jamie was kind to me. He made me feel good about myself.''

Hayes didn't say anything.

''I wanted you to know that,'' she added, ''so you'd understand why it's important to me to write a truthful account of his life. This book finally gives me the chance to pay him back for his kindness that day.''

Hayes stood quietly, motionless for a long time, then nodded slowly and raised his hand in farewell. She raised hers. He turned and walked away.

Kate went into her room and closed the door. A hot bath would feel good. So would going home. Until that moment she hadn't known she *was* going home. But without hope of an interview, she really had no reason to stick around. Hayes wasn't willing to cooperate. He'd made that perfectly clear.

Taking off her dirty clothes, she wrapped herself in a red silk robe. She was about to check her messages when a hard knock sounded at the door. She looked through the peephole and her stomach turned a somersault. Despite her disheveled appearance, she unlocked the door and jerked it open.

''Can you ride a horse?'' Hayes asked.

''Of course.''

''Be ready at one o'clock tomorrow and wear something practical.'' He wheeled abruptly, walked out to his idling truck and drove away.

Kate closed the door and leaned against it. ''Well, I'll be…'' She squealed with glee. Then a thought suddenly struck her and her glee changed to horror. Oh, no! Where, between now and one o'clock tomorrow, was she going to learn to ride a horse?

CHAPTER FIVE

"YOU LIED to me, Morgan," Bret said, hands on his hips. The blasted woman couldn't even *sit* on the horse without looking like she was about to fall off. "You don't know the front end of a horse from the back."

"I most certainly do. The front end is the one that bites, and the back end is the one that…doesn't."

The children sitting atop the fence at Pine Acres giggled. They watched as the woman attempted to ride around the large corral without mishap. Every time the horse trotted, she shrieked, Bret lost his temper and the children got more amused. Twice she'd almost taken a tumble.

"Hang in there, Miss Kate. You're gettin' it," shouted twelve-year-old Kevin.

Bret shook his head, not believing what he'd just heard. The boy hadn't said that many words in the six months since he'd arrived at the ranch.

Surprisingly, all the kids were animated today. Morgan's antics were the cause, and that made Bret feel a little better about his insane decision to bring her. None here could claim a happy childhood, but this bunch from Dorm K, they'd had it rougher than most. Tom, seventeen, had lost his family in a freak accident. Melissa, thirteen, and LaKeisha, nine, had been abandoned by teenage mothers. Shondra, seven, had been abused from the time she was born, as had Kevin. The twins, Adam and Keith, also seven, had seen their father kill their mother, and little Henry, who'd recently turned two, had almost been a murder victim himself.

Bret constantly reminded himself not too get too attached to any of these children, but he'd fallen hard for all eight of them.

"Hey, Mr. Bret," Melissa called out. She pointed at Morgan, hanging precariously off the saddle, even though the horse wasn't moving. "Maybe you should tie her on. Or at least put her on old Slowpoke."

"Or Patch," volunteered LaKeisha, setting off a round of giggling among the other children.

Bret looked over at Patch, the Shetland pony he'd bought for the smallest children at the ranch. The tiny animal barely came to his waist. If he sat on it, he could probably touch the ground flat-footed.

"What about it, Morgan? Am I gonna have to stick you on Patch?"

"I refuse to ride anything shorter than I am," she said, her voice indignant.

"Ride? You're not riding. You've been on that horse forty-five minutes and you haven't gone three feet without dropping the reins and grabbing the saddle horn. You have to be in control of an animal to ride."

"If you could shorten the stirrups a bit more, I think I could do it."

He sighed loudly and shook his head, then walked over and began shortening the stirrups for the fifth time. He helped her right herself in the saddle. "Your dang legs are too short," he grumbled.

"They are not. I have great legs." She stuck one out. It was bare between her white shorts and tennis shoes. Tan and sleek, it was also very nicely curved.

He looked away swiftly, unintentionally making a noise deep in his throat he prayed she couldn't interpret. Turning his attention back to the stirrup, he took out his knife and began twisting another hole in the leather strap with the point of the blade.

"You shouldn't have lied to me," he muttered.

"Hayes, if you'd asked me at that moment if I knew how to wrestle an alligator, I would have said yes."

He snorted. "Pity the poor alligator."

She took off the cap he'd given her to keep the sun off her face and used it to slap him playfully on the head. "Be nice," she warned, putting the cap back on, "or I might have to wrestle *you*."

Bret went deathly still at the thought of that, her on top of him, pinning him to the ground, doing more than wrestling. *Hell!*

Shaking off the image before his body embarrassed him in front of the kids, he hurriedly completed the hole and adjusted both stirrups.

"Okay, this time if she trots and you don't want her to, pull back on the reins—but gently. Make her obey you. And don't yell like that again. You nearly busted my eardrum."

The onlookers tittered.

"Sorry," she said, exchanging a funny, *Well, excuse me* face with the children.

He walked out to the center of the corral. "All

right, this is your last chance. Ride her this far so I'll know you won't kill yourself when we go out to the pasture."

Whispering loudly, the children took bets on whether she'd make it.

"I say she drops the reins," Tom predicted.

"Nah, she'll fall off," Adam said.

"Betcha she drops the reins *and* falls off," Keith said.

The toddler, Henry, who thought she was purposely putting on a show, clapped his hands excitedly in anticipation of the next trick. "Faw," he begged.

Morgan rolled her eyes. "Don't you little maggots have homework or something?"

"It's summer vacation," Melissa said. "School won't start till next week."

"Chores?" Morgan asked.

"We did them when we got out of church," LaKeisha told her.

"If I give you money, will you go away?"

They giggled. "No, ma'am," answered Shondra. "We wanna stay here and watch you fall off."

"Faw," Henry squealed, clapping his hands more rapidly.

Bret interrupted by calling out, "Come on, Morgan, we don't have all day to watch you make a fool of yourself."

"Don't rush me!"

"I should've known you couldn't do it," he said with a smirk. "You're all bluff and no guts."

"I might have to make you eat those words, Hayes."

"Yeah? Well, you have to ride over here first," he pointed out.

"Come on, Miss Kate," Shondra yelled. "You can do it." She started clapping and chanting, "Go… go…go…" The others quickly joined in.

She touched her heels to the horse's sides and loosened the tension on the reins. The horse began to move. When it tried to break into a trot, she pulled back gently and it slowed to a walk. When she reached Bret, still mounted and still holding the reins, the children whooped their delight. Even those who'd bet against her clapped.

"Well, it's about time," he said. "At least you didn't fall on your—" he remembered the kids were listening "—backside."

"Gee, Hayes, watch out. All that lavish praise might go to my head."

"You did okay."

"Okay? Is that the best compliment you can come up with?" She looked to the children for help. "Was it just *okay?*" she asked them.

"You were super-endous," one child yelled.

"Outta sight," said another.

"See," Morgan told him smugly. "I was super-endous."

Bret smiled. He couldn't help himself. She was so damn outrageous at times.

She gasped. "Well, I'll be… You actually have teeth!"

His brow wrinkled in confusion. "Wh-what?"

"You hardly ever smile. You always look like you've gotten a whiff of something foul. I was beginning to think your teeth were bad, or maybe you'd irritated the wrong person and he—or she—knocked them out.''

"I've occasionally had people threaten to knock them out, but I assure you they're intact." He gave her his best fake smile.

"Oh, very nice. Perfect, as a matter of fact."

"Thanks. My stepfather would be overjoyed to hear you say that, considering how much work he did on them.''

"Oh, that's right, he's a dentist, isn't he?"

"Uh, yeah. Retired now." He cleared his throat with nervousness. That was a stupid mistake. "You have a nice smile, too."

She cocked her head and grinned. "Why, thank you.''

The children giggled and made smooching sounds.

"All right, cut it out," he warned them good-naturedly. He steered the conversation toward a more comfortable topic, patting the horse and telling Kate they'd ride out so he could show her the rest of the ranch.

"Am I ready for that?'' she asked.

"Yeah, but listen to what I tell you and do exactly as I say. *Exactly.* No goofing off for the kids.''

"Okay. You're the boss."

He lifted a dark eyebrow at the comment.

"A mere slip of the tongue," she said quickly.

TOM OPENED the gate and the "wagon train," as one of the kids called it, began its journey. Hayes went out first, with Henry sitting on the horse in front of him. Kate moved to his left side, wanting him close in case her horse decided to act up.

"Don't go too fast," he warned as the other children passed them and took off at breakneck speed.

The road wound through pastures where round bales of freshly cut hay dotted the ground, and more hay, waiting to be cut, rippled in the wind. Henry, Kate quickly discovered, could be counted on to fill the brief moments of silence. His fascination with the scenery exceeded his vocabulary. He entertained them by periodically calling out the names of things he saw.

"Burrrd," he said when a colorful bird flew past and landed on the barbed-wire fence.

"Eastern bluebird," Hayes said. "And what sound does a bird make?"

"*Tweee,*" Henry answered.

Farther down the road Hayes motioned to the right. "We lease the hay fields to a cattle farm nearby, and, over that rise, is a pecan orchard that produces a good crop and income for the ranch each year."

"I'm impressed," she told him, a major understatement. From everything she'd seen, the ranch ran efficiently and utilized its natural resources. The administrator, Jane Logan, had given Kate a tour, and she appeared competent and genuinely enthusiastic about her job. The children seemed well cared for. "Do you spend much time out here? The children all seem to know you."

"I'm out a couple of times a week, sometimes more."

"Why kids?"

"Why kids what?"

"Why did you choose to support a charity for kids? A guy like you. Seems out of character."

"Maybe you don't know my character as well as you think."

"I admit I find it hard to believe that you're the same surly guy who yelled at me last night."

"I apologize for that. I was out of line for losing my temper."

"And I apologize for following you. I was wrong to take it to such lengths. Do you think we might call a truce? I really don't want to fight with you, and despite the crack I made about your character, you don't seem like a bad guy."

"If we call a truce, does that mean you'll leave me alone?"

"Yes, if I can solicit two promises from you."

"Which are?"

"First, that you'll reconsider my request for help with my book."

"Don't—"

"Wait a minute, now. Let me finish. If you'll *seriously* think about my request for...oh...three days, I'll stay at the motel and won't bother you. But you have to put aside your dislike for me and not make a decision based on that."

"And if I still say no at the end of three days?"

"I'll go away."

"Forever?"

"Forever."

He thought about it for all of two seconds. "That's too good to pass up. What's the second promise?"

"That sometime today you give me ten minutes to at least try to convince you to cooperate on the book, *without* your getting all surly and wanting to strangle me."

He flashed a quick grin, gone as quickly as it came. "How did you know I wanted to strangle you?"

"Believe me, I've seen that look before on the faces of at least a hundred different men, my father and brothers included."

"Morgan, sometimes you're too much." This time he didn't bother to hide his smile. "Okay, you've got a deal. Ten minutes, and I'll try my best to stay calm."

"How about now?"

"Not while we're with the kids."

"Okay, I can wait. Where are we headed, by the way?"

"The pond first and then the orchard. I want to show you the different ways we're making money and moving toward being self-sufficient. We keep bees and sell the honey. We grow muscadines and scuppernongs and we sell them to a small outfit locally that makes jelly. The pond is stocked with catfish and we open it for public fishing every Saturday during the warm months."

"For a fee?"

"No, not for fishing, but we charge per pound for the fish caught."

"Pish," Henry said.

"Catfish," Hayes corrected. "And what sound does a catfish make?"

"*Gur-ak,*" Henry said proudly.

Kate decided, after hearing Henry imitate various animals at Hayes's prompting, that this had to be a game they'd played many times before.

As they continued to the pond, the child ran through the rest of his imitations—sheep, cows, horses, bees and something called a ruby-throated brew guzzler that Hayes swore was a real bird native to the South, but whose call sounded suspiciously like a belch to Kate.

"Oh, let me guess," she said, laughing despite her efforts not to. "It guzzles beer and is identified by its *red neck.*"

Hayes grinned impishly.

She groaned. "You should be ashamed of yourself for trying to corrupt this child."

"Wasn't me," he said innocently.

"I believe that about as much as I believe…ruby-throated brew guzzlers really fly."

He had anticipated her answer. With a mischievous gleam in his eye he bent his head and said, "Henry, let a brew guzzler fly."

Henry swallowed air. "*Bu-rp,*" he said, belching loudly.

BRET LIKED her laugh. He found it soothing. He knew in the last several years he hadn't been the kind of man who inspired women to laughter. He was too somber. *Depressing,* was the word one woman had used. But today he seemed to amuse this woman a great deal, even when he wasn't trying.

She laughed often. Loudly. Wonderfully. She made *him* laugh, something he hadn't felt like doing in a long time.

He was having trouble remembering she was the enemy. And even more disturbing, he was having *no* trouble remembering she was a woman.

They sat on the pond's wooden pier, Bret with his back against a piling, Morgan uncomfortably close, so close he could smell the light flowery fragrance that seemed to be a natural part of her. Unable to resist the lure of the water, she had slipped off her shoes and now dangled her feet in it.

It was one of the few times they'd been alone that afternoon. The children had reached the pond ahead of them and were busy skipping rocks at the far end. Tom had sensed the adults' need for privacy and had assumed supervision of little Henry.

Bret looked not at the woman, but out over the glassy sun-lit surface of the pond, trying to keep from being distracted by that stretchy red top she had on and the way it showed off her curves.

Funny. Smart. Interesting. Attractive. And the kids had taken to her immediately. If she were anyone but Kathryn Morgan...

"So," he said casually, "you mentioned last night that you knew my brother. How well?"

"Not well. I spent a few hours with him one weekend at Columbia in 1987."

"Were you lovers?"

Her eyes narrowed. She hadn't liked the question. "No, we weren't lovers. What made you think we had a sexual relationship?"

"Because that was the only kind of relationship James had with women."

"Well, he didn't with me. Besides, I wasn't a woman. I was a kid, a teenager with zero experience."

"How did you meet?"

"A reporter from *The New York Post* was writing an article covering one of his concerts, and apparently James's manager convinced her to include some of the fellowship students from the university in the photographs. I was among the five or so they brought in to meet him. James and I talked, swapped family stories, and then we went our separate ways. He was extremely nice to me when he didn't have to be, and I've never forgotten it. Period. End of story. No sex involved.''

"And you said this was at Columbia?"

"I was in graduate school and he was playing a concert in Manhattan that weekend."

"Graduate school? I thought you said you were still a kid."

"I was."

"You must have been a really smart kid."

She simply shrugged.

"And you never saw James again after that day?"

"Nope." She turned to him and folded her legs underneath her. "You know, you could have asked me this last night and saved yourself the trouble of bringing me here today."

"I didn't bring you here to ask about that."

"Then why? Last night you were ready to boil me in oil, and then suddenly you're at my door asking me to go riding. What gives?"

"You tell me."

"I'm not sure. I told you I knew about Pine Acres, and maybe you were afraid I'd show up here. Or you wanted to find out what I might write about you in the book. Is that it? Those are the only two things that make sense to me. Did you think by bringing me out here I'd present you and the ranch in a more favorable light?"

"You read people pretty well."

She looked directly at him. "A lot of the time. But you're harder to read than most."

"Oh? And why's that?"

"I haven't quite figured that out yet. But I will. You're a contradiction, Hayes. You send out so many conflicting signals I'm not sure what to think of you."

"Conflicting how?"

"Well, for example, you claim not to care what people think of you, yet everywhere you've donated money around town, you have plaques acknowledging the contributions. I'm not criticizing your generosity, but that seems a little self-serving to me, and the plaques...well, tacky. You've also had your name put on the front wall of this place as the major contributor. For a man who doesn't encourage visitors and doesn't seem to want friends, you're going out of your way to ensure your name will be remembered in this town. Very contradictory."

"You really think the plaques are tacky?"

"A little."

"I suppose they are."

"Am I right about your reasons for asking me here today?"

He nodded. "When you mentioned Pine Acres, it made me uneasy. I decided you might be less likely to hurt my kids if you came out here and got to know them. And, too, by showing you the ranch I hoped to change your opinion of me. I was suddenly reminded of that old saying, 'Never argue with a man who buys his ink by the barrel.'"

That made her smile. "I'd never burn you in print for being nasty to me. That's not my style. But I am glad you invited me here. I can't remember when I've had a more enjoyable afternoon. The ranch is incredible, and so are the kids. I'd like to know more about them, if you don't mind telling me.''

''Is your interest personal or professional?''

''Both, I guess. I'm interested in the ranch because I think you used some of the money you inherited from James to build it.'' She paused, apparently offering him the opportunity to deny or confirm her statement. He did neither. ''If it's true,'' she continued, ''that *does* make Pine Acres a part of my story.''

''See, that's what I was afraid of. You're jumping to conclusions about things you know nothing about. I don't want you writing something that might make the ranch look bad.''

She gave him a reassuring smile. ''There's no reason to be concerned. I can't imagine anyone finding fault with what you've done here, including me, and the only reason I asked about the kids is because I'm interested as a person, not as a writer. Will you tell me about them?''

He hesitated.

''I swear I'm only asking because I like them.''

''All right, but you can't use anything I say about any individual child. I can't stop you from mentioning the ranch in your book, but I don't want the kids hurt by the public knowing the intimate details of their lives.''

''You have my word. I won't include them.''

He took off his cap and played with it as he talked, telling her first about some of the children she'd met but who hadn't come to the pond with them.

''Now tell me about Tom,'' she prodded.

''Tom's had it hard. His parents and two sisters

died a few years ago from carbon-monoxide poisoning caused by a faulty heater. He was spending the night at a friend's house and came home to find the bodies. He lived in six foster homes before he came to the ranch last spring.''

''Why has he lived in so many places? He's so polite and sweet. I can't understand why a family wouldn't want him.''

''Because he's a teenager. They're more trouble, and they cost more money to care for. Some people don't want to deal with that extra expense.''

''Are they all orphans like him?''

''No, the majority have at least one living parent, but due to neglect, abuse or some other reason, the kids have been removed from the home. Some have emotional problems brought on by what's happened to them, and finding adoptive families is next to impossible.''

''Those scars on Shondra's arm. How did she get them?''

''Her mother's an addict. When she got high she used Shondra as an ashtray.''

''Dear God.''

''Keith and Adam, the twins with all the freckles, their father's in prison.''

''What for?''

''Blowing their mother's head off in front of them.''

He winced when he saw what his words did to her. He'd deliberately been crude to shock her and gauge her reaction. But seeing her distressed look, he felt ashamed of himself.

"Are you sure you want to hear this?" he asked quietly.

She was silent for a long time. She looked at the water, the pier, everywhere but at him. Finally she spoke. "Yes, I want to know. I want to understand how these children came to be here."

He debated whether he should go on. He knew the horror stories, the kids used as punching bags or pawns in dirty divorces, the ones treated worse than animals or as property. But for someone who wasn't familiar with the realities of child abuse and neglect, hearing what little value some parents place on the lives of their children could be unsettling.

"Please," she urged.

"Melissa's mother was only fourteen when she gave her up. LaKeisha's mother was also a teenager. She already had two other illegitimate children by two different men, so she wasn't able to take care of her."

"And the shy boy with the drawings of sports heroes in his room?"

"That's Kevin. He was abandoned in a bus station. We still don't know the extent of the trauma he's been through because he won't talk about it. He was sexually abused and was probably forced by his father to act as a prostitute."

"But he's a baby! How could a parent do that to a child?"

"We've seen them as young as nine and ten selling themselves to finance their parents' drug habits."

"How is that possible?"

"I know it's hard to believe. I had trouble believing it myself, but it happens, and more often than you'd imagine."

"And Henry? What's his story?"

He shifted on the pier, making the old boards creak. This story he wasn't sure he could share without breaking down.

"Henry's mother…" He stopped and swallowed as the bile rose in his throat. "Henry's mother had a new boyfriend, and having the kids cramped her style. She was also heavily in debt. So she talked the boyfriend into helping her set fire to the house, a little two-for-one special. Her idea was to collect the insurance money and get rid of the kids at the same time. They tried to make the fire look like an accident, set by the kids playing with matches. As best we can figure, she told four-year-old Sarah that some bad men wanted to hurt them and she should take Henry and hide in the closet and not come out until she came for them. Because she trusted her mother, Sarah did it. Then they set fire to the adjoining bedroom."

"What happened to Sarah?"

"She died a few hours after the fire of smoke inhalation and burns. Henry spent nearly two months in the hospital recovering from pneumonia and the damage the smoke did to his lungs, but thankfully, he wasn't badly burned. Sarah had shielded him from the fire with her own body."

"What happened to his mother and her boyfriend?"

"He made a deal with the district attorney to testify against her and got fifteen years. She pleaded not guilty, and her trial comes up in a couple of months. It's a capital-murder case, so she's still in jail, but that hasn't stopped her from using Henry to get sympathy from the court. She won't sign over custody of him because it would hurt her case, and the state won't sever her parental rights because, until she's convicted, she's considered innocent."

"So Henry's in legal limbo because the state can't place him until there's a disposition of the case?"

"Yes," Bret said, slipping his cap back on. "It stinks because her rights are being placed above Henry's."

"And Henry's father? Where is he?"

"He was a one-night stand she picked up in a bar. I doubt she even knows the guy's name."

The laughter of the children drifted toward them on the gentle breeze. He smiled as he watched Henry toddling after the older kids in their game of tag.

"Will you adopt him when he becomes available?" she asked.

"I can't."

"But single men can adopt. These days it's done all the time."

"I know, but it's not an option for me." He stood abruptly, wishing he'd never allowed her to pursue this. He walked toward the tree where they'd tied the horses. She ran to catch up with him.

"Hey, wait! I don't understand. Why isn't it an option for you? Anyone with eyes can see you love that little boy and he loves you. He hangs on every word you say."

"I can't adopt him. Drop the subject." They had reached the horses and he snatched down the reins, which had been looped over a branch. He put his foot in the stirrup and started to mount, but she touched his arm.

"But if you love—"

He whirled and grabbed her by the shoulders. "I said I can't," he yelled, making both her and the horse jump. "Why won't you listen to me, Morgan? I can't adopt him. I can never adopt him. I'm no better than his mother."

"Why do you say that?"

His face contorted with the pain he felt in his heart. "Because," he said in anguish, "I killed my own brother."

CHAPTER SIX

HE'D NEVER MEANT to tell her. For six years he'd lived with the guilt of having sent his brother to a fiery death, and not once had he shared his pain with anyone outside the family. But she'd pushed until the pain had boiled over. She'd dug until the wound that had festered for years broke open.

Adopt Henry? Dear God, he prayed every day for it. He'd take him in a minute. And Tom. And Melissa. And LaKeisha. And as many others as he could make room for. If it was only possible.

But it wasn't. And it never would be. He'd resigned himself to that a long time ago.

He leaned one hand against the tree with his back to the woman and his head down, trying to bring his raw emotions under control. He knew he'd frightened her. He'd seen her fear. Then shock had replaced it. And finally repulsion.

She'd been so repulsed after he'd blurted his admission that she'd stepped back, not wanting to be touched by him.

"Hayes..." Her soft whisper jarred him. Her hand began to rub his back with the same comforting motion a mother might use to console a crying child. "Are you all right?"

"I'm okay," he said, clearing his throat. His voice was shaky. "Give me a minute."

"Do you want me to leave you alone?"

He shook his head. He found her presence and her touch oddly soothing.

She stood quietly while her hand continued its slow journey across the center of his back. It slid upward to stroke his shoulders and the nape of his neck, to brush lightly through his hair. So many years had passed since anyone had touched him this way that even after he'd calmed himself, he didn't move. He closed his eyes. He relaxed his body. He concentrated only on her hand and the pleasure it gave.

"I'm sorry," she whispered several minutes later, and his eyes blinked open. "I should never have kept after you about Henry. What you do about him is your business, and I had no right to say anything."

With regret he straightened and her hand fell away. But he didn't turn. He couldn't look at her. Not yet. Not when he'd made such a fool of himself.

He swiped his free hand across one eye and then the other. "The kids?" he asked, afraid he'd really screwed up. "Did they hear me?"

"No. I don't think so. They're playing some kind of game. They don't appear to be paying us any attention."

His shoulders sagged in relief. If they'd heard, if they'd understood what kind of man he was, he couldn't survive it. He'd lost so much. To lose the love of the children would leave him nothing.

"Hayes...Bret, please look at me," she begged softly. "I can't talk to you like this." When he didn't move, she took him gently by the arm and forced him to turn around. He saw her tearstained face and realized, she, too, had wept, but silently so as not to intrude on his grief. "How can you imagine yourself responsible for James's death?"

He lowered his gaze to the ground. She expected an explanation, and damned if he knew how he was going to give it.

A part of him longed to tell her everything, to confess the terrible wrong he'd committed against his brother and to finally face the consequences for what he'd done after his death. But his family...he had to think of them. Did he have the right to jeopardize their happiness just because happiness had eluded him?

"I..." He shook his head and expelled a breath, angry that he'd placed himself in such an awkward predicament. When he looked back up, she gave him a smile that said she understood his unwillingness to talk.

She reached over and took his hand, squeezing it lightly. "I know I'm the last person on earth you'd listen to, but I probably know as much—or more—about your brother as anyone. So will you listen to me for a minute, please?"

He nodded.

"You are *not* responsible for James's death. The crash that killed James and the band was an accident, the result of a thunderstorm. I saw the report from the Federal Aviation Administration. I interviewed the investigators and dozens of people who were at the airport that night, and the evidence was conclusive."

"You don't understand."

"No, I don't. I don't know what you think you did

or should have done, but it's obvious to me that you're still hurting very deeply.'' She let go of his hand. ''I can't say I understand why you didn't go to his funeral, but I believe you loved your brother. I can't imagine you hurting him intentionally.''

Her expression held such compassion that it made him ache. How could this woman express such unwavering faith in him when he had so little in himself?

''I want to tell you what happened the night James died....''

Her lips parted in surprise. ''I don't have to know this,'' she whispered, offering him the chance to change his mind.

''No, but I have to tell it.''

''I *WAS THERE* that night.''

His revelation sent Kate's heart fluttering. ''I don't understand what you mean when you say you were 'there.' Were you at the airport?''

''No, at the concert. And later I was at the hotel.''

Kate thought back to her interview the day before with the local librarian. ''Miss Emma,'' as she'd instructed Kate to call her, said Bret had been at the library returning books when they heard the news about his brother's death, more than sixteen hours after it happened.

Kate quickly calculated the distance from Bret's farm to Rome, Georgia—not more than four or five hours by car. Okay, that was feasible. He could've easily driven over that Friday night for the concert, talked to James, then driven home, unaware until he and Miss Emma heard it Saturday afternoon that the plane had gone down.

But why hadn't his family notified him of James's death Friday night, instead of letting him find out secondhand a day later? That didn't make sense.

"If you did go to that concert, you were one of the last people to talk to James," she said more to herself than to him.

"If you want to call screaming at each other talking, then I guess so. I told him he was killing himself with the crap he was putting into his body, but as usual he wouldn't listen to me. So I came home."

"By 'crap' you mean drugs?"

"Yes."

Kate briefly closed her eyes to regather her strength. So it was true. James had been using drugs. She'd refused to believe it even after the autopsy turned up diethyltryptamine, a synthetic hallucinogen. She'd held on to the slender possibility that somehow James had ingested the DET by accident.

"Did you know before that night that he was using drugs?"

"I suspected it for a long time because of the way he acted. One minute he was depressed and angry with the whole world, and the next he acted like nothing bothered him. I confronted him a couple of times and he swore he was clean."

"Like he swore to his fans and the media."

"I'd never seen any evidence, no needles or pills. I had to try to believe him, although I think a part of me knew he was lying."

"How did he ingest it?"

"On blotting paper. He had several squares of it. I walked in on him putting one in his mouth."

"What did you do?"

His eyes watered and he looked away. Kate understood his pain. She had six brothers and thought them all perfect. To catch one using drugs would shatter her. To discover a brother on drugs and then to lose him in the tragic way Bret Hayes had lost his…that, was inconceivable.

"You don't have to tell me the rest of it," she said.

"I want to tell you, but I need time to ease into it. Do you mind walking for a while?"

"No, not at all."

He called to Tom, telling him they'd be back in a little while and to watch the children. Tom waved that he understood.

"I still own the land adjacent to the ranch," he said. "Through these woods is a place that's very special to me. I'd like to share it with you if you're interested."

The offer touched her. "I'd like that very much."

THE OLD HOMESTEAD was beyond a locked gate and cleverly hidden on all sides by thickly planted pines. A crumbling rock chimney stood in a sea of yellow field grass and wildflowers of every conceivable hue. The house once attached to the chimney had long ago given in to the assault of time; it rested among the flowers, now just bits of decaying wood and tin rusted to a color an artist would have difficulty re-creating.

Kate marveled at the contrast, the weathered gray of the wood, the tan of the rocks among the red, yellow and green of the vegetation.

"This is lovely."

"I think so." Hayes stood on a low rock wall that ran for thirty feet along one side of the ruins. He offered her a hand and pulled her up beside him. "Originally there was a two-room log house chinked with grass and mud, but over time, as the family grew, they replaced it with a larger house that had a tin roof and clapboard sides. Come on and I'll introduce you to them."

Kate followed him into the tall grass. The air held a pungent but pleasant odor. "That's rosemary I smell. Where's it coming from?"

"All over. The lady who lived here believed some superstition about growing it near the house."

"The woman rules where rosemary flourishes."

"That's it. She made her husband plant tons of the stuff."

"Hedging her bets," Kate said. "I like this woman."

The graves were beyond the field in the quiet cool of the trees. Joshua and Elizabeth Satterfield rested under a common headstone dark with age and covered with lichen. Kate knelt and brushed away the dirt that partly obscured the inscription. Using her fingers to feel the words, she was able to read it.

Death is only a shadow across the path to heaven.
"How beautiful."

"Joshua died during the Civil War," Bret said. He gestured to the graves on the left. "These three children were stillborn and never named. The two over here were boys—five and seven. They died when the barn caught fire and they were trapped inside."

"And this one?" she asked, pointing to the grave

of the couple's infant daughter, Nancy Mary. The crude gravestone said she'd been born in January 1861 and had died in April that same year. "She was only three months old."

"She died of pneumonia."

"So many children lost." She stood and wiped the dirt off her hand onto the seat of her shorts. "How do you know about the family?"

"Elizabeth's granddaughter told me. When she was a child, she and the other grandchildren would sit on the front porch at Elizabeth's feet, listening to her talk about how the family had lived through the war."

"Is this granddaughter still living?"

"No, she died several years ago." He smiled with remembrance. "She was really something special. Feisty. Funny. You never knew what she was going to say next, and you didn't dare argue with her because she always won."

"You sound as if you cared about her."

"Yes, very much. She was an important part of my life. Her name was Margaret, but everybody, even her children, called her—"

"Granny Mag," Kate finished for him, suddenly realizing the significance of his story and this place. "Margaret Taylor Bridges. Your maternal grandmother."

"You've done your homework."

"Obviously not well enough. I didn't trace your family history on your mother's side beyond your grandparents." She looked at the graves with renewed interest. "These people—Joshua and Elizabeth Satterfield—were your great-great-grandparents, weren't they?"

"Yes. The farm passed out of the family and became pastureland after Elizabeth died in 1915. I bought it back a few years ago. Most of it ended up as Pine Acres, but I kept fifty acres, intending to build a house for myself. I'd grown up hearing wonderful stories about the place from Granny Mag, and I got this crazy idea that I should settle on the same spot where Joshua and Elizabeth's house had been and live a simple life like them."

"A return to your roots?"

"Something like that."

So that was why he was living here, in Alabama. "Why didn't you build a house here?"

The shadow of regret for desires unfulfilled passed slowly across his face. She recognized it, having seen it in her mirror.

"Dreams die, I guess," he said softly. "People die. And what seems simple never really is."

His terse sentences said what poets have attempted to describe for hundreds of years—the ironies of life—but Kate heard no poetry in his words, only sorrow for the loss of a dream and the loss of a brother, who'd died much too soon.

Unintentionally, Bret Hayes had also described himself—a man whose simple facade hid a soul of great complexity. In this respect, at least, the brothers were very much alike.

Kate was beginning to understand him. And yet today he'd repeatedly surprised her. In bringing her here, in showing her this private place that meant so much to him, he'd given her an unexpected gift. The idea overwhelmed and confused her.

Crouching at the foot of one of the graves, he

picked up a clump of dry pine needles and nervously twisted it with one hand. He didn't look at her, never looked at her when the conversation grew serious. His face betrayed him when he tried to hide his feelings. She knew that embarrassed him, and so he glanced away or lowered his head, even turned his back to her so she couldn't look into his eyes.

"Thank you for sharing this place with me," she told him.

"You understand you can't write about it, don't you?" he asked, seemingly mesmerized by the circular movement of the brown needles. "If fans knew James's ancestors were buried here, they might desecrate the graves in search of souvenirs, like they did at the family plot in Chattanooga."

"I understand. I was furious when I saw the damage they did to the headstones, and so thankful when your family built the mausoleum and moved the graves. It's a beautiful resting place for James, don't you think?"

"I guess so."

Kate's intuition kicked in. "You have seen it, haven't you?"

"Sure." His tone was convincing, but something about his answer made her doubt the credibility of it. If she could catch a glimpse of his face...

She dropped down in front of him and took the pine needles away. She held his hands within her own. Earlier she'd watched him lift a heavy saddle with one hand, as if it weighed nothing. Moments later that same hand had lightly, lovingly, rubbed across the head of a child. The hands were like the man, she decided. They possessed both strength and gentleness.

He'd stiffened when she touched him, and he watched her in silence as she turned his hands over and lightly brushed her thumbs across his skin. Hands always told a story. His spoke of hard work outdoors. The palms were rough, as were the pads of his fingers. A ridge of tiny calluses marred the tips of the fingers on his left hand, and cuts, not quite healed, ran across the second joint of the two middle ones. The stained skin told her he often worked in the dirt.

She had his attention now. She looked into his eyes.

"You've never seen the mausoleum, have you?" she asked, fearing she already knew the answer.

Silent seconds passed. Indecision showed on his face.

"I've never been there in person," he said finally. "Only seen pictures of it."

"Why haven't you visited?"

"I haven't found the time to go."

"I don't believe that." He looked away. "No, please don't hide from me," she pleaded, making his gaze come back to her face. "You don't have to hide your feelings from me or lie to me."

"What makes you think I'm lying? I work hard. The horses have to be fed twice a day and I can't leave that responsibility to anyone else. I don't have time to take off."

"Now, Hayes…"

"Well, I don't," he said defensively.

He stood abruptly. Kate also rose.

"You've gone to elaborate measures here to protect

the graves of relatives you never knew. Yet you want me to believe you haven't visited the tomb that holds your brother, father and grandparents because in the four years since your family built it you haven't found the time? That makes no sense."

He scowled, unable to deny the logic of her words.

"What keeps you away?"

"My conscience," he said, his voice filled with self-loathing. "I can't force myself to visit my brother's tomb because I know I put him there."

"That's not true. A freak of nature…God's will…something…I don't know…made that plane crash. But you're not responsible. You didn't kill him."

"I *did* kill him. I was so angry he'd lied to me about taking drugs that I…" The painful memories etched his face with agony. Kate held her breath and prayed he'd go on. He needed to face the bad memories before he could get past them.

"You what? What did you do that makes you feel responsible for James's death?"

"I told him…he was dead to me, that I no longer had a brother and nothing he said or did would ever change that. And I hit him. Not once, but over and over until I had to be pulled off. I'd never hit my brother in anger before in my life, but that night I wanted to kill him."

"But you didn't kill him," she repeated.

"No, not with my hands. With my anger. He begged me to listen to him, to stay and try to work things out, but I refused."

"He had to know you didn't mean what you said."

"I *did* mean it. When we were growing up, we

were very close, but we'd lost that somehow and it was too late get it back. I didn't want to get it back.''

Kate's heart skipped a beat. ''No. I can't accept that.'' She shook her head, although his face told her he spoke the truth. ''But he was your brother. You loved him. You'd never have walked away from him or given up trying to help him.''

''I did walk away. I meant what I told him and he knew it. I'd watched drugs kill or destroy the minds of too many people I cared about, and I wasn't going to go through it again, not with him. He got on that plane because I left him no choice. I refused to forgive him or give him the help he begged me for. And he died because of it.''

Kate didn't speak, but the tears that escaped against her will and slowly moved down her cheek conveyed her feelings better than words. He reached out and gently put his hand against her face, wiping a tear away with his thumb.

''Do you cry for him, Kate?'' he whispered.

She drew a ragged breath. Giving in to the overwhelming desire to hold him and be held, she wrapped her arms around him and put her head against his chest. Both brothers had suffered so much because of a few words hurled in anger. One brother was dead and could never be returned to her. The comfort she offered the other would never match his pain, but it was all she had to give.

''No, Bret, not for him,'' she lied. ''Only for you.''

SHE WAS SILENT in the truck on the way home, something Bret decided didn't happen too often. Twice today he'd upset her enough to make her cry, and that was probably a rare thing, as well.

The tears she'd shed for him had not only been a surprise, but had touched him deep inside. When she'd clung to him and whispered those tender words, he'd almost fallen apart.

But now the tender words had been replaced with silence, and the eyes that had looked upon him with compassion avoided him. She stared out the front window, thinking...what? He didn't know. The awkwardness that had shadowed them at times throughout the day had returned to settle itself on the seat between them. Since leaving the ranch, they'd exchanged only a handful of sentences, and those had been mere pleasantries. Fifteen minutes had gone by without a word spoken.

They were back to being "Hayes" and "Morgan," and the intimacy they'd shared at the graves was gone.

He supposed she regretted revealing her soft side. A woman like Kate, whose job required her to be tough and unbending, would equate softness with weakness and consider both a liability. She wouldn't understand how appealing that softness was.

His gaze moved over her, lingering on her pensive face before returning to the road. He'd spent the day trying to keep his raging desire in check, but he was failing miserably at the moment.

Her clothes were dirty, and her cap was on backward. The Kool-Aid the children had brought her when they'd returned from their ride had given her a cherry-colored mustache that matched the sunburn on her nose. She was irresistible, and he ached to touch that stain with his lips.

He chided himself for the disturbing thought. Things were becoming too complicated. She was the enemy. He couldn't be attracted to her.

If he was smart, he'd take her back to the motel right now, tell her their deal was off and let that be it. But he hadn't acted wisely yet where she was concerned. Maybe one more stupid act wouldn't hurt.

"I'm going to drop by my house and unhitch the trailer and then I'll buy you supper," he said, determined to breach the wall she'd erected. After tonight he never had to see her again, but he wanted tonight. For once, he wanted to end his day not feeling so damned empty.

"I don't expect you to feed me."

"It's nearly eight. Aren't you hungry?"

"I'm always hungry."

"Then let me buy you supper before I drive you back to the motel."

"You wouldn't offer to do that if you knew how much I can eat," she said, finally looking at him.

"So, if you eat like a pig I'll make you pay for your own meal." That forced a whisper of a smile from her. "Deal?"

"My arms are filthy."

"You can wash up at my house. And over supper you can have your ten minutes to make your pitch."

"All right, but I'm not getting out unless you tie up your dog. I like my ankles and I want to keep them."

He turned into the driveway as the sun sank below the horizon and the trees became silhouettes against the sky. An excited Sallie raced the truck to the house. The mares in the pasture trotted to the fence and called a welcome to Bret's gelding in the trailer.

"Do you want to come up to the barn with me?" he asked.

"No, I'll wait here."

"I have fillies and colts in the corral on the other side of the barn." Maybe that would tempt her out of her somber mood.

She perked up. "Can I pet them?"

"All you want. I'll even let you help me feed them." He stopped the truck, slid it into Reverse and carefully backed the trailer into its grassy parking place near the fence. "I'll go tie up Sallie."

He fastened Sallie to a clothesline post with a rope, then dashed in the back door to the kitchen to hide the dirty glasses left in the sink. Maybe she wouldn't notice the cobwebs in the corners of the kitchen or the muddy boot marks on the floor.

A pile of freshly washed laundry—underwear and socks—lay on the kitchen table. He hurriedly carried them to the bedroom and threw them on the unmade bed.

How long had it been since anyone other than him had set foot in this house? He wasn't sure. When his hands, Willie and Aubrey, were working, they preferred to put their lunches and drinks in the refrigerator at the barn rather than walk to the house. He never invited anyone to visit. His few encounters with women during the past few years had purposely been elsewhere.

He glanced in the bathroom, thankful to find it fairly clean. After opening the windows wider and turning on the ceiling fan in the living room to chase out the stagnant air, he left the house through the front door. Kate had climbed out of the truck and stood under the halogen yard light, looking at what remained of the garden on the other side of the driveway.

"Very artistic," she said, pointing to the scarecrow.

"That's Henry's creation. It's supposed to frighten the deer so they won't eat my peas."

"Does it work?"

"No, but he's proud of it so I leave it up." He opened the door of the trailer, and his gelding backed out without prompting. "How about holding him while I unhitch the trailer?" He handed her the lead rope and she accepted with reluctance, nervously staring up at the big horse.

"He's not going to try anything, is he?"

"No, he's gentle."

"Do you think he'd let me touch him?"

"Sure. He likes you to rub that blaze on his nose."

Bret smiled to himself as she inched her hand slowly toward Dusty's head while begging the horse not to trample her to death.

It didn't take him long to unhitch the trailer and grab a flashlight off the dashboard, but that was all the time she and Dusty needed to get acquainted. When he walked to the back of the trailer, the horse had lowered his head so she could scratch him behind the ears.

"I found something else he likes," she said, grinning with pleasure.

"So I see."

"His ears are soft, almost like a puppy's. And you're right—he's very gentle."

"Not all of them are. They have different personalities. Some, like him, enjoy being around people and being touched. Others don't. Would you like to lead him?"

"Could I?"

"If you're careful. He gets anxious sometimes when he's close to the other horses, and he'll step on you if you don't watch out."

She became more animated on the walk up the dirt road that led from the house to the barn, fully exercising her innate curiosity about everything. She made him explain what horses eat and how much, how they're trained and what diseases they can catch. It amazed him that her brain could store the answers to the millions of questions she'd probably asked over the years.

He didn't mind the questions. One of the few subjects he could talk about with some authority was horses, and it had been a long time since anyone— any woman—had shown an interest in what he did.

When they got to the barn, he flipped on the lights in the wide alley that divided the stalls. He should have known she'd walk immediately to the one thing he didn't want to answer questions about.

"What's this contraption?"

"A mount."

She ran her hand over the hard rubber and into the tubular hole at the end. "A mount for what?"

"Breeding. That's what we use to collect the semen for artificial insemination."

She jerked her hand out of the artificial vagina.

"You mean they don't actually…and that's where he puts his…?"

"Uh-huh," he said, trying not to laugh.

"Oh, nasty." She wiped her hand on her shirt. "You could have told me what it was before I stuck my hand in there."

"Don't worry, it's clean. We disinfect the tube every time we use it."

He turned on the lights over the corral so she could see "the babies," as she called them, although most of them had been born in late winter and were already six months old.

When she saw the long-legged colts and fillies, she went all sweet and motherly. They came to the fence and she had to stroke each one, immediately forgetting Bret's existence.

"Do you want to help me feed Dusty?" he asked, trying to win back her attention.

She didn't even look at him before she waved him away. "No, go ahead." One of the colts stuck its head through the fence and nudged her. "Oh, you're a little doll," she cooed. "Will you give me a kiss? How darling you are."

Bret glowered. He wondered what he'd have to do to get her to talk to *him* like that. For the first time in his life he was jealous of a horse.

Leading Dusty into the barn, he tied him outside one of the stalls and went to the feed room where he began filling buckets with a high-protein mixture of grain.

Feeding was a major undertaking twice a day. During the week he had Willie and Aubrey to help, but weekends it was just him. He'd never minded the work, but tonight he was resentful of the time it took because the woman intrigued him. If he didn't hurry, the grill would be closed and he'd have to take Kate straight back to the motel, losing the extra hour he might spend with her over supper.

His mind was on that hour and not on what he was doing when he opened Dusty's stall and followed him in. Had he been thinking straight, instead of day-dreaming like a moon-eyed kid, he'd have checked the stall to make sure that pesky raccoon hadn't slipped under the door again to scrounge for leftover feed.

That thought hit him about the same time the cor-nered coon hissed and Dusty screamed in terror. Bret lunged to the side as the horse reared. The front hooves missed him when Dusty whirled and bolted out the door, but the horse went out kicking, catching Bret solidly on his left thigh and cutting the left side of his chest, under his ribs. The frightened coon also made a hasty exit out the open door.

"Hayes? Where are you? Why is the horse loose?" Through his veil of pain, her anxious voice seemed miles away. "Hayes, answer me!"

He tried but he couldn't. The floor of the stall was designed to be easy on the feet of confined horses, but underneath the three-inch rubber surface was con-crete. When he'd fallen on his side, the jolt had knocked the breath out of him.

He struggled to sit up. His chest ached and his leg felt worse, but he was more worried about his gelding than himself. Had he closed the gate in the yard when he and Kate had come through it? With great relief he remembered that he had. Dusty was trapped in the corridor between the gate and the barn. Even if he jumped either fence that bordered the dirt road, he'd be in the pasture with the mares. He couldn't get out onto the highway.

"Hayes?"

"I'm in here," he called when he was able to sit up and catch his breath. Even talking hurt.

She appeared in the doorway, eyes wild with fear. "What happened? I heard this awful noise and the horse came running out of the barn and... Oh, my God, you're bleeding! Did he run over you?"

"Kicked me."

"Where?" He showed her the two places and she rubbed her hands gently across them, forcing a groan of pain he couldn't stifle when she touched the one on his leg. "Is it broken?"

"I don't think so."

"You need a doctor."

"No, no doctor. I'm okay. Help me get up."

"But you shouldn't move."

"Help me stand up," he insisted.

When she saw he was determined to do it, she relented, hooking his arm over her shoulder. But she thought he was crazy and she told him so in one of her rambling soliloquies; it made him wonder how she could talk for so long without taking a breath.

Several minutes later he managed to get to his feet. He was afraid to depend too much on her fragile frame for support. He was dripping with sweat by the time he made it. He tried to take a step, but the injured leg rebelled. Had he not grabbed the hay rack with his free hand, he and Kate would've both gone down.

"This is ridiculous," she said, trying to steady him.

"You might be hemorrhaging. I'll get the truck and take you to the hospital."

"We don't have a hospital."

She swore. "Where's the nearest one?"

"Cloverton. But it's fifty miles from here."

"I don't care how far it is. We're going to Cloverton."

CHAPTER SEVEN

THE CEILING of the waiting room at Cloverton Hospital had 316 tiles, and if you were imaginative or extremely bored, you could pick out shapes in their roughened surface. Kate had counted the tiles twice, horizontally, then vertically, skipping the spaces where the tiles were missing. That was after she'd read all the dog-eared magazines, finding out more than she wanted to know about skin care, bass fishing and Prince Charles.

She looked at her watch. Two hours! What could be taking them so long? Surely the doctor had examined Bret by now.

He'd been very pale when they reached the hospital, and the leg had begun to swell noticeably against his slim-fitting jeans, causing him agony every time he moved. The ride had seemed endless, although she'd driven like a madwoman and covered the fifty-plus miles in under sixty minutes.

Every foot of the way she'd struggled to remain calm. That calm had deserted her when she'd pulled up outside and seen the single dilapidated building with its torn awning.

"Please tell me this isn't the right place," she'd begged him. "This doesn't qualify as a hospital—it's some Civil War relic. We have to find you a real one.''

''Kate…''

''What?''

''I can't go any farther.''

That had decided it. Reluctantly she'd helped him inside.

That had been around nine-fifteen. It was now eleven-thirty, and she hadn't been told a thing about his condition.

Unable to sit still any longer, she got up and paced the tiny room. It was empty except for the college kid at the reception window. No other patients had come in. Aside from a security guard, who ambled through every thirty minutes or so, Kate had been alone since she and Bret arrived.

She walked to the window and tapped. The kid looked up from his textbook and frowned, letting her know he wasn't happy about being bothered again.

''I want you to go back there and find out what's going on,'' she told him through the round hole in the glass.

''Ma'am, as I explained before, when Doc Burman knows anything, he'll let *you* know.''

''It's been hours.''

''Yes, ma'am, but we only have one doctor tonight to work on all the patients.''

''What patients? There's no one else here. And no one else has been here all night.''

''Well, yes, ma'am, that's true. I meant the other patients.''

''In the hospital?''

''Yes, ma'am.''

"You mean there's only one doctor in this entire hospital?"

"Well, yes, ma'am, Doc Burman, but he's the best there is."

"Please ask this Dr. Burman to step out here for a minute so I can talk to him."

"No, ma'am, I can't bother Doc when he's with a patient."

"Then let me go back there."

"No, ma'am, I can't do that until he says it's okay."

"Why?"

He looked perplexed. "Because…well, it's the rule."

"Why is it the rule?"

"Well, I don't know. It just is. Always has been."

"So, although the man I brought in may be seriously injured, I'm not allowed to see him or talk with the doctor because of a vague rule you're determined to enforce but you don't know why?"

He frowned. "Well, yes, ma'am, I guess so."

"Look—" she glanced at his name tag "—Randy. I'm trying to be reasonable here. Please walk down the hall and get a condition report on the man I brought in. That's not too much to ask, is it?"

"Ma'am, I'm sorry, but I'm not supposed to leave the desk. You'll have to wait." He turned his attention back to his textbook. Kate tapped on the glass again, but he ignored her. College kids. Sheesh.

Frustrated, she walked to the double doors on the right and looked through one of the small windows. She saw nothing but the same empty hall and stark white walls she'd seen the ten previous times she'd looked through the window.

Bret was down there somewhere. Alone. In pain. Probably being doctored by the Beverly Hillbillies.

She jerked open the door and walked through.

"Hey, wait," Randy yelled as she passed his cubicle. "Ma'am, you can't come back here. I told you it's not allowed."

"I'm rewriting the rules."

Small examining rooms flanked the hall. Kate checked the first one. Bret wasn't there, so she systematically began to check the others in a zigzag pattern. Randy continued to whine, but he didn't try to stop her. Finally he gave up trying to coax her back to the waiting room and returned to his desk.

Kate found Bret in the fourth room on the right. He lay on a gurney with his hurt leg elevated on pillows and his arm thrown over his eyes to shield them from the bright light overhead. His shirt was off and his jeans, too, she guessed. A sheet covered him from the waist down, but his leg protruded from it, revealing a ghastly purple bruise on his thigh that extended far beyond the ice pack on top of it. A second smaller bruise and a gash marred the left side of his chest.

"Are you terrorizing the hired help, Morgan?" he asked without moving or opening his eyes.

She said a silent prayer as she walked to his side, thankful he felt well enough to joke. "How did you know it was me?"

"Because you're a born troublemaker. You're not happy unless you're driving some poor soul crazy."

"It's a gift."

"How about doing me a favor and waiting until

these people are through checking me out before you irritate them too much?''

"Okay, I'll try." She leaned over, picked up the edge of the ice pack and looked more closely at his leg. "Ugh! Did they x-ray it?"

He peeked at her from under his arm. "Yeah. It's only bruised."

"And your side?"

"Bruised and cut. Nothing broken."

She let out a breath. "Thank, goodness. I was afraid you might have broken a rib. You know, we could have punctured a lung moving you like that, or caused you to bleed internally. You could have died on the way over here."

"Is this how you cheer sick people up?"

She grimaced. "Sorry."

He shifted his arm, then winced when the light hit his eyes. "Flip off that light, will you?"

She turned it off, then turned on the smaller one over the sink. "How's that?"

"Better." He folded the disposable pillow and stuffed it under his neck so he could talk to her without straining. The tightness around his mouth indicated that he was in pain. He didn't say anything, only looked at her. The intensity of his gaze made her suddenly self-conscious about her appearance. She nervously touched her hair.

When they'd brought him back here, she'd gone to the ladies' room and washed her face and arms. Her hair was a disaster, though. She'd taken off the cap and tried to force her curls into a braid, but they refused to cooperate. They fell in a tangled mess across her shoulders.

He, on the other hand, was disturbingly attractive.
Taut. Muscular. Tanned to the waist from working
outside without a shirt. The men at her gym paid a
fortune to work out every day and their upper bodies
didn't look half that good. She willed her eyes not to
leave his face. They wanted to follow that intriguing
line of hair that ran down the center of his abdomen
and disappeared beneath the sheet.

"Are you in pain?" she asked, trying to focus on
anything other than how low the sheet had slipped on
his hips and why she was seeing skin below his waist,
instead of underwear.

"A little," he said.

"Where's the doctor?"

"I'm here, I'm here," came a voice from the doorway. An elderly man wearing a tweed suit and bow
tie shuffled in. He was bent with age and leaning on
a cane. A nurse followed him into the room.

This was the doctor? He was older than the hospital!

"Glad you're here," he said to Kate, gripping her
hand with surprising strength. "I'm sorry it took so
long, but we wanted to cool that leg awhile to reduce
the swelling. He's pretty banged up, but I don't think
there's any need to admit him. Watch him closely and
call us if there's a problem." He looked at Bret. "Are
you allergic to penicillin, son?"

"No, sir."

He handed Kate a bottle of pills. "I think as a
precaution we'll give him some. Be sure he follows
the directions and takes the whole prescription. Make
him stay off that leg for a couple of weeks. We'll
give him some crutches to get around the house, but

keep him immobile as much as possible.'' He looked at Bret and smiled. ''You won't mind having your pretty little wife fuss over you in bed for a few days, will you? No, of course you won't.''

Kate's gaze met Bret's, and they both turned crimson.

The doctor pulled a prescription pad out of his coat pocket and scribbled on it while the nurse fixed a hypodermic. ''Janice is going to give you a shot to ease your discomfort. That ought to last until morning. If you're still in a lot of pain tomorrow, you can have this filled.'' He tore the prescription off the pad and passed it to Kate. ''You take it easy, son,'' he told Bret.

Kate followed him out into the hall. ''He is all right, isn't he?'' she asked. ''He hasn't suffered any permanent damage?''

''Oh, he'll be fine,'' he assured her with a fatherly pat on the arm. ''He's in more pain than he's admitting, so if he's a little grumpy, ignore it. Pamper him. But I'd hold off on any hanky-panky until he feels better.''

Kate had trouble keeping a straight face. ''Oh, no,'' she said, trying to explain that she and Bret weren't having any hanky-panky, but the doctor misinterpreted her words.

''Now, I know it's hard for you young people to stay away from each other for long, but I really think it's best.''

''No, you don't understand...''

He chuckled and shook his head. ''Ah, you kids. Don't know where you get all that energy.'' A voice over the intercom announced that Dr. Burman was needed on the second floor. "Oh, dear, that's me. Got to run." He turned and shuffled very slowly down the hall, still chuckling.

Kate walked back into the room. The nurse had moved to the other side of the examining table and was standing over Bret with the needle raised in one hand. Before Kate realized what she was about to do, the woman already had her hand on the sheet. "Okay, hon," she said, flipping it back. "Which cheek do you want it in?"

"IF YOU DON'T STOP laughing…" Bret warned across the cab of the truck.

Kate blotted the tears from her face, but they fell more quickly than she could blot. Lord, she'd never laughed this hard. Her stomach hurt. Her sides felt like someone had used them for a punching bag.

She fumbled with the ring of keys, finally getting the right one in the ignition, and the truck started. "I'm sorry. I can't help it. When that nurse yanked the sheet back and I saw your face…"

"My face wasn't what I was worried about you seeing," he said, his voice almost a growl.

That set her off again. She collapsed against the steering wheel in an uncontrollable fit. Her right arm hit the horn, her left bumped the lever that started the wipers moving and turn signal blinking. The wipers scraped across the dry windshield a couple of times with a slow irritating screech before she could shut them off.

"Damn. Enough! Get out of the way and I'll drive."

He opened the door and tried to climb out, but the

tip of one crutch caught on the floor mat. He wrestled with it, banging himself on the head and letting out a string of obscenities crude enough to make even Kate blush.

He was in danger of falling out the door when she got hold of herself and reached across the seat, grabbing him by the arm and pulling him back inside. "Will you stay still before you hurt yourself worse than you already have?"

"I'm tired, I'm hurt and I want to go home," he said shortly. "And it wasn't that funny to begin with."

"I'm sorry. I know you're hurting."

"Do you expect me to sit here all night listening to you cackle like a hen trying to lay an egg?"

"No, of course not. I promise, I'll quit. Now please get back in the truck before you fall on your head and I have to take you into the hospital again."

He hesitated, as if not trusting her to keep her promise. "The flashing of a man's private parts shouldn't be a source of amusement."

The comment wasn't supposed to be funny, but it took all of Kate's willpower not to laugh. Poor man. He was physically hurt and embarrassed. She'd never forget his look of horror when the nurse had yanked that sheet off him. Immediately Kate had whirled and left the room, but her departure had been a little too late, allowing her to see more of Bret Hayes than she'd ever intended.

"I really am sorry," she told him again, praying she could control her expression. "The nurse assumed I was your wife."

He snorted, as if the possibility of their being married was ludicrous.

"Please, get back in." She was sure he stalled just to make her feel bad. "Please. I promise I won't laugh again."

He lifted his hurt leg into the truck, then slammed the door and glared at her, clearly wanting her to know she wasn't forgiven. She buckled him into the seat belt and moved the crutches to the middle so he wouldn't have to hold them.

"Now, that's better," she said in syrupy-sweet voice, fussing over him as the doctor had suggested. "Are you comfortable?"

"Humph."

"Do you want something to put behind your head so you can go to sleep? How about this shirt? I can fold it up and—"

"I'm not going to sleep," he snapped, but five minutes later he conked out, his chin resting against his chest and his big body held upright in the seat only by the shoulder strap.

Kate was grateful for the short respite from his foul mood. She intentionally didn't wake him until they got home, after she'd parked the truck and unlocked the front door of his house. She found the switch for the flood lights and turned them on. Sallie, still tied in the backyard, pitched a fit, howling to be set free.

Bret rubbed his eyes with the base of his palms and let out a long noisy yawn that made Sallie yodel a response. "We can't be home so soon. What time is it?"

"After midnight."

"Can't be." He looked at his watch and blinked,

trying to focus with eyes that obviously didn't want to focus.

She unbuckled the seat belt for him. "Are you going to be able to make it to the house? I parked as close as I could, but I didn't want to run over your flowers."

He yawned again loudly and clasped his hands behind his head to stretch. "I'll be okay. Go on home. I'll send one of my men to the motel tomorrow to pick up my truck."

"I thought I'd sleep over."

He stopped abruptly with his elbows in the air and his mouth open. His eyebrows rose in surprise. "Sleep over?"

"On your couch," she hurriedly explained. "In case you need something during the night."

"Oh," he said, dropping his arms.

"You don't mind, do you?"

"That's not necessary."

"I think it is. You're hurt and you can't take care of yourself."

"I can take care of myself just fine."

"Maybe so, but there's no way I could sleep at that motel tonight knowing you were here to fend for yourself."

"This isn't some ploy to get on my good side so I'll help you with your book, is it?"

"No, I'm worried about you being alone and needing help. That's all. Let me stay, okay?"

He sighed. "Okay, you can use the front bedroom."

"Thank you."

"You might as well go on in. I've got to turn Sallie

loose and feed her and the colts, and that's going to take some time."

"Hayes, it's dark, you can hardly walk and you're drowsy from that shot. Sallie's okay where she is for tonight, and so are the horses. Be smart about this and let me get you to bed before anything else happens."

He agreed, reluctantly. It took him several minutes to hobble to the house and considerably more time to climb the concrete steps to the porch. Crossing the threshold, he swayed, reducing her life by at least ten years. She didn't breathe normally until he'd safely reached the bedroom.

"Let me fix these covers," she said, moving a pile of underwear to the antique dresser. The bed was unmade and the top sheet lay partly on the floor. She found the pillows wedged between the old iron bedstead and the wall.

Either he'd had a restless sleep the night before or he'd been playing with someone in bed. She could easily imagine it, that exquisite body of his in motion, thrusting, driven by passion, bringing some woman to the pinnacle of ecstasy.

"I can do that," he said suddenly.

Her eyes widened.

"Do what?"

"Fix the bed."

"Oh." She almost laughed out loud at her foolishness. "That's okay. I'll do it."

She quickly straightened the bed and helped him sit. He put the toe of one boot on the heel of the other and pushed it off his foot. "Oh, man, that hurts."

"You'll likely be sore for a long time. Are you going to need help getting undressed?"

His face reflected his amusement at the offer. "No, but I can pretend if you want me to."

"Very funny."

HIS HOUSE WAS OLD but hospitable. Kate went to the kitchen to get water so he could take his pill. She found ancient linoleum on the floor, so worn that in spots the rose-colored flowers in the pattern were no longer visible and the edges that met the baseboard had started to curl back and split.

Purple and pink African violets bloomed in small clay pots on the windowsill over the sink. A large wooden table took up most of the center of the room. Chairs, in a mishmash of styles and colors, flanked it.

Compared to Kate's modern kitchen, the room was shabby, but she liked it better. This place had a feeling of home that her kitchen, her entire condo, had never given her, despite countless changes of decor.

Crayon pictures by some of the younger children at Pine Acres covered the refrigerator—drawings of horses and stick people with smiling faces, the sun peeking out from clouds above crudely drawn houses.

Kari loves Mr. Hayes, one child had scrawled across her drawing of a dog that looked like the ugly one still whining in the backyard.

Happy Father's Day, another had wished him in carefully printed block letters.

Most of these children had reason never to trust an adult again, much less love one, yet it seemed Bret Hayes had somehow broken through their barriers of pain, sorrow and neglect.

"Finding everything?" he called from the bedroom.

"Yes, coming."

Surprised to discover tears on her face, she wiped them away. She opened the refrigerator, intending to fix him something to eat, but it only held raw vegetables, a few condiments, a tub of butter and some canned drinks. Frozen microwave dinners packed the freezer compartment, but she didn't think he was up to eating anything that heavy.

She smeared butter across some crackers she found in the cabinet and arranged them on a paper plate.

When she took him the crackers and a glass of water, he was sitting on the middle of the bed with his back against the headboard and his eyes closed, but he wasn't asleep. He turned his head and looked at her as she approached.

She sat on the edge of the bed where she could face him. She put the plate in his lap, but she kept the glass, afraid he was too sleepy and might spill the water on the bed. "Here. Eat these. Taking medicine on an empty stomach isn't good for you. I can fix you something more substantial if you think you can eat it."

"No, don't bother." He ate one cracker with little enthusiasm and couldn't eat another. "I can't." He sat the plate on the bedside table.

"Maybe that was enough." She opened the bottle of pills and shook one of the gray-and-red capsules into his palm.

"What is this again?" he asked, peering down at it.

"Penicillin. To keep that gash from getting infected."

"I'll pass."

"Come on. It won't hurt you to take this, especially when you think of all the germs in a horse barn. All that manure. Ticks. Lice. Flies carrying all kinds of horrible—"

"All right, all right. Damn! I'll take the pill. Would you mind putting some ice in this water? I'm hot."

He did seem a little clammy. Beads of sweat had formed on his upper lip and his face looked flushed. "Do you have a fever?" Kate asked.

"No, it's hot in here."

"It isn't really. A little stuffy, maybe, but there's a cool breeze coming in the window." She stood and pulled the string to the old fan overhead, putting it on the high setting. "How's that?"

"Better, but maybe if I had something cool on my face…"

"Like a cool cloth?"

"Yeah, that sounds good."

"Okay, I'll get you one."

She went to the kitchen for his ice water and a small bowl, throwing the crackers he hadn't eaten out the back door. Sallie stopped growling to gobble them up. Kate felt sorry for her and threw out a few more. Then the rest in the pack. Then the rest in the box.

In the bathroom, she filled the bowl with cool water and found a washcloth. Quietly she opened the medicine cabinet to take a quick look. Nothing unusual there. The cabinet under the sink was the same way, cluttered and uninteresting. It looked like hers, except she didn't buy adhesive bandages with cartoon characters on them.

She felt a bit guilty about prying, but this might be her one chance to have a look around.

Hurrying back to the bedroom, she searched for the pills, then remembered they'd been in her hand when she'd gone to get the water. "I guess I left your pills in the kitchen. Did I give you one already?"

"Mm-hmm." He pointed to his mouth to let her know the pill was inside. When he'd washed it down, she wrung out the cloth and offered it to him to wipe his face.

"Do you mind doing it?" he asked. "My arms feel like lead."

"No, I guess not." Gently she wiped his brow, jaw and down both sides of his neck.

He'd unbuttoned his shirt while she was out of the room but hadn't taken it off. His tanned chest glistened with sweat and drew her gaze to its muscular contours like metal to a magnet. She dared not look at it for long. And touching it with the cloth, even if it was only to help cool him, would surely unravel her already frayed emotions.

Repeatedly she went through the routine of dipping the cloth in the water, wringing it and wiping his skin. He watched her face, making her uncomfortable, but she pretended detachment. Follow the movement of the cloth was wiser than looking too long into his eyes.

"You're not what I expected," he said. "Sometimes you can be so hard to get along with, and other times, like now, you can be incredibly sweet."

"Please don't tell anyone about my sweet side. I wouldn't want it to get around."

He smiled. "Your secret's safe with me," he said. "Nobody would believe me, anyway."

"Probably not. They'd swear the horse kicked you in the head, instead of the leg."

"I'm not so sure he didn't. Isn't fraternizing with the enemy against the rules of war?"

"I believe so." She tossed the cloth into the bowl. "But we have a truce, remember?"

"So we do."

She glanced at her watch. "It's after midnight. Did I miss my chance to make my pitch, or will you honor our deal?"

"Pitch away."

"Now?"

"I'm not going anywhere."

"But you're groggy from that medication. I was thinking tomorrow."

"Take your shot, Morgan. Tomorrow may be too late."

"Okay, well…you were pretty candid today about your brother, and that tells me you might not be totally against helping me. So let me start by reminding you that I'm very good at what I do, my reputation is already established and I'm not out to make a fast buck or a name for myself like the writers who've told his story in the past."

"If I say yes, what would I be committing myself to and what could I expect in return?"

"Talk to me and tell me the truth, and I'll promise to leave your mother and sister alone and not to call them again for interviews. I'll also let you read—for accuracy only—what I've already written and you can review the edited manuscript. You'll know what's in it before it hits the bookstores.''

"What if I don't like something or don't want it included?"

"Then we discuss it. If the information didn't come from a confidential source, I'll tell you where I got it and give you the opportunity to respond to it and even present your case to my publisher for excluding it from the book."

"And if we still disagree?"

"Well, I can't let you tell me what to publish, but I'll seriously consider your arguments. And if after that I still feel the information is important and has to be included, I give you my word I'll present it as fairly and honestly as I can."

He took one of the pillows from behind his back and used it to support his leg. "This deal favors your side."

"No, it doesn't. Rejecting my offer won't stop publication of the book. You already know I plan to go ahead. But accepting it will give you the power to influence what will be in it. I think that greatly favors *your* side."

"What do you want from me? I've already told you what happened the night James died. Why isn't that enough?"

"I need more. I believe he went through hell those last few years with the band, because of Lenny having to be institutionalized and Lauren's suicide, and that's why he turned to drugs. But I'm only guessing at the reasons. And I want to know more about his personal life."

Bret's guarded expression prevented her from reading his thoughts. She wondered if she'd killed her chances by mentioning Lauren Davis. More than once the gossip columns had linked the backup singer's name with Bret's, although she was also known to have been romantically involved with James.

"I promise I only want to write a balanced account of your brother's life, and I believe I can do that without hurting you or your family. Deep down, don't you believe that, too? Otherwise, why would you have volunteered so much information today?"

"Maybe I believe it, and maybe I don't. You have a solid reputation, Morgan. I'll give you that much. But I'm not sure I *want* to help you."

"Don't give me an answer now. Think about it for a few days, and when you're feeling better, we'll talk again."

"I want to read the manuscript before I make up my mind."

"I can arrange that."

He shifted and winced, grabbing his hurt leg. "Damn."

"Shouldn't you call your mother and stepfather and tell them what's happened to you?"

"No, they'll only worry."

"Someone else, then. A friend? Miss Emma?"

"No."

"What about one of the hired men you mentioned?"

"They have work to do, and with me out, that work is going to double."

"You should have help. Can't you think of anyone?"

He looked away to hide the truth, but she saw it. He didn't have anyone, other than his family. Not a soul here cared enough about him to lend him a hand. How incredibly sad. Her heart went out to him.

She felt his face. He was still hot, so she began the ritual again—dipping the cloth in the water, wringing it and pressing it to his skin. The rhythmic noise of the fan and her touch must have had a lulling effect; before long his eyelids fluttered, then closed.

She kept up her gentle attentions for a long time after he'd fallen asleep, unwilling to wake him now that he'd finally found relief from his pain. And she found she liked touching him. She liked looking at him when he didn't know she was doing it.

A shadow of a beard had begun to show along his jaw and above his mouth, and his hair rejected style to fall in wayward curls across his forehead. Occasionally, when he smiled or made a certain gesture, his resemblance to James was uncanny. The shape of his head was the same. He had the same long dark lashes.

But Bret had a maturity that fate had denied James, and it was that maturity, or perhaps her own, that made him as attractive to a woman of thirty-three as James had been to a girl of nineteen.

James. Thoughts of him had sneaked into her head more than usual today. Putting the bowl aside, she eased carefully off the bed. The movement was still enough to wake Bret.

"Get some sleep," she told him. "I'm going to bed, too. Call me if you need anything during the night."

He said he would.

Once alone in the spare bedroom, she tried to wind down, but her emotions were in turmoil. As she often did late at night, she took out the *Post* article she kept in her wallet. The copy had creases and was falling apart; over the years she'd opened and refolded it a thousand times.

The accompanying photograph was of her and James. How young they both looked. Back then, Kate would never have guessed his fate, or that she'd write a book about him. She certainly would never have imagined she'd one day sleep in his brother's house.

She put away the article, undressed and turned off the light. The bed was old, but comfortable.

She'd started this day not liking Bret, but had come to realize there was much about him *to* like—his dedication to the kids at Pine Acres, for one.

His reasons for not adopting didn't make sense, though. He was hiding something, something she was determined to ferret out. If she could keep her mild attraction for him under control, she might succeed.

He was cute. Okay, she admitted with a sigh, more than cute. And she was more than *mildly* attracted. But she couldn't let either interfere with the job she had to do here.

Maybe she was allowing her admiration for James to trick her into feeling something for Bret that didn't exist. James's friendship, although it had only lasted a few hours, had meant a great deal to her. She could be transferring her admiration for one brother to the other.

That was probably it. Or maybe she'd *wanted* to be charmed. Heaven knows, she was long overdue. She hadn't felt such curiosity about a man in a long time. Not since…

Closing her eyes, she tried to call up Bret's face, but it was James who appeared.

"Please, not tonight," she whispered to him in the dark, knowing it would do no good. He would invariably haunt her dreams…as he'd haunted them so often in the past fourteen years.

CHAPTER EIGHT

SHE'D BEEN NINETEEN and James twenty-four the weekend he gave a concert in Manhattan and came into her life, unknowingly altering it. One day, just one tiny thread in the unending fabric of time, but she'd carry the memory in her head and her heart forever.

Away from home, living in a strange city and dealing with the recent death of her mother from cancer, she'd never felt more alone or afraid. In James, she'd seen herself as she might be: confident, fearless, able to handle the problems that came with being considered gifted.

He'd offered her friendship when no one wanted to be her friend. And brief as that friendship had been, it had gotten her through one of the most difficult periods of her life.

Having graduated with highest honors from DePaul University two years early, she'd entered the Graduate School of Journalism at Columbia University, still in her teens, way too bright and too young to ever hope to fit in. She'd begun to see her intelligence as a curse. Always on display, humiliated if she made a mistake, she learned not to make mistakes.

Outwardly, she was an adult, but emotionally she was still a child. When things got too rough, she lost herself in the music of James Hayes, because she believed he somehow understood her pain. She conjured up a mystical connection with him through his music, and that connection sustained her during the bleakest moments.

The things some people said about him, that he was a little wild and drank too much and always had a different woman at his side, didn't matter. In truth, those things were exciting. Everything about him was exciting, from the way he looked to the timbre of his voice. But it was his talent Kate admired the most. His lyrics were poetry and the music touched her soul. He spoke to her directly in his songs; she was certain of that.

To meet him, to be able to sit and talk to him face-to-face, was a dream she harbored but never expected to come true. When it happened, she convinced herself that divine intervention was the cause. In reality, it was nothing more than his band manager Malcolm Elliot's idea of a publicity stunt....

PEOPLE FROM THE college and members of Hayes's band and entourage packed the suite. "I see him," one of the other students said with excitement, craning his neck to look over the crowd. The others surged forward. Kate fought to retain her position in front, but she was soon at the back of the group.

"Everyone," she heard Mr. Elliot say, "this is James Hayes. Jamie, these are the scholarship students I told you about." At the man's prompting, four of them rattled off their names and hometowns. "And...where'd the young kid go? There she is." He reached through the other people, grabbed her above the elbow and pulled her forcefully toward him.

Someone stuck a foot out, or maybe she simply stumbled. With the sickening realization that she was about to make a fool of herself, Kate flew forward and out of Mr. Elliot's grasp. She landed hard against the chest of James Hayes, nearly knocking him down.

"Whoa!" he said. His arms came up to steady her.

She looked up to find herself staring into extraordinary eyes that reminded her of a cloudless sky on a warm spring day. The apology she should have offered flew right out of her head. "Stupid idiot," she blurted, instead.

Until one of the other students groaned, she didn't realize she'd said the words out loud.

"Oh, no, I meant me!" she explained, horrified.

James smiled softly with understanding. "I can't think of a nicer way to meet a pretty lady than to have her fall into my arms."

He thought she was pretty? Against her will, she smiled.

"Ah," he said, "and look at that fantastic smile. Lady, you're breakin' my heart."

She knew she should thank him for the compliment, but she had difficulty thinking or speaking when he still had his arms around her and his face was so close. His dark hair fell straight and shiny to his shoulders from a center part. An intriguing dimple in his chin called out for her to touch it, to put her fingers there and play with it.

He didn't appear in a hurry to let her go, and she couldn't have moved if the building was on fire. But then, to her disappointment, Mr. Elliot interrupted to suggest they sit while the photographer took her shots for the article.

Kate pulled out of James's arms and stepped back. He was taller than she'd imagined he'd be, and thinner in person than in his photographs. The black T-shirt and black jeans gave him no definition, but in her eyes, he was absolutely perfect.

Mr. Elliot guided them to a sofa at the other end of the room. Everyone waited for James to sit, then Mr. Elliot arranged the rest of them around him—the two other girls on either side of him, one boy in a chair pulled up on the right, and the other boy sitting on the floor.

"We'll shoot you and Jamie separately," he told Kate, making her heart flutter. "Genius meets genius. The fans will love it."

This couldn't be real. Any minute she was going to wake up and realize she'd only been dreaming about James again, that he wasn't really sitting ten feet away, that he hadn't just winked at her.

When the photographer finished the group shots, Mr. Elliot ushered the other students across the room to meet the band. Kate took her place next to James.

"What's your name?" he asked.

"Kathryn."

"Kathryn. That's an awfully formal name, isn't it?"

"Some people call me Kate."

"Kind of severe. How about…Katie? That fits you."

She nodded. "My dad sometimes calls me that."

"You can call me Jamie like my friends do. So, Katie, do you like going to school here?"

"It's okay, I guess. Sometimes."

"You don't seem sure."

She shrugged. "School's okay, but a few of the people are a little unfriendly. They don't seem to like me very much."

"That's hard to believe. What do they do?"

"Ignore me mostly, but that doesn't bother me too much because I've gotten used to it. Only…a few have made a career out of trying to embarrass me in class, to make me look foolish or stupid in front of my instructors. Because I'm younger, I guess. They don't think I should be here. They make my life hell."

"They're jealous you're so bright."

"I guess that's part of it. I'm an easy target." And this article would only make things worse, but she wouldn't ever have turned down the opportunity. "Sometimes I think I…" She shook her head. "I'm sorry. This is crazy. You're James Hayes! I shouldn't be boring *you* with the problems of my crappy little life."

"You're not boring me. I'm interested. What were you about to say?"

"Really? You really want to hear it?"

"I really do. It's been a lifetime since I've sat down with a nice girl and had a normal conversation. I'm enjoying myself. Now, tell me what you were going to say."

"That I'm thinking about dropping out of school and returning home. I'm not happy here. I feel so…I don't know…out of place."

"Hey, now, wait a minute. I'm really sorry you're having such a rotten time, but I'd hate to see you do something drastic like drop out when you obviously have so much going for you. You can get through this rough spell, can't you? Everybody has one now and then.''

"Have you?''

"Yeah, sure. More than one. When my first album went double platinum, practically every reviewer in the country said it was a fluke and predicted I'd be a one-shot wonder. Certain people can always find something they don't like about you. And when they can't find something bad, they make it up. It happens to me all the time.''

"What do you do about it? Doesn't it hurt? I can't stand it when someone talks bad about me or excludes me.''

"Oh, yeah, it hurts like hell, but I like what I'm doing, so I keep going and I ignore what people say. That's what you have to do. Believe in yourself. You're the only person you have to please.''

She sighed. "You make it sound so easy.''

"It's not. Being different means you have to put up with a lot, especially from people who are ordinary. A time will come, though, when you'll be glad you're special.''

"I wish I believed that. Sometimes I feel like such a freak.''

"Trust me when I say that a few years from now you'll wonder why the opinion of these people ever mattered.''

"So you think I should tough it out?''

"Yeah, I do. People can't hurt you unless you give them the power to hurt you. Be strong, and don't let those jerks get away with making you feel bad about yourself. You don't *really* want to drop out of school, do you?''

"No,'' she said, shaking her head. "Not really. I want to be a journalist. I like finding out about people and telling their stories. And the program here is really good. I'm learning a lot.''

"Then don't let anybody push you into giving up your dream.'' He put his finger under her chin. "Now, show me that pretty smile of yours, and promise me you'll never again give anyone the power to hurt you.''

She smiled, and for once didn't feel as if her smile was ugly. "I promise.''

"That's my girl.''

Once the interviewer was finished with her questions, Kate and James talked for a couple of hours more. He shared stories about his half sister, Ellen, and he showed her a photograph of his brother, Bret, when he was younger, holding up a huge catfish he'd caught in their grandfather's pond.

"Jamie,'' Mr. Elliot called, and they both looked up. He tapped his watch.

"I guess Malcolm's trying to tell me I need to get ready for rehearsal. You're coming to hear us play tonight, aren't you? I'm giving a special concert for the students and faculty.''

"I don't have a ticket. I camped out for two days before they went on sale last month so I'd be sure to get one, but when the box office opened, they were gone in fifteen minutes.''

"Would you still like to come? I can have Malcolm arrange it.''

Her pulse leaped with expectation. "Are you serious? He can do that?"

"Malcolm can do almost anything." He motioned for Mr. Elliot, who immediately walked over. "Malcolm, I'd like Katie to be my guest at the concert tonight. Fix it for me, would you?"

"Sure thing, Jamie."

"And you'd better arrange for a chaperon. I don't want to destroy the young lady's reputation."

"Good idea." He scurried off.

"Okay, then," James told Kate, laughing at her stunned expression. "It's a date."

It's a date.

He meant it as a figure of speech, not a real date, but that didn't stop Kate from pretending as she sat in the audience that night, listening to James sing. He actually invited her up on stage, introduced her as his friend and sang a song to her. She didn't think she cared about anyone at that precise moment as much as she did him.

When the song ended, the audience went wild. James leaned over and gave her a kiss on the cheek, then escorted her to some steps at the side of the stage. "We're leaving right after the show," he said in her ear as the applause continued. "I won't see you again. You take care. And remember…be proud of your gifts."

"I will." As she looked at him, she knew the admiration and physical desire she felt for him showed openly in her face. All he had to do was ask her to stay with him and she would.

He smiled. "Go on, now. My world is no place for you."

She nodded, knowing he was right. "I'll never forget you, Jamie. I swear it."

"Sweet Katie, I envy the man who one day really steals your heart."

As SHE'D PROMISED, she never forgot him. He'd given her a precious gift that night. By singling her out, by announcing she was his friend, he'd elevated her to a position of importance. Most of the students who'd teased her stopped. Two or three treated her no differently, but it didn't matter because James had given her the power to disregard their pettiness.

She'd taken his advice and stopped apologizing for her intelligence. Instead, she'd made it work for her, first in her career as a journalist and later as a biographer.

For years after that she considered contacting him, to let him know how much his kindness that day had meant to her. But she knew he wouldn't remember her or might confuse her with one of a thousand other girls he'd met on the road, and she didn't want anything to spoil the magic of the most wonderful day of her life.

The idea of returning his kindness never left her, but offering James something that his fame and fortune couldn't provide seemed impossible. Now, at last, she could repay the debt, even if it *was* after his death. She was at the peak of her career, and her name on the cover of a book guaranteed it would be read by millions. With the twentieth anniversary of the release of his first album approaching, the timing was perfect. This was a chance to remind the world of his talent, rather than his vices.

Everything was coming together—finally. The only obstacle to her project and her peace of mind was a teenager holding a big fish—a kid who'd grown up to become a handsome, stubborn and confusing man. And Lord help her, he was every bit as fascinating as his older brother.

CHAPTER NINE

HE AWOKE DISORIENTED from a vivid dream. He sat up slowly, wondering where he'd been and how much he'd drunk to make him feel so bad. Images flashed in his brain but refused to stay long enough to capture. He remembered a woman. Sweet-smelling. An incredible mouth.

Mouth. That word stuck with him for some reason. He couldn't remember kissing her on the mouth or kissing her at all, only wanting to—badly. Something about her mouth, about the woman, was important. The answer teased him, then moved out of his reach.

Pulling the sheet away from his body, he looked down and swore. A quick glance at the other side of the bed was more comforting. He was buck naked and had a wound on his ribs he couldn't remember getting, but at least he was alone.

He tried to shake the dullness from his mind and concentrate on the woman's face. Her eyes had been green and her hair…brown. Or maybe red. It had been long. He was sure of only that, but the rest of it…her features…her name…continued to elude him.

He remembered her hair spread out across the pillow beside him, but had that really happened or was it part of the dream? He wasn't sure.

He yawned and ran a hand through his own hair.

The front was oily and plastered to his head. At the crown it stood up as it did every morning like the backward feathers on a Frizzle chicken. He needed a shower to clear his brain and get rid of the cloying smell of sweat that cloaked his aching body. Only he wasn't sure where the shower was, where *he* was.

He moved to get out of the bed and understood finally why he felt so awful. He was hurt. The pain shot through his leg from ankle to groin. He examined the bruise on his thigh. The leg was grossly swollen. Looking at it made him remember small pieces of the night before. The injury involved animals, but that made no sense. And it had something to do with the woman whose face he couldn't recall, which made even less sense.

The woman. His thoughts kept coming back to her, her laugh, her smell. Lavender, he thought the fragrance was. For reasons he couldn't explain, the memories were frightening, as well as pleasant. She posed some threat to him, this woman.

Confusing. Too much for his brain to sort out at the moment.

A gentle knock at the door had him scrambling to cover himself. He dragged the sheet to his waist as a head popped around the door. *Her* head. The woman who haunted him.

"I'm glad to see you finally decided to wake up. I was getting worried."

When he didn't speak she opened the door wider and came in. The shirt she wore had to be his. The tail hung to her knees and the short sleeves fell below her elbows. Her legs were bare below the shirt, leaving him to wonder what she had on under it. Her hair flowed in waves over her shoulders and a becoming blush marked her cheeks.

From the look of her, they'd had sex. From the instant reaction of his body to her presence in the room, the sex had been good. Damn good. Too bad he couldn't remember it.

She'd stopped inside the doorway, obviously waiting for him to say something.

"Bret?"

His memory came rushing back to assault him, and the pain was worse than the kick of the horse. He knew now where he was. And he knew why the lovely woman in front of him filled him with both lust and dread.

"Are you okay?"

Several seconds passed before he could answer. "Yeah," he managed to croak out, surprised he could find his voice at all. "Just a little out of it."

She gave him a sympathetic smile, one corner of her mouth rising higher than the other. "Maybe you'll feel better once you've had something to eat and you clean up. Are you okay to take a shower?"

"I think so."

"Let me know when you're through and I'll bring you some food."

When she'd gone, he fell back on the bed with a groan, putting his forearm over his eyes. Kathryn Morgan. Here! In his house!

And walking around half-naked.

He didn't have to lift up the sheet again to know he was fully aroused. *Hell!*

A SMELL EMBRACED HIM when he finished his shower and hobbled into the hall. This smell he dearly loved, but it had never filled the air in this house in all the years he'd lived here—bacon frying.

He made his way to the kitchen as fast as the crutches would allow. The sight that met him made him stop abruptly. Kate was standing at the stove with her back to him, swishing her hips from side to side to a classic Fleetwood Mac song on the radio. She had a fork in her hand that she banged in rhythm on the old iron skillet.

She bent over to check something in the oven and the shirt eased up the backs of her thighs.

"Nice outfit," he said, startling her. She shot upward and whirled, self-consciously yanking down the shirt.

"Do you always sneak up on people like that?"

"Only when they're wearing my clothes and dancing in my kitchen."

She glanced down at the shirt and grimaced. "I hope you don't mind. My clothes had blood on them and smelled like horse. I washed them and hung them outside, but they aren't quite dry yet."

The back door was open and he could see the shorts, red top and two scraps of white skimpy underwear flapping in the breeze on his clothesline. If all her clothes were out there, then under that shirt she had on... His gaze went down her body and back to her face, which had suddenly taken on the color of a ripe plum.

"You really shouldn't be walking around on that leg," she said. "Go back to bed and I'll bring you a tray."

"I need to sit up awhile."

"Okay, but if you're going to stay in here, at least sit down so you won't fall."

Bret limped over to the table, putting his crutches under the chair, out of the way. A Mystic Waters song began to play on the radio on the counter, and he reached over and switched it off.

She watched him until he was seated, then turned back to the stove to slide something around in the pan he hoped really was bacon.

"Time for another pill," she said. "Would you like some orange juice with it?"

"I'll take one in a minute. I didn't think I had any orange juice."

"Aubrey was nice enough to run to the store this morning and pick up a few things. I knew you'd be hungry when you woke up since you didn't eat last night. Do you want me to pour you some juice? We also have coffee and milk."

"I'll take coffee," he said without hesitation. Bacon *and* decent coffee? And he was pretty certain she had biscuits in the oven. The woman was becoming more attractive by the minute.

She took the percolator from the counter and filled his cup. "I assumed you like it perked when I went looking for a coffeemaker and could only find this. Which reminds me, are you in the habit of keeping your dirty glasses under the sink?"

"I wasn't expecting you to be here long enough to look under my sink. I was hiding them."

"Oh," she said, chuckling. "Well, I was afraid you'd get bugs, so I washed them and put them away."

"You didn't have to do that."

"I didn't mind. I needed something to keep me busy while I was waiting for you to wake up."

He watched as she skillfully cracked eggs with one hand and stirred something on the stove with the other. Five minutes later she set a plate of food in front of him that rivaled anything served at the grill—bacon, scrambled eggs, grits and homemade biscuits with gravy.

When he'd eaten almost everything in sight, he leaned back in the chair, put his hands on his middle and groaned. By his best estimate, he'd eaten five eggs, at least eight pieces of bacon, and half a dozen biscuits. He'd washed it all down with three cups of coffee.

They sat for a while, sipping coffee in companionable silence, Bret thinking how strange it was to be doing so, given the events of the past forty-eight hours.

"Aubrey also went to the post office and got your mail." She stood and got it from the counter, then began clearing the table. "If you'll tell me what you'd like to eat, I'll go to the store and get more groceries. And make of list of anything else you need done while I'm in town."

"Look, just because you were there when I got hurt doesn't mean you have to take care of me."

She stopped clearing and sat back down. "I know, but it seems to me that it's the ideal arrangement, since I'm in town for the next few days, anyway. I need something to keep me from getting bored, and you need someone to take care of you."

"I can take care of myself."

"But it's silly for me to sit around in the motel

when I could come over here and work on my laptop just as easily. Plus, I can cook for you.''

''I don't need you to cook for me, Morgan.''

''Judging by the look of your refrigerator and freezer, somebody should. Do you eat everything raw or d'you live off frozen microwave dinners?''

''I can cook okay.'' It was a good thing Sallie couldn't talk and dispute that.

''Hayes, I'm better than okay, I'm fabulous. I learned the basics from my grandmother who grew up in Mississippi, and I've even taken classes. So I can cook anything, including the home-style kinds of things you probably go for...like, oh, country-fried steak, barbecued pork, mashed potatoes with gravy, peas, turnip greens and cornbread made with buttermilk. Doesn't that sound good?''

''No,'' he said, but with little conviction, starting to fantasize about that country-fried steak.

''How about pork chops stuffed with mushrooms? Or pot roast with potatoes, carrots and onions? I'm great with breakfast dishes, too—pancakes, crepes, pecan waffles, blintzes. Don't you want me to fix you some of those?''

''No,'' he said again, but he wondered what kind of pancakes.

''My specialty is desserts—cakes, pies, brownies and different cookies. And, of course, I make a terrific homemade peach cobbler. It's the best thing you ever put in your mouth.''

She shut up then and waited for him to protest a final time, but he didn't because she'd gotten him with the peach cobbler, and they both knew it. Damn those gossiping waitresses at the grill.

"You don't play fair," he grumbled.

She smiled innocently. "Why, I have no idea what you mean."

KATE SLID COOKIES into the oven, set the timer and silently said a prayer of thanks to her grandmother for insisting she learn to cook.

Bret had gone back to bed after eating, giving her time to ride to the motel with Aubrey and pick up her car. She'd keep her room. Moving in with Bret—even temporarily—wouldn't be appropriate, but he'd agreed she could spend the daylight hours at his house. At night she'd return to the motel to work and sleep.

She'd changed into slacks and a sleeveless top, checked to see if there were any messages and retrieved her computer, also stopping at the pharmacy to fill the prescription for pain medicine Bret needed but swore he didn't.

His house was now clean and stocked with enough groceries to last a couple of weeks. A supply of bones in the refrigerator would distract Sallie and guarantee Kate safe passage to and from her car.

She turned down the flame on the beef stew she'd planned for his dinner, then went to the bedroom to check on him. He was sprawled on top of the sheet wearing nothing but cutoff sweatpants that he hadn't even bothered to tie. They drooped precariously off his slim hips and outlined every curve and bulge.

Quietly she picked up the clothes he'd taken off last night and discarded on the chair. He probably couldn't wear jeans until the swelling went down, but these needed soaking to keep the bloodstains from setting.

Back in the kitchen she emptied his pants pockets. Wallet, comb, string, nails, pieces of hay. She put the hay in the trash and the other things on the counter. She dug into the small front pocket, and her fingers touched something little and plastic. No, not plastic, gelatin, she realized when she pulled out the gray-and-red capsule.

The medication the doctor had given Bret was on the table, and she opened the bottle and shook one of the capsules into her palm. Gray and red. The man-ufacturer's name inscribed on both capsules was the same. This had to be the penicillin pill she'd given him last night and he'd said he'd taken. But why had he put it in his pocket and then lied about it?

She wrapped the pill in a paper towel and stuck it in her purse.

Bret slept for several hours. She passed the time by tidying up his house and browsing through the books in his living room. She was surprised to find two of her own—the biography on Tipper Gore and the one she'd written on the terrorist group Shining Path as an extension of her Pulitzer prize–winning newspaper articles.

She opened the doors to the lower shelves, expect-ing more books, and found stacks of video cassette tapes. The dates and cities on the labels, she realized suddenly, corresponded to major concerts of Mystic Waters.

Kate had some of the same tapes in her office, cop-ied from film so she could play them on the VCR. Many were from her private collection. The others, she and Marcus had spent countless hours searching for in the film archives of the universities where the band had performed, and in the holdings of independent filmmakers.

The band's record company had videotapes of every performance, but Marianne Hayes Conner had issued an edict denying Kate access to her son's work.

One label in particular caught her attention. Greensboro, 1991. She'd never watched this entire concert, only pieces of it in fifteen-second sound bites on the evening news. She popped the tape in the VCR and pushed Play.

A ripple of something powerful yet difficult to define moved through her as James appeared and his sweet clear voice filled the air.

Kate couldn't see the audience, but she knew what it was experiencing. James didn't just sing; James set emotion to music. He seemed to be able to look inside your soul, read what was there and then express your feelings in a way you never could.

At sixteen he'd put together a garage band with his childhood friend, Lenny Dean, and began playing clubs around Chattanooga and Nashville. At nineteen he released *Free Fall*. The eclectic little album used the best elements of rock, folk, blues and pop, and was so unique that it sold more than a million copies the first week.

Like his music, James was also appealingly different. Young people found someone to admire and imitate, a voice that represented their collective conscience. In a decade defined by money and self-gratification, James often sang about the environment, the plight of farmers and human rights. Most importantly, he *lived* according to his beliefs. At least, he'd appeared to.

She pressed Fast Forward and moved to a point later in the concert, where the band was rocking and a camera pan of the audience showed thousands of kids dancing and screaming. She had to be pretty close to the spot where—

"You won't see anything on the tape," Bret said from behind her. She jumped, embarrassed at being caught looking at his personal things.

He moved unsteadily through the doorway on his crutches and across the room to where she stood. But instead of stopping the tape, he advanced it and said, "Right about here was where those kids got killed, but you won't see anything out of the ordinary. I've never been able to see anything, anyway."

Silently they watched for several minutes, but Bret was right. All Kate saw was enthusiastic fans having a good time. The band hadn't known until later that three girls had been crushed as the crowd—whipped into a frenzy by the music—had tried to press too close to the stage.

"I was told that James was pretty shaken up when he found out," Kate said.

He nodded, not taking his eyes from the screen. "I don't think he ever got over it. He felt guilty, depressed, angry. And he believed the deaths were an omen."

Kate had never heard this before. "An omen of what?"

"Of even worse things to come." He stopped the tape and pushed the button to rewind it. "He was convinced something else bad was going happen. He just didn't know what.''

''Are you saying he had some sort of premonition?''

He hesitated, then shook his head. ''No, not really a premonition, but a feeling that things were never going to be the same. He thought what happened to those girls was not only a tragedy, but a sign that what he and Lenny had envisioned when they formed the band had somehow gotten distorted. The music was supposed to be good, not destructive.''

''Is that why he spoke of quitting?''

''Partly. He had other reasons.''

''Lenny's illness.''

''Yes, that was one of them. When Lenny started having psychotic episodes and had to be institutionalized, James was really...distraught. He and Lenny had been best friends since they were kids, yet he'd had no idea the guy was in such bad shape. But it wasn't only Lenny that made him think about giving it all up. After the concert where those girls died, things started to unravel and he felt responsible.''

''When Lauren killed herself, did he blame himself for that, too?''

He swallowed hard before answering. ''I guess he did. We didn't talk about Lauren. She was a touchy subject between us.''

''Because you were both in love with her?''

Kate waited for his answer without taking a breath, watching the emotions reflected in his eyes. ''Yes,'' he said finally, confirming what she'd suspected for many years. ''Because we were both in love with her.''

The tape stopped. He ejected it and returned it to its case. Kate followed him as he took it across the room and put it back on the shelf.

"Then Lauren's suicide must have been as difficult for you as it was for James," she said. "I'm sorry."

"Don't be. I dealt with it a long time ago."

He closed the cabinet abruptly and headed toward the kitchen with his slow awkward gait. Kate walked silently behind him, although she was burning with questions about Lauren and the singer's relationship with the Hayes brothers.

Her curiosity went beyond needing answers for the book. As a woman, she wanted to know what was so special about Lauren that two very different yet equally impressive men like James and Bret had both fallen in love with her.

Lauren had certainly been beautiful and a good backup singer, but she hadn't had the talent for the solo career she wanted. Without James's help, Lauren would never have achieved any recognition at all. The reviews of her two solos on the last Mystic Waters album had been brutal.

Kate's empathy, though, wasn't with Lauren and her failed dreams, and she was surprised to find it wasn't even with James.

When she looked back on those tragic events, the person she felt sorry for was Bret. The woman he loved had killed herself after realizing she'd never be a star. Then, eight months later his brother had died, and in a way that left Bret feeling responsible. That was too much pain for any one person to handle.

CHAPTER TEN

TWO DAYS LATER, Kate's manuscript arrived from her brother by courier, and Bret settled in the swing on the front porch to read it. When she came to the door for the tenth time in an hour to peek out at him, he wondered what excuse she'd offer to justify the interruption. Were there any she hadn't used yet? He didn't have to wait long to find out.

"Just straightening up in the living room and thought I'd check on you," she said, talking to him through the screen.

He shifted in the swing with a "Uh-huh," not looking up from the page but resisting the urge to laugh. Out of the corner of his eye, he watched her move nervously from foot to foot. He couldn't see her hands, but on one of her earlier trips, he'd noticed she'd already chewed off her fingernail polish and started on the nails.

And he was only on page 308. By the time he'd finished the more than six hundred pages, she'd likely have chewed right up to her elbows.

"How's it coming?" she asked.

"Get lost, Morgan."

"But I—"

"Get lost."

"Oh, all right." The bare feet and legs disappeared

from his peripheral vision without further comment from their owner, leaving Bret and Sallie alone on the porch—for the moment. He was certain it wouldn't be long before some other excuse would bring Kate to the screen door again.

First, there'd been the pillow for his back, the glass of tea in case he got thirsty, followed by the pencil to mark any parts of the manuscript he thought they should talk about. Then she'd made three trips to find out if the pillow was soft enough, the tea sweet enough and to ask whether he wanted a pen instead of the pencil.

After that, the cleaning frenzy had begun: chairs, porch floor, steps. She'd pinched the dead leaves from the hanging plants and rubbed the windows so hard that the squeaking had almost driven him insane. Unfortunately that hadn't been the end of it.

When she'd run out of reasons for being on the porch, she'd moved her base of attack to the living room so she could peek out the door every few minutes and see how far along he was in his reading. In the past hour she'd rearranged the books in his bookshelf, swept the floor, dusted, taken down the curtains for a trip to the dry cleaners and gathered his throw rugs for torture on the clothesline with a stiff brush.

"Hey, don't worry," he told a trembling Sallie, who had pressed herself tightly against his side. "I swear I won't let her get you."

The normally ferocious dog had watched the activity with growing alarm, apparently deciding she was next in line for a good cleaning. The intensity of her growls had lessened with each of Kate's appearances until the only sound she made was a low pitiful whimper.

He patted her reassuringly. "It's okay. I understand. She scares the hell out of me, too."

He found his place and went back to reading, knowing that the only cure for Kate's ailment was for him to finish. So far he'd been mesmerized. She'd captured his and his brother's childhood on paper with such clarity that reading the accounts was like reliving it.

It bothered him to destroy what she'd worked so hard to create. Sadly, he realized he had no choice.

The screen door squeaked and he looked up, expecting Kate. His hired hands, Aubrey and Willie, each carried a bowl.

"Man, look at you," Aubrey said with a grin, shaking his head. "Feet propped up, a big pillow behind your back. A couple more days of this and you ain't gonna want to git back to work."

"You know me better than that."

"Yep, I do."

Aubrey folded his tall lanky frame into a nearby rocking chair. Willie, in his usual way of trying not to be obtrusive, chose to sit on the steps and quietly eat.

Bret eyed the contents of Aubrey's bowl. "Is that my peach cobbler you're eating up?"

"We figured we better eat it to keep you from gettin' fat, seein' as how you're not doin' any work."

"You better have left me some, you sorry rascal."

"Well, now, maybe we did and maybe we didn't. Can't rightly remember if we got the last of it or not." He took off his cap and scratched his head in feigned confusion. "Seems to me we scraped the bottom of that bowl. Ain't that right, brother?" Willie snickered and bobbed his head in agreement. "Maybe if you snuggle up to that pretty little gal, she might cook you another one."

Bret shook his head, used to Aubrey's good-natured ribbing. "You're so full of shit sometimes."

"Well, now, that's true, but if I had a woman who looked like that waitin' on me like she's waitin' on you, I'd sure be doin' me some snugglin'. More than snugglin', if you catch my drift."

Bret did. And while he'd never admit it to Aubrey, the idea had crossed his mind with alarming frequency the past few days. He'd been in a state of partial arousal ever since Kate had walked in this morning in blue-jean shorts and her hair spilling all loose and shining across her shoulders.

When she'd bent over him a little while ago to put the pillow behind his back, her top had gaped open at the neck and he'd had lace-covered breasts staring him right in the face. That was too much temptation for a man who'd spent more time with horses than women in the past few years, and had nearly forgotten what breasts looked like.

"Brother, I do believe he's givin' it a hard think," Aubrey said, making Bret realize he'd been doing exactly that.

Bret growled, "Quit your jawin'," making both Aubrey and Willie chuckle. Heat rose noticeably to Bret's face.

"Gettin' hot imagining it?" Aubrey asked.

The door opened again and Kate came out, wearing her shoes and carrying her billfold and keys. She had books under her arm and his living-room curtains in a big ball. Aubrey and Willie both shot up and almost ran into each other trying to help her. Sallie whimpered, jumped down and scampered off the porch with her tail between her legs.

"Here, ma'am, let us tote that for you," Aubrey said, taking the curtains and books, then immediately passing them to Willie.

"Thank you, Aubrey, and I want to thank you again for bringing the oysters. That was very thoughtful of you."

"My pleasure ma'am. Hope you enjoy 'em."

"Oysters?" Bret asked.

"Yes," Kate said with a nod. "He brought us some mountain oysters to warm up for our dinner."

Aubrey grinned.

"Do you like mountain oysters?" Bret asked her.

"Well, I don't know, because I've never eaten any, but the idea of oysters grown in freshwater ponds sounds intriguing."

Aubrey's grin grew wider.

"Well," Kate said. "Bret, will you be all right for a little while?"

"I think I can take care of myself for an hour."

"It may be a little longer than that. I had Marcus throw in some extra copies of my books in that package he sent. I want to drop them off at the library for Miss Emma."

"I'll manage."

"I made your lunch and left it in the oven." She looked at him oddly, walked over and gently felt his forehead and cheek. "You look flushed. You aren't getting too hot out here, are you?"

Aubrey and Willie exchanged grins behind her back, making Bret narrow his eyes at them in warning. "I'm fine," he told her. "Go on and run your errands. These two comedians and I have business to discuss, anyway."

"Okay, I'll be back in a little while." She turned to leave, then stopped. "Oh, while I'm in town I might go by the courthouse to see if I can look at the file on Henry's mother. Do you have any problem with me doing that? I'm curious about what's happening with her case and what motions her attorney might have filed. I used to cover a court beat for the newspaper, so I could decipher the legal mumbo jumbo for you if you'd like."

"Go ahead. I'd be thankful for the information." He gave her the name of the mother and boyfriend.

Bret turned in the swing and watched while she and Willie walked to the car. His gaze went to her denim-clad behind and the alluring way it swayed when she moved.

"I might have to kill you over those oysters," he told Aubrey casually, not taking his eyes off Kate. She bent over and arranged the curtains on the back seat, putting a twist in his gut that would take a tractor to yank out. "She has no idea what they are."

Aubrey chuckled. "A man's gotta have a little fun now and then."

"Yeah, well, it seems to me you have more than your share of fun."

"Ain't *my* fun I'm worried about, boss man, it's yours."

Bret turned and looked at him. "Meaning?"

"Ain't you ever heard? Mountain oysters is supposed to be one of them afra-dizziacks."

RECORDS OF THE CIRCUIT court weren't computerized, and it took the clerk a while to locate the files Kate requested on Henry's mother and her ex-boyfriend.

Next she went to the probate and tax assessor's offices to check Bret's land records. He'd seemed forthright about his life here, but she wouldn't make the mistake of not confirming what he'd told her. Erroneous information, sometimes given unintentionally by a source, was a biographer's nightmare if it appeared in print; it could taint the entire book.

She quickly located the records, comparing the descriptions to the assessed value of the property. In March of 1992 he'd bought his farm and the old family homestead, valued collectively at $750,000. Where had he gotten that kind of money? From James? His brother was still living then. From George Conner? His stepfather had a lucrative dental practice at the time.

Someone must have helped him with the purchase. He'd been twenty-five with no college degree and a less-than-stellar employment history. She made a note to herself to check where Bret was working that specific year.

He'd subdivided the more valuable property—the homestead—four years later, retaining ownership of fifty acres, as he'd told her. Getting down another index, she followed the paper trail for the remaining six hundred acres, the land he'd donated for Pine Acres. The current owner was listed as...the Mason Bret Hayes Foundation.

"Well, well," she muttered. "You're simply full of surprises, aren't you?"

He'd set up a foundation to operate the ranch. Why go through the red tape and tax hassle of that when he could have used the foundation his mother had created in James's name?

She paid for copies, dropped the signed books off at the library and went to the motel room. Cell phones were insecure for the kind of information she and Marcus often swapped, so she'd told him to call her room with any messages. He'd left five. She dialed her office.

"Kate, how about checking in more often?" Marcus said. "I don't like not hearing from you for days."

"But I've e-mailed you every night."

"Doesn't count. I need to hear a real voice once in a while."

"I'm sorry. What was so urgent that you had to leave me this many messages?"

"I dug up a few things you'll be interested in. Nothing on the drug allergies you asked me to look into, but the rest of what I have you'll want right away. Do you want to download?"

She looked at the clock on the bedside table and saw that she'd been gone from Bret's for more than two hours. Before she left, she wanted to go on-line to check the law on capital murder in Alabama. She'd better hurry.

"No, I'm pressed for time. Tell me briefly what you found, then put everything in a file on my hard drive with today's date and I'll dial in tonight and get it."

"Will do."

He gave her a brief account of what it cost to run a breeding farm the size of Bret's and how much he could expect to net each year.

"From what I've been able to find out, Hayes has a good reputation, his stock is excellent and he probably makes a fair income, but he could do a lot better if he wanted to. I talked to some of his competitors and they say he'd have a first-class operation if he'd expand and stop turning down business."

"Probably worried about losing his privacy if he gets too big. Or maybe he doesn't need to work. Conceivably he could be living modestly on what's left of his inheritance."

"I'm pretty sure he's not."

"What makes you say that?"

"I found news stories on seventeen other ranches he's set up."

"Seventeen?" Kate's surprise made her bolt into a sitting position on the bed. "There are seventeen more of them?"

"Yep, they're all over the South. Hayes built them through a separate foundation, and that's why we didn't pick up on them until now."

"The Mason Bret Hayes Foundation."

"Yeah, how'd you know?"

She outlined what she'd learned at the courthouse.

"I never dreamed there was more than one ranch, Marcus. If he's supporting seventeen, this goes beyond a local project. We're looking at a major charity using an incredible amount of money, possibly even more than Bret had to begin with. Where's he getting it?"

"I think I've figured that out. Up until today I thought the entire seventy-two million his mother and sister got after taxes went to set up the James Hayes Foundation."

She frowned. "That's not the case?"

"No, I don't think so, and I don't think all the annual income from investments and music royalties is going into that foundation, either. I can't be absolutely sure because the records aren't open, but working backward and using what I could find through public sources, I added up the contributions the foundation's made to university music programs, scholarship funds and other charities. Then I factored in what I estimate the investments should be bringing in annually. The revenue's coming up short of the expenditures."

"How short?" She picked up a pen and started jotting notes.

"Way short. A minimum of twenty-five million a year."

She stopped writing, stunned. "That can't be right."

"Sis, either that money *isn't* being invested, which is fiscally irresponsible, or it's going somewhere else."

"And you think they're giving it to Bret's foundation?"

"I do. While he probably used his inheritance to build the first few ranches, I think he's maintaining them and building new ones using the income from James's music royalties. He's also made several large donations there in Alabama."

"I know about those. They all benefit children in some way."

"That family's funneling money right and left, and it's got my radar hoppin', but I'll be damned if I can find even one instance where they've used any of it for personal gain. Why set up this second foundation? They're both being funded from the same source. Why don't they throw all the money into the original foundation and dole it out for their individual pet projects?"

Because, she suddenly realized, Bret wanted *his* name on the ranches. Could he really be that self-absorbed? Maybe he hadn't changed at all.

But if *that* was true, why build the ranches in the first place?

They were missing something, something important, and until they had it, none of this would fall into place.

"I don't get it, either," Kate told Marcus, "but at least one mystery is solved. We now know why Bret lives the way he does. He controls a fortune, but he gives away every penny."

"Yeah, great guy. I might be impressed if he'd earned it."

BRET GOT ANXIOUS as lunchtime came and went, and Kate failed to return. He ate some of the lasagna she'd left in the oven, a double helping of cobbler, then hobbled back out to the porch.

She hadn't returned by one o'clock. Or by two. She'd be hard-pressed to find any trouble in this town, so he had no reason to worry about her. Which meant that he missed her. And that didn't sit well with him at all.

The sound of a car on the dirt road made him look up. In a few seconds he could see flashes of white as Kate's rental made its way along the pine-bordered drive to the yard. He put down the manuscript and used the crutches to push himself onto his feet as she stopped and got out. Sallie instinctively ran snarling toward the intruder. Kate froze, but before Bret could react, Sallie saw who it was, whimpered and crawled under the porch.

"What's wrong with that crazy dog?" Kate asked, retrieving a stack of papers from the back seat. She closed the door, jogged up the walk and the steps. "She's been acting weird all day."

"She's afraid of you."

"Oh, sure."

Bret opened the door for her and followed her in. Depositing the papers and herself on the couch, she took off her tennis shoes and folded her legs under her. Bret remained standing but leaned heavily on the crutches.

"Only one thing terrifies Sallie and that's a bath. With you running around cleaning everything this morning, she thought she was next."

Kate seemed to consider that.

"Oh, no," he warned her. "Don't get any ideas."

"Okay. No bath for Sallie. How's the reading? Get much done while I was gone?"

"Some."

"And do you like it?" Her eyes shone with hope. "Are you going to help me?"

"I'll let you know when I finish."

"When will that be? Are you purposely reading slowly just to aggravate me?"

He glanced at her pointedly.

"Okay, okay," she said, "I promise I won't bug you about it again. I'm eager to hear what you think, and I guess I'm a little nervous about you reading the parts where you're mentioned. Some are a bit... harsh."

"More than a bit."

She grimaced. "I see you've gotten to them already."

"I've hit a few."

"And I can tell you're ticked off. You're grinding your teeth."

"I'm not happy with them, but I'll comment when I've read them all."

"I'm sure you will." She stood and gathered up her shoes. "Well, I think I'll work while you read. The papers on Henry's mother are here, too, if you want to take a look. The motions are all pretty routine, but it's an interesting case. I did a little research online when I stopped at the motel to get my messages. If the boyfriend's going to testify that she set the fire, she'd better plea bargain if she wants to make sure she doesn't meet Big Yellow Mama."

"What's that?"

"That's what they call the electric chair in this state."

"You think they'll execute her?"

"Well, it's unlikely, but it could happen. You never know what a judge or a jury's going to do. I wouldn't want to gamble my life on what twelve strangers might recommend to a court, and with the victim being a small child, she can't hope for any public sympathy. While the odds are she won't get a death sentence, the only way she can be sure is to make a plea in exchange for life without parole. Of course, there's always the possibility she could go to trial and get acquitted.''

"Please tell me that can't happen.''

''That can happen in any case, but I don't think it'll happen here. The boyfriend's the key, though. If he comes through as promised, then I think everything will be okay. The case looks good from a prosecution standpoint.''

''Explain.''

''Well, even if she didn't intend to kill the children when she committed arson, it won't help her. As long as she started the fire, a child died in the fire and the state can prove it, her intent to kill or lack of intent isn't an issue. By law, she committed capital murder.''

''So her pretending she didn't know the kids were in the house won't matter?''

''Right. As far as the prosecution's case is concerned, it makes no difference.''

''I'd be satisfied to see her in jail for the rest of her life.''

''Me, too.'' Kate headed for the kitchen, then stopped and turned. ''Oh, before I forget…I went to the library and was reminded of something Miss Emma told me last week. Can I ask you about it? It has me stumped.''

''What?''

''She said you got the news of your brother's death

Tyler Brides

It happened one weekend...

Quinn and Molly Spencer are delighted to accept three bookings for their newly opened B&B, Breakfast Inn Bed, located in America's favorite hometown, Tyler, Wisconsin.

But Gina Santori is anything but thrilled to discover her best friend has tricked her into sharing a room with the man who broke her heart eight years ago....

And Delia Mayhew can hardly believe that she's gotten herself locked in the Breakfast Inn Bed basement with the sexiest man in America.

Then there's Rebecca Salter. She's turned up at the Inn in her wedding gown. Minus her groom.

Come home to Tyler for three delightful novellas by three of your favorite authors: Kristine Rolofson, Heather MacAllister and Jacqueline Diamond.

HARLEQUIN®
Makes any time special ™

PHTB

Play **LUCKY HEARTS** for this...

exciting FREE gift!
This surprise mystery gift could be yours free

when you play **LUCKY HEARTS!**
...then continue your lucky streak with a sweetheart of a deal!

1. Play Lucky Hearts as instructed on the opposite page.

2. Send back this card and you'll receive 2 brand-new Harlequin Superromance® novels. These books have a cover price of $4.50 each in the U.S. and $5.25 each in Canada, but they are yours to keep absolutely free.

3. There's no catch! You're under no obligation to buy anything. We charge nothing—ZERO—for your first shipment. And you don't have to make any minimum number of purchases—not even one!

4. The fact is thousands of readers enjoy receiving their books by mail from the Harlequin Reader Service®. They enjoy the convenience of home delivery...they like getting the best new novels at discount prices, BEFORE they're available in stores...and they love their *Heart to Heart* subscriber newsletter featuring author news, horoscopes, recipes, book reviews and much more!

5. We hope that after receiving your free books you'll want to remain a subscriber. But the choice is yours—to continue or cancel, any time at all! So why not take us up on our invitation, with no risk of any kind. You'll be glad you did!

Visit us online at
www.eHarlequin.com

The Harlequin Reader Service®—Here's how it works:

Accepting your 2 free books and gift places you under no obligation to buy anything. You may keep the books and gift and return the shipping statement marked "cancel." If you do not cancel, about a month later we'll send you 6 additional novels and bill you just $3.80 each in the U.S., or $4.21 each in Canada, plus 25¢ shipping & handling delivery per book and applicable taxes if any.* That's the complete price and — compared to cover prices of $4.50 each in the U.S. and $5.25 each in Canada — it's quite a bargain! You may cancel at any time, but if you choose to continue, every month we'll send you 6 more books, which you may either purchase at the discount price or return to us and cancel your subscription.

*Terms and prices subject to change without notice. Sales tax applicable in N.Y. Canadian residents will be charged applicable provincial taxes and GST.

while you were with her the next day. Why didn't your mother contact you earlier?''

''You and Miss Emma must have gotten along pretty well. She sure has been talkative.''

''She likes me. She's read all my books.''

''Just my luck.''

''So what happened? Why didn't your family call you?''

''They tried to call Friday night, but I unplugged the phone when I got in from the concert. I was still angry at Jamie and sick emotionally. I thought he might call, and I couldn't go through a repeat of our fight.''

''I figured there was a logical explanation.''

''I slept in Saturday morning and didn't think about the phone still being unplugged when I went to town to return my overdue books. Some people came in while I was at the library and they'd heard the news on the radio. They started telling Miss Emma while I was standing at the counter. They didn't realize they were talking about my brother.''

''That must have been horrible for you.''

His voice cracked when he said truthfully, ''It was the worst day of my life.''

BRET WENT BACK to the porch to read while Kate worked at the kitchen table on her laptop. At six-thirty he finished, but he didn't go inside immediately. He needed time to get himself under control. Her words were too powerful, her descriptions so vivid that for the past few hours he'd been transported to the past. And it wasn't a friendly place for him.

As she'd said, she'd been harsh. Everything he

wished he could erase was there in damning detail: the bar fights, the inability to keep a job, the petty jealousies. They would overshadow the ranches. Pine Acres and the other good things he'd accomplished in the past few years would all be for nothing.

In the kitchen he found her engrossed in the words on the computer screen, her legs tucked under her in the chair and her hair pulled into a big knot on top of her head. Pencils stuck out of the knot at weird angles, and she wore glasses, which he'd never seen on her.

He watched for several minutes. Seeing Kate like this, he could imagine her as a little girl with a big brain, probably talking foreign policy while other children dressed dolls and had tea parties. That child was still very much a part of her, despite the toughened hide she'd developed as she grew. The vulnerability he'd seen in her expression when she'd asked what he thought of her manuscript pulled at his insides. He'd wanted to hold her, to protect the child hiding within.

God, that was a laughable notion. Him? The protector? Hell, he resembled the dragon more than he did the knight. During some of his worst times with a bottle, he'd probably breathed fire and devoured a few virgin sacrifices.

She paused in her typing and looked up, but her mind was still somewhere else and her gaze remained distant and unfocused.

"Hey," he said, startling her.

She jumped, noticed him and smiled. "You scared me," she said, quickly taking off the glasses. She

patted her hair, found the pencils and removed them, also untying the knot to let her hair fall free.

He hopped to the table on one foot and sat down across from her, hooking one forearm through the wooden crutches and using them as an armrest. "My eyes have given out for the day. How about we both knock off, have a leisurely supper and relax with a movie or some music?"

"You want me to stay after we eat?"

"Why not? Are you so crazy about that motel?"

"Hardly. Even the roaches refuse to stay there."

"Then spend the evening with me."

She glanced at the screen. "I usually work for a few hours when I leave here."

"Can't it wait?"

"I suppose so, but I normally don't hang out with people I want to interview. Being too friendly with a source gives the appearance that I could be influenced."

"Wait a minute," he said, leaning forward. "Are you saying you *can* be influenced?"

"Of course not. I would never let my personal feelings color my professional judgment."

"Then it's a moot point. I'll make the salad if you'll get me the lettuce and tomatoes out of the refrigerator." She didn't move, so he appealed to her sympathy. "Well, go on. I'm injured and you're supposed to be taking care of me."

She sighed, got out of the chair and went to the refrigerator, but she threw him a look over her shoulder that said she was humoring him.

Nonetheless, an hour later they'd baked potatoes

and a green-bean casserole, fixed a salad and warmed the mountain oysters.

"Mmm, these oysters are wonderful," she said, picking up another one with her fingers and taking a bite. "They look and taste a little like fried chicken livers."

She chewed a few seconds, then in a provocative way that had Bret writhing in his chair, she moaned and sucked the juice off her fingertips.

"Some people believe mountain oysters are an aphrodisiac," he said. "That's what Aubrey believes, anyway, although I've never heard that before today. I guess it's an old wives' tale."

"You know what they say about old wives' tales, don't you?"

"What's that?"

She wiggled her eyebrows and said, "Old wives ought to know."

They both laughed and she bit into another oyster.

Bret cleared his throat. "Aubrey's also of the opinion that I'm lacking in female attention. I think he's decided we'd be good together."

Their eyes met and the unspoken question hung between them: *Could* they be good together?

"Ridiculous notion," she said, looking away.

"Ridiculous," he echoed.

"But it's sweet of Aubrey to do this."

Bret chuckled. Then the chuckle turned into a deep laugh as he thought about what "sweet" Aubrey had done.

"What's so funny?" she asked.

"This wasn't only an attempt to get us together. Aubrey saw it as a way to play a little practical joke."

She helped herself to another oyster, and out of dev-
ilment he waited until she'd put it in her mouth and
started to chew. "He lied to you about where mountain oysters come from. They aren't really oysters or
grown in ponds. They're from bulls, the parts they
snip off when they're castrated."

The chewing stopped abruptly, and disbelief, or
maybe it was horror, replaced her look of enjoyment.
Her mouth was too full to talk, so she grunted what
he interpreted as an appeal to admit he was joking.

"Sorry." He shook his head. "That's what they
are. Some people around here consider them a deli-
cacy."

She politely covered her mouth with her napkin and
spit the offending meat into it, then drank a full glass
of tea in a few deep swallows.

"I can't believe you sat there and let me eat these
things and didn't tell me."

"You just got through saying how good they are."

"That was before I knew what I was eating!" She
picked up one of the pot holders she'd used earlier
and threw it at him. It missed by a foot, sailing over
his left shoulder and landing on the floor.

"It's no different from eating fish eggs or snails in
some fancy restaurant," he told her.

"I suppose not, but those poor bulls."

"Steers now," he corrected.

"Sorry. Steers."

"Do you know what sound a steer makes?"

"I don't know. Moo?"

"Ouch!"

She broke down and laughed, and he told her another joke, then another, so he could hear the sound

again and again, and watch the way her eyes sparkled and the way her mouth crooked up and her nose wrinkled.

He waited until dessert, when the mood was more serious, to break his news. "I'm finished with your book. Overall, it's very good, but there are errors."

"Errors?" She seemed to slump. "Not serious ones, I hope."

"Nothing we can't fix."

"*We?*"

"Since you won't give up on it, I'd better help you make sure it's accurate. Maybe I can even minimize the damage. You tell me what you need, and I'll do my best to provide it."

For a moment she didn't respond, only stared at him.

"This is a new twist," he said finally. "*You* speechless for all of—" he looked at his watch "—fifteen seconds."

"I don't know what to say." She smiled widely. "Thank you. I promise you won't regret it."

He was sure he would when he had to tell his family what he was doing. They wouldn't understand the necessity of killing James Hayes a second time.

AFTER SHE CLEANED UP the dishes, Kate followed him to the living room. He had a wonderful collection of classic-rock record albums he'd inherited from his brother, and she flipped through the selections with awe.

"Three Dog Night. Lynyrd Skynyrd. Queen. Chicago. Jimi Hendrix. Oh, my goodnesss! Pink Floyd. Can we play these or are they only to look at?"

"Play any you want."

Thrilled, she pulled out several and stacked them on the stereo. After setting the volume low enough so they could talk, she joined him on the couch, but she wished there was another place to sit. He'd eased down in the middle so he could rest his leg on the big trunk he used as a coffee table, but that meant she had to wedge herself between him and the arm.

"Sorry for the cramped quarters. With only me here, I never saw a need to have much furniture. I can move the trunk over, if that helps."

"That's okay. Don't bother." She didn't want him straining himself, and she wasn't certain she could move the thing by herself.

She was acutely conscious of his bare leg resting against hers, his muscular hip pressing against her more rounded one, but it wasn't long before she relaxed and stopped worrying about the intimacy of the position. He really did have a wonderful sense of humor when he allowed himself to show it, and he kept her laughing nearly continuously as he told her about some of the practical jokes Aubrey had pulled on him over the years. She found herself entertaining him, too, with stories about the antics of her brothers growing up.

Before she realized it, hours had passed. She couldn't remember when she'd enjoyed herself more. Maybe she was still giddy from what he'd told her over dinner, or that old wives' tale about mountain oysters being an aphrodisiac was true, but she didn't want to leave. She had to, of course.

"Well, it's nearly eleven, and I should go." Regretfully she packed up her computer and got her bill-

fold and keys. "I had a nice time tonight," she told him, leading the way to the front door. "I'm glad you talked me into staying."

"Me, too."

His gaze touched her hair, slid over her cheek and lingered on her lips before going back to her eyes. The caress was visual, but no less powerful than if he'd dragged his work-roughened fingers across her skin.

"Well…" she said, then totally lost her concentration in the fullness of his bottom lip, in the lock of dark hair that fell across his brow.

Like any woman, she reacted to a handsome face, but this man got to her, somehow, on a deeper level. He could move her to tears with only a few words, simply smile at her and make her want to giggle like a teenager. When he looked at her a certain way, like now, as if he wanted to kiss her, it hurt as much as a physical blow.

Seconds passed when he didn't move or speak, when the demons of indecision and desire taunted him, and the battle he fought showed openly in his face.

Kate fought her own demons. Lust. Fear. Regret for what could never be. To care about this man, to let him touch her physically or emotionally, meant crossing a line she'd never crossed, jeopardizing the integrity of the most important work she'd ever done.

He made the decision for both of them, reaching past her to open the screen door and hold it open.

"Sleep well," he said.

CHAPTER ELEVEN

"COME ON. Let me touch you. I'll rub your stomach if you want. Or scratch your back. Wouldn't that feel good? Don't you want to come over here and let me see that pretty tail of yours?"

Sitting in a chair in the middle of Bret's kitchen floor a week later, Kate tried to coax Sallie to come to her. Bret watched unnoticed from the doorway of the living room. The dog cowered by the back door and whimpered, looking first at Kate and then with longing out the screen door into the backyard.

"I don't understand why you won't let me touch you. I swear I won't give you a bath, although I've got to tell you I think it would greatly enhance your appeal."

Bret nearly had to bite his lip to keep from laughing out loud and alerting Kate to his presence. Every day she'd gone through this ritual so Sallie would get used to her and the sound of her voice. He admired her determination to win the dog's trust, but it was downright comical listening to Kate talk to her as though they were girlfriends. And it was interesting, too. He'd learned quite a bit by eavesdropping.

"I really didn't mean it when I told Bret you were ugly. I was mad that day because you ate my shoes and they were new, but that doesn't mean I *believe*

what I said about you. You're really very…unusual-looking—particularly the way your bottom teeth jut out and can be seen even when your mouth is closed.''

Sallie whined.

''Oh, I'm not making fun of your mouth. I've got an ugly mouth myself.''

Bret's forehead furrowed with disbelief. An ugly mouth? She had a beautiful mouth. It tormented the hell out of him.

Kate opened the can of dog food she'd been holding on her lap, shook it into a bowl at her feet and cut it into pieces, using the can as a knife. ''How about something to eat?''

Sallie lifted her nose and sniffed the air.

''Mmm. Smell that?''

The dog took a tentative step forward.

''Big chucks of meat. Gravy. Looks so good I might eat it myself.''

Another step.

Bret held his breath as the dog eased to the bowl and cautiously began to eat. Kate reached out her hand and touched the dog's head. Sallie jerked, but she didn't move away, allowing Kate to stroke her.

''That's a good girl. Now see, I wouldn't hurt you for anything in this world. We're going to be good friends.''

Bret cleared his throat. ''She's not so bad once she gets to know you,'' he said. ''She's been mistreated, so she doesn't trust people easily. Somebody tied her to a tree at the garbage dump. Left her without food or water. She was in bad shape when I found her.''

''And you rescued her?''

"More like…she rescued me. She came into my life in the aftermath of my brother's death. Helping her recover forced me to focus on something positive." He walked slowly over to where she was sitting, finally able to put a little weight on his leg and needing only one crutch. He pulled a chair around next to her and sat down. "And for the record, Kate, you don't have an ugly mouth."

"How long were you eavesdropping?"

"Long enough to find out a few things I didn't know."

"Didn't your mother teach you it's impolite to lurk and listen to other people's conversations?"

"If I don't lurk, I don't find out anything. You won't talk to me like you talk to Sallie."

"I talk to you all day long. Don't be ridiculous."

"Yeah, you talk. About the book. About writing. About business. But the minute I ask you anything about yourself, you get that no-nonsense reporter look of yours."

"I don't have a 'no-nonsense reporter' look."

"Yeah, you do. You're wearing it now. It matches that silly business suit and the braid."

For the past week, she'd arrived precisely at eight every morning, looking like a corporate executive dressed for a power lunch, in a suit, heels and tailored blouse. Lord, it was awful. The heat forced her to shed her jacket every day and helped lessen the severity of her appearance, but not by much.

Armor. That was it. After the night he'd nearly kissed her, she'd reverted to the all-business Kathryn Morgan, and the sweet woman he'd come to know had been swallowed up. But the good Kate was in

there somewhere, and by God, he was going to find her.

He grabbed her braid with one hand and pulled off the rubber band that secured it with the other.

"Ow! What are you doing?" Her squeal sent Sallie scurrying for the back door. Kate tried to move away from him, prompting a tug-of-war with her hair as he unbraided it. He held the rubber band out of her reach. "Give that back."

"Nope."

"Hayes, give it to me right now!"

He stuck it in the pocket of his shorts, where he knew she wouldn't attempt to get it.

"Have you lost your mind?"

"No, but I might if I have to look at you trussed up in those ridiculous clothes and wearing your hair like that one more day."

Sallie pawed the door and yodeled to get out, drawing their attention. "Now, see what you've done," Kate said.

Bret got up, took the empty dog-food can from her hand and walked slowly across to the back door. He tossed the can in the trash and let Sallie out.

"We should get back to work," she told him.

"No more work. We're through for the day."

"Through? We only got a few hours in."

"It'll have to be enough. I talked to Henry on the phone last night, and he's upset because I haven't been out to the ranch. I need to spend time with him."

"Do you want me to drive you?"

"I was hoping you'd pick him up and bring him back here so the three of us could spend the afternoon together."

"I don't know…"

"I can't guarantee excitement. Henry's a cartoon freak, so we usually pop one of his favorite tapes in the VCR, lie on the couch and drink chocolate milk. How does that sound?"

"Nice, actually."

"Then you'll stay?"

She hesitated.

"Kate, you run out of here every afternoon the minute we're done. When I try to talk to you about things that don't have to do with the book, you change the subject. I'm going insane closed up in this house all day. I can't drive. Take pity on me and stay for a few hours, okay?"

She pulled at her bottom lip with her teeth. "All right," she finally said. "We can't have you going insane."

"Great. Run by your motel on the way and change, though. I'm tired of you looking like my mother."

BRET AND SALLIE were in the garden when Kate drove up with Henry. She muttered a curse. He'd been foolish to come down the concrete steps alone.

She lifted Henry from the car seat she'd borrowed from the truck. He hit the ground running, ignoring her warning to wait. When he threw himself at Bret's legs, her breath stopped. In one fluid movement Bret grabbed him and lifted him easily with his free arm.

"Mo bing me see Bet," Henry said.

"Mo?"

Henry pointed at Kate, making Bret laugh.

Kate walked to the edge of the garden, not daring to step off the grass into the soft dirt with her heels

on. "I was trying to teach him to say my name and somehow the Morgan part ended up as Mo."

"I like it." He looked at the suit Kate still wore and frowned. "I thought you were going to change clothes before you came back."

"Well, I didn't." In truth, she'd gone by the motel and picked up shorts, a top and her tennis shoes, but she was still undecided about whether or not to change into them. "What are you doing out here?"

"Trying to find some decent tomatoes. I've let most of them dry up or rot."

He leaned over to set Henry on the ground.

"Wait!" Kate yelled. "Don't put him down!"

He stopped in midair. "Why not?"

"The dog's loose."

"She won't hurt him." He set Henry down. "She's crazy about him."

Kate watched in disbelief as Henry went down on both knees in the dirt and Sallie lavished his face with licks.

"Don't let that dog kiss you," Bret gently scolded. "You'll give her a disease." Henry giggled and got up. Bret dropped a tomato into a plastic grocery sack. "I need somebody strong to hold this for me while I put the tomatoes in it," he told the child. "I don't think Mo's strong enough. What do you think?"

"Uh-uh," Henry said.

"You might be, though. Think you can do it?"

Henry nodded. "Bet hurd leg," he told Kate. He pointed to Bret's bruised thigh.

"Yeah, I'm hurt." He ruffled the boy's hair. "But I'm feeling a lot better now that you're here to help me."

He picked two more tomatoes, discarded one and dropped the other in Henry's sack. The next two he started to toss away, then stopped. He looked Kate up and down and grinned.

"What?" she asked, not understanding what he intended to do until a rotten tomato splattered against her chest. The second one hit her in the stomach before she could react.

"Guess you'll have to change now." He roared with laughter.

Kate was initially too stunned to move. She stood with her mouth open and her arms raised in the air like the nearby scarecrow, shocked that he'd actually hit her with rotten tomatoes. The smell was horrible. The liquid immediately seeped through the fabric to wet her skin.

"I can't believe you did that!" She stared down at her skirt and blouse.

"I warned you to change into playclothes."

"Is this your idea of playing?"

"Yeah," he said, grinning. "Among other things. But I doubt you'd let me do those."

Her mind went through and discarded various forms of retaliation. Slipping out of her shoes, she stepped into the garden and carefully chose two of the rotten tomatoes.

His eyes widened. "Whoa, wait a minute," he said, sobering, trying to retreat as she advanced on him. "No fair. I can't run away from you."

"You should've thought of that *before* you used me for target practice." She raised her hand.

"You throw that at me and you'll be sorry."

"I'm really scared. Let me show you how scared

I am.'' She heaved it at his chest, but it hit him on the shoulder, splattering over the side of his face. Henry squealed and clapped his hands. Sallie let out an excited yodel.

Bret wiped the dripping juice off his face with his sleeve. "Oh, you're asking for it now, Morgan. I think you've been asking for it ever since you met me." His expression told her the double meaning of his words was intended.

Kate decided she could also play this game. She put her hands on her hips and taunted him. "Oh? And you think *you're* going to be the one to give it to me?"

"I think I'm exactly the one who's going to give it to you."

"We'll see about that."

A battle erupted, one in which there was no hope of a winner. Bret flung down his crutch and pelted her unmercifully with tomatoes. Kate gave back as good as she got. Her aim wasn't as accurate as his, but she was able to move, while he had to remain stationary.

Within a couple of minutes, they were both covered with the stinking liquid. So was Henry, who had jumped into the game with enthusiasm.

Kate threw a tomato and accidentally grazed Bret on his bruised thigh. He yelped in pain and fell backward into the dirt. "Oh, Bret, I'm sorry!" She dropped her other tomato and rushed to him, keeling at his side. He had his eyes closed and was groaning. "I'm so sorry. I didn't mean to hit you on your sore leg. I was aiming for your head."

"Bet hurd?" Henry asked, leaning over to look at him.

Bret opened his eyes, grinned and grabbed them both, making them shriek in unison. "Gotcha." He pulled them down on top of him, then bellowed, "Whew-ee, somebody stinks!"

AFTER KATE HAD CLEANED UP Henry and herself and changed their clothes, he led her by the hand into the living room and pointed at one of the tapes on top of the VCR. "This one?" she asked, and he nodded.

She'd dressed him in one of Bret's T-shirts while she washed his jeans and shirt, tying the bottom so it wouldn't drag on the floor. He looked like one of Snow White's dwarves.

"Hi-Ho, Hi-Ho," she said, tweaking his nose.

He laughed and pulled on hers. "Mo."

"That's me. Old Mo. Are you hungry, sweetie?" He nodded again. "Okay, you watch your show and I'll fix us something good to eat."

She put his tape in and adjusted the volume while Henry settled on the couch. Bret was still taking his shower, so she headed to the kitchen sink to wash the handful of tomatoes he'd picked. She made sandwiches and got out some of the peanut-butter cookies she'd baked that Bret liked so much.

When he came up behind her and asked what she was fixing, she told him ham-and-tomato sandwiches. She turned and handed him a cookie. "Where's your crutch?"

"I left it in the bathroom."

He wore only gym shorts and he was still damp

from the shower. She tried to look away, but all that taut glistening skin wouldn't let her.

She watched with fascination as a bead of water at his throat started to roll slowly downward through the hair at the center of his chest.

"You're still wet."

"Uh-uh," he said nonchalantly, taking a bite of cookie. He didn't understand what he was doing to her, how that damn bead of moisture was torturing her.

She reached out with her finger, meaning only to wipe it away, but the skin was warm and too inviting. An invisible force drew her. And it was much stronger than her will.

Lightly she placed her palm on the spot, feeling not only his strong chest but the beating heart below. For an eternity she didn't move it, couldn't move it, but then it moved of its own volition across the width of his chest...once...twice...many times in an almost loving caress, the fingertips grazing the skin and the springy hair that covered it.

"Go put on a shirt, or I'm likely to do something crazy," she told him.

"I'm about to beat you to it."

His left hand covered hers on his chest. His right reached behind her neck to slowly pull her body forward and her mouth to his. The kiss was gentle, the lightest brush of his lips to test her willingness. He tasted faintly of peanut-butter cookie and smelled of her father's favorite aftershave lotion. Innocuous unromantic things in any other man. In this man, they were endearing and strangely erotic.

He touched his lips to hers again, but no gentleness

guided him this time. The kiss was long and hot, and melted her reservations one by one. Before long, she couldn't remember that she had reservations. She forgot about the book, about James, about everything but how wonderful it felt to be kissed so thoroughly.

"Mmm." The sound escaped her throat to fuel the fire.

His hands moved to her back to bring her closer. He trembled, telling her of his struggle for control, and it was more flattering than all the honeyed words men had used on her over the years.

This man needed no words to express his feelings. His body spoke eloquently. The labored breathing, the fingers that had worked their way under her shirt to caress her fevered skin—they said he wanted her. The repeated assaults on her mouth said he enjoyed kissing her as much as she enjoyed kissing him.

He was a paradise of hard angles and muscle, and she let her hand roam freely over his supple skin, something—she admitted to herself now—she'd wanted to do from the first time she'd seen him.

His hand was also moving, touching her hair, her throat, her breasts. She could imagine him touching her even more intimately, fingers stroking, tongues seeking moistened places.

"We shouldn't be doing this," she whispered.

"I know, but heaven help me, Katie, I want it."

The nickname pierced her heart as it always did when anyone used it, and she shut her eyes to fight back the emotion that suddenly overwhelmed her. James's voice from so long ago filled her head.

Kathryn. That's an awfully formal name, isn't it? How about...Katie? That fits you.

"Kate." Her eyes popped open. "What's wrong? I thought you wanted this, wanted me."

"I do, but it's wrong."

She began to pull out of his embrace, but he stopped her.

"How can it be wrong when it feels so good?"

"Because it is. We both know it is. My work is important to me, and I don't want to jeopardize it or lose my objectivity, but I feel that happening. And you...I'm sure I'm the last person in the world you imagined getting involved with. My being here has turned into such a mistake."

"What are you saying?"

"That maybe we should do our interviews another way. Over the telephone. Through written questions. Tapes. When I came here, I never expected to like you or be physically attracted to you. I'm considering going home."

"No," he said sharply. "You're not going anywhere."

"But—"

"No!"

"Bet play me!" Henry demanded from the doorway, interrupting. "Bet no play Mo."

Bret turned her loose and groaned. "This conversation isn't over," he told her under his breath.

"Yes, it is."

She watched him as he made his way slowly—too slowly—into the living room to watch cartoons with Henry. He was obviously hurting and didn't want to admit it. When she went in to tell them lunch was on the table, she found Bret lying on the couch with

Henry on his chest, both of them asleep. The TV blared and she turned down the volume.

She gazed at the two of them with an odd feeling of joy and pain. They were both so innocent in sleep, so appealing. She patted Henry's back and brushed a lock of hair off Bret's forehead. He opened his eyes and looked at her sleepily.

''Promise you won't go back to Chicago,'' he said, hardly able to keep his eyes open. ''We can work this out.'' He took her hand.

She nodded reluctantly. ''Okay, I promise.'' He closed his eyes and drifted back to sleep with a smile of relief on his face.

Carefully she disentangled her fingers from his and draped his arm across Henry. Watching them made something break loose inside her, something that had been held prisoner for too many years, and she broke down and cried, tears falling faster than she could wipe them away.

No, she wouldn't leave. She'd been afraid Bret would somehow make a place for himself in her heart if she stayed much longer, but staying made no difference now.

It was already too late.

CHAPTER TWELVE

"No, DAMMIT, that's not the way it happened! Why won't you listen to me?" Bret couldn't believe this. He'd never met a more pigheaded, singularly focused woman in his life. "Look," he said, trying once again. "James wasn't really sick. He only pretended to be."

Kate threw her pen on the table. "You must have it mixed up with some other time. I have statements from the organizers of the charity event saying he had the flu and was in bed and that's why he didn't attend like he promised."

"Oh, he was in bed, all right. He picked himself up a couple of groupies and spent the night with them."

Her face practically turned purple as she fought not to lose her temper, although why any of it mattered now, he didn't know. She'd been like a she-cat today with her claws extended, and every time he said something about the mighty James Hayes she didn't like, she raked him. His ego was in shreds.

"Do you want to know what I think?" she asked.

No, he didn't. Not really. But he was stupid enough to say, "What do you think?"

"That deep down you're jealous of him and don't even realize it. I think it's skewed your perspective."

He dropped his head to the kitchen table and banged it a couple of times. Why, why, did she have to argue with him on every blasted point? Not once today had she simply accepted something he'd told her.

Destroying her image of her hero had seemed such a practical plan when he'd conceived it, but it had backfired on him. He hadn't counted on the depth of her admiration for James Hayes or how much it would rankle him whenever she jumped to James's defense.

"I was *not* jealous of him," he mumbled to the tablecloth, which appeared to be the only thing in the room that was listening.

"Don't be ashamed of it. He was brilliant and handsome. Anyone with a brother like that would be crazy not to feel some jealousy."

He raised his head. "Handsome? He was a string bean and so clumsy he used to fall over his own feet. He was not handsome!"

"See, there you go again. Every time I say anything nice about him, you contradict me."

"No, you've got it backward. Every time I try to tell you the truth about him, you refuse to believe it. You're the one with the skewed perspective. Why are you so determined to turn him into a martyr?"

"I'm not, but I also don't believe he was the pitiful excuse for a human being you make him out to be. Drunk all the time. Staying up every night making love with two and three women. He couldn't possibly have written such exquisite music if he was living that kind of life."

"Well, maybe he didn't write as much of it as everybody thinks."

That statement was the most absurd thing he'd come up with yet, but he was a desperate man running out of ideas. Nothing else was working. Maybe a little shock treatment would.

Her initial reaction was disbelief, but in her expression he also saw a hint of curiosity. He took advantage of it. "Haven't you ever heard the rumors that Webb Anderson wrote most of the band's songs those last few years and James took credit for them?"

"I've heard the rumors. Are you telling me they're true?"

He shrugged, deciding to play it cool. "I don't really know, but I got an indication from James that he and Webb weren't getting along. They argued a lot. Especially in those last months. And a couple of times their arguments came to blows."

"They actually fought?"

"Yeah. And I know that's true because I saw it with my own eyes."

She frowned. "When was that, exactly? Let me pull up a file." She typed something into the portable computer in front of her, and he groaned to himself. He didn't know which he was more frightened of— Kate's brain or that stupid computer.

"Okay," she said. "Where and when did this happen?"

He pretended to think. "I'm not sure."

"Well, give me a guess. Was it in the six months before James died?"

He shook his head, looking pensive.

"In the last twelve months?"

"Probably."

She scrolled through the file. "Okay, I've called up

the chronology of his life. Tell me where this fight took place, and let's see if we can use that to figure out the date.''

Oh, hell! "You have a chronology? Like a day-by-day list of where he was his whole life?"

"Well, not every day, no, but from his teenage years on I can narrow any event down to about a two- or three-month span.''

"Where did you get all that stuff?''

"Various places. Interviews, newspaper clippings. I've spent more than ten years gathering this information.''

"Ten years? You can't have been working on this book for ten years!'' He couldn't hide his disbelief.

"Well, no, not technically. But I guess, in the back of my mind, I always knew I'd write a book about him one day, so it became a habit to clip articles I saw and to save information I ran across. When I became proficient enough to write the story, I was already years ahead of where I would've been in my research. That's why I think I'm uniquely qualified to write this book. Nobody on earth knows as much about him as I do.''

Now he was the one frowning. "What do you mean, when you became proficient enough? You won a Pulitzer, for God's sake. I'd guess that makes you pretty proficient.''

She shrugged modestly. "Yes, but thankfully, writing is something you get better at the more you do it. I'm still young compared to most of the writers in my field, but as I've gotten older my writing has matured. Until I gained that maturity, I didn't want to write James's story because—''

"I know, because you admired him," he finished with disdain.

She gave him a look that said he was acting jealous again. "Yes, and because I didn't want to write this book and not have it be my best work."

He picked up the diskette next to her laptop and studied it. "Do you have my whole life captured on one of these little things, too?" Thinking of what might be on there made him sick to his stomach.

"Some of it. The parts that are important to James's story."

"He always comes first with you, doesn't he?" The minute the words were out, Bret regretted them. He tossed the disk back on the table and rubbed his hand across his eyes. "Forget I said that."

"What's with you today? You're so ill-tempered, even for you."

"I am not ill-tempered, dammit." He sighed at her amused expression. "Okay, so I'm a *little* ill-tempered."

"Is your leg bothering you?"

"No."

"Then what is it?"

"Nothing's wrong that getting out of this house wouldn't cure. I'm not used to being shut up. I need fresh air." He looked over her head and stared longingly out the window. The day was beautiful and they'd wasted it inside. "I know it's going to be dark soon, but how about we move this interview outside? We can pack some sandwiches and go down to the pond for an hour. I've got to get out of this house."

"Will that improve your nasty disposition?"

"Yeah, a hundred percent."

"Then, by all means, lead the way."

THE POND WASN'T BIG, but it provided him with some excellent catfish and the perfect place to be lazy when he felt like it. He didn't sneak off and fish often, but the lure of it on a warm day was sometimes more than he could resist. After all, it was why he'd bought the place.

He'd stood in the driveway all those years ago, looked at the pond and imagined himself on the bank with a cane pole in his hand. He'd immediately called the agent listed on the For Sale sign and made what was probably too generous an offer for the farm, given the fact that he'd never been inside the house or walked over the property. Plus, he'd only intended to use it temporarily.

As it turned out, he'd abandoned his plans to build a house on his ancestors' land, and this farm had become his permanent home. The house was small, but solidly built and in good shape. The pond and a nice-size stream in the back pasture provided plenty of water for the stock.

He had a beautiful place and he was proud of it. But something was missing from his life and that, regardless of what he'd told Kate, was why he'd felt ill today. He'd gotten a taste of how much better things would be if he had a woman—this particular woman—around all the time. Thinking about that, about Kate going home when her interviews were over, made him feel low. Knowing he'd probably never see her again—and would be crazy to try—left him feeling downright depressed.

He was falling in love with a woman he couldn't have.

The sun was slowly inching its way toward the horizon, coloring the sky and water crimson, settling a peacefulness over the land that bolstered his sagging spirits. The night insects hadn't yet begun their sweet symphony. Only an occasional splash disturbed the quiet. Even Sallie was enjoying the outing. Slowly becoming less fearful of Kate, she'd stretched out on her side a few feet away from them to take a nap.

"The lightning bugs are out," he said, relaxing on the quilt they'd spread out.

"Lightning bugs?" Kate asked, not looking up.

She was lying on her stomach next to him, going over the notes she'd made at the house. He let his gaze wander leisurely over her shoulders and across the soft curve of her backside. He'd already noticed how the shorts hugged her slender body, how they outlined the feminine parts of her.

He'd always appreciated nice breasts or a good set of legs on a woman. This one had both, along with a perfect little ass that put a tightness in his groin every time he looked at it.

"Lightning bugs," he repeated, gently closing his hand over one as it blinked in front of his face. "See?" He scooted next to her and opened his hand. The tiny beetle fluttered, then flew away.

"That's a firefly," she said casually, returning to her notes. "Family *Lampyridae. Genera Photernus* and *Photuris.*"

"No, city girl, that's a lightning bug," he insisted, to get some attention.

"Firefly."

"Lightning bug."

"Firefly." She turned her head and looked into his face. When he grinned, she slapped him playfully on the shoulder. "Why are you baiting me?"

"Because you're ignoring me and I don't like it." He took the notebook out of her hand and threw it over his head.

"Bret!" She tried to get up to go after it, but he grabbed her ankle and pulled her back down.

"Leave it. We'll find it later."

"But we still have a hundred things to discuss today. And we never did settle that question about the arguments between James and Webb. We need to pin down that date."

"I'll answer all your questions later."

"You keep saying that, but you always find some way to avoid answering the tough ones. And I'm beginning to wonder why."

"Maybe I'm becoming so attached to you I'm trying to string this out so you'll stay longer."

His teasing held a certain amount of truth, and because she knew it, it flustered her. "You're being silly now." She tried to cover her uneasiness by sitting to gather the plastic wrap and the remains of their sandwiches.

"I'm not trying to avoid your questions, Kate. But I like spending time with you when the conversation doesn't revolve around my brother. Other topics are a lot more interesting."

"Such as?"

"My place. What do you think of it?"

She looked out over the placid water at the horses grazing quietly on the tender grass across from them.

"I think it's beautiful. Aubrey told me you've worked hard fixing it up. Did you really dig every hole for the fence posts by hand?"

"Manual labor builds character."

"And muscle," she said, poking his biceps with one finger.

"Yeah. The place was pretty rough when I bought it. The house had been vacant for about five years, and kudzu had nearly covered it. But I knew it had potential the minute I saw it. Fate brought me down this road."

"Did you come here to find your family's old homestead?" She lay down on her side, facing him, her head propped on her hand.

"That, and just looking around. I liked the town and decided this farm was as good a place as any to live while I built a house. I had a little money stashed away. Not much, but enough for a down payment on this property and the other one."

"Did James give—?" She waved the thought away with her hand. "Never mind."

"James didn't buy it for me. That's what you were going to ask, wasn't it?"

"I thought he might have given you the money."

"Kate, I wasn't always the most reliable person when I was younger, and I admit I went through a few jobs before I found something I love—horse breeding. But I've always worked and I've always paid my own way."

"Sorry."

"I didn't depend on James to take care of me. He'd probably have given me the money, but it was *his* money, and I didn't feel I was entitled to it."

"Is that why you and your family set up two foundations and donated all his millions to charity? You don't feel you're entitled to the money?"

He looked away momentarily. Damn! He'd expected her to find out eventually, but still he was unnerved and had to fight to keep it from showing. He kept forgetting who she was, how dangerous she was. That sweet face had a way of lulling him into thinking she was like everyone else, that she didn't have the power to destroy all their lives if he slipped up and said the wrong thing.

"Why have you been looking at my finances?"

"Because you obviously aren't living on the money you inherited. I was curious about where it went."

"You could have asked me."

"Okay, I'm asking now. Why have you given all of it away? And why set up a separate foundation to do it? Isn't the money coming from James's royalties?"

"I didn't use the money for myself because I didn't want to profit from my brother's death. And yes, the money comes from James's royalties. But my mother and I have different ideas about how it should be used, so rather than battling each time one of us wants to support a project, we came up with this split. That's the reason we have two foundations. She and Ellen fund their charities and I fund mine. They have no problems with the arrangement, so you shouldn't, either."

She nodded, but he could almost hear her brain working, weighing his explanation against what she knew. He could tell his answer bothered her. Or

maybe, he thought with alarm, there was something else she hadn't mentioned.

"We're talking about him again," he said. "Somehow the conversation always gets back to my brother, regardless of what subject we start out with. Now how do you suppose that happens?"

"I'm sorry. When I'm working on a book, I tend to let it take over my thoughts."

"Maybe you need a diversion."

She glanced at him suspiciously. "What kind of diversion did you have in mind?"

"Fishing."

"Oh," she said, visibly relaxing.

Quickly, while her guard was down, he closed the few inches between them and covered her mouth with his, taking advantage of her surprise to slip his tongue inside her slightly parted lips. She stiffened, but he refused to let her pull away, and gradually her lips softened under his, opening wider. Damn, she tasted good. Why hadn't he done this an hour ago?

He used pressure on her lower back to bring her body into contact with his, reveling in the feel of her soft breasts against his chest, her stomach pressed against his own. Arousal, warm and potent, wound its way from his head to his belly.

For several minutes his mouth continued its expert assault while his hand moved lazily over her hip and back. When he grew bolder, moving his hand between them to touch her breast, she dragged her mouth from his and gasped for air. "This is *not* fishing."

"No, but it's a lot more fun."

He bent and put his mouth over her nipple, teasing it through the cotton of her shirt until it was rigid and

she began to moan and squirm. Her hand went to the back of his head and held him in place. "We can't do this," she whispered.

"We already are."

He kissed her again, rolling her onto her back where his hands could have better access to the places he longed to touch. Her own hands began to move, tormenting him as they skimmed his back and buttocks, working their way under his shirt to touch his bare skin.

He quickly pulled the shirt over his head and discarded it so she could touch him more easily. When he unhooked the clasp on her bra, she didn't protest.

"God, you're beautiful," he said, taking off her shirt and bra to look at her. Her lips were red and swollen with his kisses, her nipples hard with arousal. The hunger in her eyes—hunger for him—was blatant.

He put his hand between her legs, stroking her while he watched the play of emotions on her face: the surprise turning to passion, the passion to white-hot fire that threatened to burn her alive. But it wasn't enough for him. He wanted to touch her without the barrier of her clothes. He wanted to put his mouth there and drive her mad until she climaxed a hundred times and screamed his name with every one.

He slipped his hand under the elastic waistband of her shorts and inside her underwear. The curls between her legs were the gateway to a tantalizing array of surfaces and temperatures, and he wasted no time in exploring everything. She writhed beneath his hand as he stroked the swollen nub, and she arched into him in a gesture of supplication.

"Oh, James…"

His heart stopped and his hand stilled.

"What did you call me?"

She opened her eyes and blinked in confusion. "What?"

"He's not the one making love to you. I am. Can't you forget him for five seconds?"

For a moment nothing registered on her face, and then the realization of what she'd said hit her. Horror distorted her perfect features. "I wasn't…I swear I wasn't thinking about anyone but you."

He sat up and reached for his shirt, tugging it on in anger. The passion he'd felt had died instantly with the whispered name.

"Bret, I'm sorry." She tried to touch him, but he pulled away.

"Put on your clothes," he snapped.

"Bret—"

"Put on your clothes! I don't want to hear any explanations."

She hurriedly dressed, then drew on her shoes.

"Go to the house," he ordered.

"Are you coming?"

"No! I'm too angry to be with you right now."

Her bottom lip trembled and tears slid silently down her cheeks. But she said nothing else. She stood, walked to where he'd earlier thrown her notebook and picked it up.

"Yeah, don't forget that," he said, his voice cracking with pain. "I wouldn't want you to miss out on getting one more detail about my brother for your book."

She opened her mouth to say something, then ap-

parently thought better of it. Turning, she started toward the house with Sallie close on her heels. When she was crossing the yard, he thought he heard her sob but he wasn't sure. And he didn't care. She'd wounded him in a way she could never begin to understand.

For a long time he stayed by the pond, until his anger left him and he thought he could talk to Kate without screaming. Night had fallen and the mosquitoes were threatening to eat him alive, so he walked slowly back to the house. As he entered, he heard no sound. Only a pale light came from the living room.

He hobbled to the doorway. Kate was on the couch in the dark, illuminated only by the light of the television screen. The volume had been turned off, and she appeared to be so entranced by the picture that she didn't know he was there. Tears streamed down her cheeks.

He came forward to where he could see the TV, but he knew already what he'd find. The face of James Hayes stared back at him.

"Damn," he said with disgust, finally drawing her attention. "Now I understand why you don't want me. You want *him*. You're in love with a dead man."

BRET HAD LITERALLY RIPPED the tape out of the VCR and thrown it across the room. He stood before her now with his face twisted in anger. It hurt her to know she'd caused it.

"Bret," she said calmly, more calmly than she felt. She stood and put her hand on his arm. "You're angry and I can't—"

"You're damn straight I'm angry! How do you expect me to feel?"

He pulled away, backing up. Had her touch become offensive to him? She couldn't stand to think that. Down by the pond she'd wanted to make love to him, show him she cared for him. She wanted to touch him now. To hold him. To soothe him. To let him know he was every bit as important to her as James had been.

"Bret, please. You don't understand."

"What don't I understand, Kate? You tell me. Explain to me why you moan his name when I touch you. Explain to me why you're sitting here in the dark crying over a man who's dead and never coming back."

She wiped the tears from her cheeks. Until that moment she hadn't realized they were even there. "I admired him. I've told you before. He was special."

"Yeah, he was special," Bret said sarcastically. "He drank and screwed his way across the country and pumped himself so full of drugs that half the time he didn't even know what was going on."

The words hurt her. But then, he knew that, didn't he? That was why he'd thrown them at her.

"Don't," she warned.

"Don't what? Remind you that he wasn't worthy of this *admiration* you feel for him?"

"Don't make up lies to hurt me."

"You don't get it, do you? You've created this huge fantasy about him and now you believe it's the truth. Do you know what you are? I've just realized it. You're the ultimate groupie. Only, you're worse than all those women who used to hang around the

motels hoping to go to bed with him. They, at least, gave him up when he died, but you're still obsessed with him. And you're using this book as a way of keeping your obsession alive. It has nothing to do with trying to restore his reputation.''

She tried to close her heart against the verbal blow, but it still struck and gravely wounded her. Without a word she walked to the kitchen, shut down her computer and packed everything in her briefcase. She had so much she wanted to say to him, but it wouldn't do any good.

He was determined to make something dirty and sick out of her feelings for James.

''Go on. Run away, rather than face the truth,'' he said from the doorway.

''I think we've said it all.''

''I'm not finished.''

''Well, I am. Completely. I'll be returning to Chicago in the morning.''

''What about your promise?''

''I see no reason to stay here.''

His jaw moved back and forth as he ground his teeth. ''No, I guess not.''

''I'll mail you a copy of the final manuscript when it's done.''

''Don't bother. It's fiction and there's nothing in it I want to read.'' He turned and limped down the hall to the bedroom, slamming the door behind him.

Kate picked up her briefcase and went out the front door, but she only made it as far as the steps before she broke down. She collapsed, put her face in her hands and wept. How had she made such a mess of things?

She couldn't blame him for being angry. If he'd called out Lauren's name during their lovemaking, she'd have been just as hurt and angry. James's name had come out of nowhere.

A wet tongue with the feel of sandpaper touched her knee and made her raise her head. Surprised, Kate lifted her arm, and Sallie wriggled next to her, covering her tear-streaked face with licks.

Kate put her arm around her and hugged her close. "Oh, great. Now that I'm leaving, you've decided to like me." She rubbed her hand across the dog's back one last time. "Take good care of him, girl. Love him for me." Standing, she retrieved her briefcase and walked to her car. She started the engine and, with a final glance at the darkened house, drove away.

CHAPTER THIRTEEN

Chicago

SHE'D BEEN STARING at the computer screen for almost two hours and hadn't written a single decent sentence.

Highlighting the last paragraph, Kate hit ''delete'' and zapped it into oblivion, thinking that was where the entire chapter needed to go, if only she had the guts to send it there.

Outside, the rain had started again, and she watched the water stream in rivulets down her office window, finding it much more interesting than work. Everything seemed more interesting than writing today— opening the mail, fielding requests for interviews, answering letters from readers.

The whole day had been a bust as far as writing went, like the rest of this week and the week before. She was having trouble reconciling her research with what Bret had told her, and the more she struggled with it, the harder it became to write. If *she* didn't understand the inconsistencies, how could she hope to present James's story in a way that readers would understand?

She used the pencil beside the keyboard to put an-

other *x* on the desk calendar. Six weeks. Bret hadn't tried to get in touch with her once.

He'd accused her of being in love with his brother, but the idea was ludicrous, especially since it was Bret who occupied her thoughts all day.

Going to Alabama had been a huge mistake. Starting to fall for him had been an even bigger one, and now she was paying dearly for her foolishness. She couldn't work. She had trouble sleeping. Her dreams were a tumble of images of both brothers that seem to swirl and intertwine.

It was almost as if... No, the idea was insane, physically impossible. Forensic reports don't lie.

She got up and walked to the window, unable to sit still. Her office was thirty-three stories high, and on a gray and rainy day like today, she was literally in the clouds. Her only view was the drab uninteresting building across the street.

Looking at the steel and glass, she thought immediately of Pine Acres and how the hay in the pastures moved in the wind. The trees would be clothed in their autumn colors and the children would be preparing for Halloween, a few days away. She thought of Henry. Was he old enough to enjoy dressing up to go trick-or-treating? Would Bret take him? In the short time she'd been with the little boy, she'd come to care about him deeply.

A knock sounded and the door opened. "Here are all the clippings we've got on Lauren's death," Marcus said, bustling in without waiting to be invited. "I've included the autopsy report, the disposition of her property and the interviews with her sister. What else do you need?"

"Nothing right now, thanks," she said without turning around, hoping he'd leave. No such luck.

"How's that chapter coming?"

"Okay."

He walked up beside her and stared out. "Nasty day." When she didn't say anything, he said, "You're still coming over to Dad's tonight, aren't you?"

"Maybe."

"Kate, it's ages since we've all been together. Dinner won't be the same if you're not there."

"Mmm," she said noncommittally. Spending time with her rowdy brothers and their families wasn't exactly what she needed right now.

He sighed with impatience. "Okay, what's wrong?"

"Nothing."

"Something is. You've been like a zombie ever since you got back from that trip south. You come in every morning with dark circles under your eyes, so I know you aren't sleeping. And you spend the day looking out the window when you're supposed to be working. What happened to you in Alabama?"

"Nothing happened. I'm simply finding it a little difficult to get focused, that's all."

"That's strange, considering how obsessed you've been with finishing this book."

Obsessed. There was that word again.

"I'm not *obsessed*. Just because I'm conscientious about my work and I want to give a fair account of the life of a man I respected, that doesn't make me obsessed. And I'm damn tired of people telling me I am!"

Marcus raised one blond eyebrow, obviously shocked by her outburst. "Okay, okay, don't get all bent out of shape. You're being conscientious. Fine."

"I'm sorry, Marcus. I'm a little tired today."

"Come to Dad's tonight. I think you need to get away from this book for a while."

"I'll try, but I won't promise."

Marcus started for the door. "I've got to take Cindy to the pediatrician this afternoon, so I'll be out of the office. Oh, and I finally found that information on drug allergies you asked for. Bret doesn't have any, but as a child James almost died from a reaction. I'll type up my notes in the morning."

"Wait!" Kate's heart had plunged to her knees, but she tried to present a calm exterior. "A reaction to what?" she asked evenly.

"Penicillin."

THE CAR STOPPED at the curb and Kate got in.

"Get down in the seat," the burly man said.

"Afraid someone will recognize me?"

"Don't want anybody seein' me riding 'round with a white woman."

Kate stifled a laugh and slid farther down. Midnight had come and gone, and it was unlikely another cop would see them at this hour, but Flapjack enjoyed playing the game. And discretion *was* called for. Her old buddy could get into serious trouble if anyone found out what he was about to do.

She hated asking for the favor. During her stint as an investigative reporter, she'd solicited his help and not worried about it. Cops and reporters swapped information under the table all the time while pretend-

ing publicly not to like each other. But this was different. She wasn't a reporter anymore; she was a private citizen.

He checked the side mirror and pulled out into the street. They would keep moving while they talked to avoid arousing suspicion from any patrol cars that happened to be in the area. And when they were finished, he'd drop her back at her car.

"Give it to me," he said.

She pulled a plastic bag containing a computer disk from her jacket. "My prints are on here, too, but those are the only two sets—his and mine. *Don't* run them. I don't want them in the system. Compare them to what you already have on file for him, and give me your expert opinion."

"You've got it."

"And Flapjack, I need this as quick as I can get it."

"You always do."

"If there was any other way, I wouldn't ask, but somebody's been nosing around my research, and I want to make sure it's not him," she lied.

"You sweet on this guy?"

"Yeah, I'm sweet on him."

He snickered. "Katie Kat's got her a man."

"Don't give me grief, okay? Just look at the prints."

"Is this the same dude you had me run DMV records on a few months ago and request files?"

"Yes."

They arrived back at her car. Flapjack pulled over to the curb in front of it. "I'll talk to you when I've had a look."

"I'll be at my condo until I hear from you. I'd rather keep Marcus out of this."

"Whatever you say."

Kate got in her car and drove home for the long wait. She didn't go to work the next day, telling her brother she had a virus and didn't want to give it to him. When the call from Flapjack finally came, she picked up the phone on the first ring.

"You can relax, Scoop," he said. "Your boy-friend's in the clear. Those prints on the disk? Not his."

Oh, God!

Kate thanked him, apologized for putting him to the trouble for nothing and pretended calm as she made arrangements to get back her disk. She even laughed, unsure how she managed it with the knot in her throat and her body shaking uncontrollably.

When she put down the phone, the first wave of nausea hit her, and she hung her head between her knees to try to get back control.

Not his. Yet the prints in the police file definitely belonged to Bret Hayes.

She took rapid breaths, drawing in air to keep her-self conscious.

Not his. If the prints on the disk didn't match those on file…

The bile surged upward. She slapped a hand over her mouth and stumbled to the bathroom, almost making it before she threw up.

THE WIND HAD RISEN steadily all afternoon and now wailed in a ghostly symphony through the cracks in Bret's barn. This was going to be one of those nights

when a man wanted to turn in early and press himself against the warm body of a woman. But the only woman he wanted was a thousand miles away. And in love with a dead man.

He stood in the barn doorway staring out, his hands in the pockets of his goose-down jacket, watching the sky with growing uneasiness. The light was fading, but the threatening clouds that had been gathering in the east for the past couple of hours were still visible above the shadowed landscape. Snow clouds, rain clouds, he couldn't tell which. But they bothered him.

He never worried about snow until late January or February, and it was only the last week of October. Most years it never snowed at all. But rain, now that was a different kind of problem. A horse was pretty sure-footed and reasonably smart, but ice on the ground could turn it into a brainless lump of uncoordination.

Everything of value he had was tied up in his horses. He couldn't afford to lose an animal because of something stupid like a broken leg. And the way his luck had been running lately, if they got rain tonight and it turned to ice, there'd be *some* kind of accident.

The weather report said a low of twenty-two degrees and no rain, but he wasn't taking any chances. With Aubrey and Willie's help he'd gone through his severe-weather checklist. They'd given all the animals an extra ration of sweet feed to help them generate more body heat, and opened the gates so the mares and colts could move out of the wind and into the shelter of the trees that fringed the grass on the hill beyond the barn.

Inside the unheated barn, they'd put blankets on the studs and set out the portable kerosene heaters in the alley between the stalls. They'd wrapped the water pipes so there was little chance they'd freeze. But still, an uneasiness had settled in Bret's bones like the cold. Something was going to happen and it was going to be something he wasn't prepared for. He felt it.

Aubrey came up beside him and scanned the sky. "Well, it don't look good."

"I might start using that as my motto," Bret said with dead seriousness.

"Thinkin' of puttin' it on a business card, are you?"

He almost smiled. "Maybe."

"You should paint it on a sign down at the road. Make sure folks know what a hard-luck guy you are. Maybe have you some flyers printed up and passed around town."

That did it. Bret's lips twitched against his will.

They'd known each other long enough that Aubrey could get away with poking fun at him and his dark moods. And he'd been in a dark one lately, the darkest he could remember in a long while, or so Aubrey kept reminding him. He could pinpoint when it started by the xs he'd drawn on the calendar in the office, one for every day of the six weeks since Kate had gone back to Chicago.

He didn't know why he bothered to count the days. She was never coming back. He hadn't heard a word from her. No apologies. No attempt to explain her feelings. But why should she when her feelings were obvious? She was in love with a rock star. And there

was no room in her heart for a simple country man, a horse-breeder.

"You want me and Willie to hang around a spell, see what the weather's gonna do?" Aubrey asked, interrupting his thoughts.

"No need. I can handle whatever happens."

"We don't mind."

"I know, and I appreciate it, but this storm will probably blow over, and even if it doesn't there's not much else we can do right now. And something tells me, the way you two have been whistling all day, you have plans tonight."

Aubrey grinned and confessed, "Promised to take a couple of fine-lookin' ladies dancin'."

Bret suppressed a chuckle at the image of a bow-legged Aubrey whirling some woman around the dance floor, and shy Willie even talking to a woman, much less dancing with one.

Aubrey leaned out the door and spit tobacco juice in an arc toward the corral. "Why don't you come along? Don't imagine we'd have too much trouble rustlin' up a female who'd mind starin' into that face of yours for one night."

Bret shook his head and gave the answer he gave every time Aubrey asked him to join them in their constant attempts to woo women. "Thanks, but some other time."

Aubrey didn't persist, having learned by now it wouldn't do any good.

They stood awhile in the gathering darkness, watching the mares slowly make their way across the pasture and up the hill, with the friskier colts and fillies trotting among them. The scene was part of a

larger picture Bret had often thought about back in those days when his life had begun to fall apart. He'd dreamed of waking up here every morning to a slower simpler existence, horses grazing peacefully on the hill. The dream had kept him going.

He'd believed that getting back to the land now and then and doing a hard day's work with his hands would right what was wrong with his life, and it almost had. But the price he'd paid—his brother's life—had been too great. And lately he'd begun to realize that heaven looked a lot like hell when there was no one to share it with you.

"You should call that little gal and tell her how you feel about her," Aubrey said, accurately reading his thoughts. "Ain't healthy for a man to brood over a woman like you've been broodin' over that one and not do somethin' about it."

Bret shifted and leaned against the doorway, crossing his arms over his chest. "I don't know what you're talking about."

"Yeah, you do. You're being your usual hard-headed self."

"Don't you have somewhere to go?"

Aubrey spit again and wiped his sleeve across his mouth. "Yeah, I reckon I do, seein' as how you're not gonna listen to me, anyway."

"Go on, then. I wouldn't want those *fine-lookin' ladies* mad at me because I made you late."

When he'd gone, Bret made a second check of all the faucets to make sure they were dripping in a steady stream, then settled in at the desk in the small room he used as an office. Bookkeeping wasn't his

specialty, but he'd learned it to avoid having to turn his books over to a stranger.

He switched on the lamp and ignored the dust that coated his desk. Maybe one day, if he ever got his life back together, he'd build a new barn at the homestead, although he had to admit this old place had served him well for a lot of years.

He was adding up his first column of figures when the sound of the wooden door opening and closing made him raise his head. He made a mental note to oil the rusty hinges.

"You forget somethin'?" he called out.

But Aubrey didn't answer.

He got up from the desk, walked to the door and looked down the dark alley. The heaters with their eerie orange glow provided the only illumination and did little to breach the darkness, but the silhouette of a figure by the door was unmistakable. "Aubrey?"

Kate stepped out of the shadows.

"You are really something," she said, the harshness to her voice letting him know this wasn't his sweet Kate talking, but the hard-edged reporter Kathryn Morgan. He could feel her anger, even from thirty feet away. "You jerked me around like a puppet. You made me doubt my own sanity when I couldn't separate the two of you in my head. You used me, lied to me, manipulated me. You made me feel cheap and dirty because I let you touch me even when I knew it was wrong."

She walked over to him and slapped him hard across the face.

"Damn you, James!"

THREE DAYS PASSED before he decided he was ready to talk. On Sunday afternoon he showed up unannounced at the motel, looking as if he hadn't slept or shaved or even eaten since she'd left him. His handsome face appeared gaunt, his eyes red-rimmed and puffy. In the instant after she opened the door, she felt remorse for the agony she was putting him through, but it was quickly replaced with the anger that had boiled within her since she'd realized who he was and how he'd manipulated her.

At the barn when she'd confronted him, he'd denied everything and refused to talk to her. He'd walked away. Three days of stewing about it had apparently convinced him she wasn't going to simply disappear.

"You have to give me the chance to convince you not to publish what you know," he said now. Not…"I'm sorry," or "Forgive me," or "I care about you," or any of the declarations her schoolgirl heart had dreamed he might make.

"I *have* to?" she repeated incredulously. "I don't have to do a damn thing."

"Let's get out of here. Will you take a ride with me?"

"I suppose."

In the truck, as they rode, the air was frigid, but not only from the weather. James became silent and morose. For the moment Kate was glad of his silence, because she didn't know how they could ever resolve this. It also gave her the opportunity to study him.

James. She still couldn't believe it, even though the evidence sat next to her. She'd wished again and again after the plane crash that some miracle would

bring him back, and here he was—older and bigger than the James she'd known, but still vital and overwhelming. A mature man had replaced the willowy long-haired youth.

"Where are we going?" she asked.

"My house. If we're going to talk, I don't want to risk someone overhearing."

"Should I be worried you'll slit my throat and dump me in a ravine somewhere?"

His gaze flicked to her and returned to the road. "That's not funny, Kate."

"It wasn't meant to be."

"You can't actually believe I'd hurt you."

She wanted to say he already had. Instead, she chose silence, turning to watch the passing scenery from the side window. Let him wonder what she thought.

A few minutes later they pulled into the yard. James parked the truck and got out, coming around to open her door. When Kate stepped down, Sallie came wriggling up, licking Kate's shoes and slacks. Kate knelt and rubbed her head. "Hey, girl. How are you?"

"She missed you," he said, making her look up. He gave her a small tentative smile. "*I* missed you."

She frowned. "Don't," she warned. "I've heard enough of your lies to last me a lifetime." Angrily she stood and walked to the front door. James had left it unlocked, and she pushed it open and went inside. He followed her in, turning up the gas heater in the living room to knock the chill out of the air. He took their jackets and threw them over the back of the couch.

They faced each other across the living room like boxers in a ring. "Do you want to hit me again?" he asked finally.

The absurd question took some of the steam out of her. "Of course not."

"Then can we talk calmly about this?"

She swallowed the anger that had settled in her throat. "I don't know. I'm so furious right now I'm not sure I can stay in the same room with you long enough to talk."

"Will you try?"

Reluctantly she made her way to the couch. He came forward, apparently intending to sit next to her, but she quickly pointed to the other end. "Down there. I don't want you touching me, trying to manipulate me."

He did as she said, leaning forward to rest his forearms on his knees. "First," he said, "I want to tell you that, although I had no choice but to mislead you, I didn't like doing it."

"You used me. You pretended to have feelings for me so I'd get distracted and you could play out this bizarre little masquerade of yours."

"You're wrong about that."

"What really infuriates me is how you compromised my book. All that stuff about what a bad guy James Hayes was. I don't know what's true and what's fiction anymore. Do you know you've ruined years of work?" She didn't give him a chance to answer. "What possible reason is there for doing that?"

"It's a long story."

"Another fictionalized one, no doubt."

"Come on, Kate, ease up."

"Ease up? You're joking. All those lies you told, and you expect me to calmly sit here and listen to more of them?"

He sprang to his feet. "This isn't getting us anywhere. How long do you intend to stay mad at me?"

"As long as I breathe."

"Ah, forget it. Talking to you is like hitting myself in the head with a baseball bat. I don't know why I was stupid enough to think you'd care about me enough to listen."

He walked with angry strides to the front door, jerked it open and walked out.

Kate ran after him and onto the porch. He was already in the yard headed toward the side of the house, with Sallie racing next to him. "Where are you going?"

"Out," he said, not stopping.

"It's freezing."

"Yeah, but that's still a lot warmer than being in there with you."

"But you forgot your—" he disappeared around the corner of the house "—jacket." She sighed, went back inside and slammed the door. Well, let him freeze.

CHAPTER FOURTEEN

PIGHEADED. RATCHET-JAWED. Temperamental. With every stroke of the brush on the horse's flank, James thought of another word to describe Kate. Annoying. Exasperating. Stubborn. He'd never met a woman who riled him more than she did.

Sallie whined at his feet a second before the barn door squeaked. James had his back to the door, but Sallie's wagging tail told him it was Kate and not the wind that had made the noise. He continued to brush the horse, his heart in his throat, and it was only a few seconds before she came and stood silently at the horse's head. He glanced at her and she held out the jacket she'd draped over her arm. He slipped it on, then immediately resumed his brushing.

"Your leg," she said stiffly. "Did it heal okay?"

"Yes."

"And your side?"

"Fine."

She said nothing else for several minutes, only watched as he worked. The horse didn't need brushing. He'd already done it once today. But he enjoyed it. And it kept his hands busy and away from that lovely throat of hers.

"You still play the guitar sometimes, don't you?" The question surprised him and he stopped brushing

to look at her. He had an old acoustic guitar in the storage room, and occasionally at night he took it out, sat on the porch and serenaded Sallie and the deer that ate his garden. But Kate couldn't possibly have known that.

"How did you know I still play?"

"The calluses on your fingertips. I noticed them that day at the ranch, when you took me to see the graves of your ancestors." He raised his hand and rubbed his thumb across the calluses made by pressing the strings. "At the time I thought it odd you'd have calluses like that on one hand and not the other, particularly on the ends and not the pads of your fingers."

"Is that what tipped you off?"

"Partly." She reached into her pocket, took out a red-and-gray capsule and gave it to him. "Then there was this. You hid it in your jeans and lied about taking it that night you got hurt. James Hayes is allergic to penicillin, but Bret Hayes wasn't."

"I was hoping that had dissolved in the washing machine."

"I found it when I emptied your pockets."

"One pill and calluses on my fingers couldn't possibly have been all that gave me away."

"No, it was a hundred little things that didn't add up. Your lifestyle, the fact that you aren't living on the money you inherited. The inconsistencies bothered me from the beginning, and they only really made sense if you were James pretending to be Bret. But that seemed so implausible I couldn't force myself to even consider it. After I did, after I accepted

it *might* be possible, I set out to prove what I suspected.''

''And how did you do that?''

She took a deep breath and swallowed, as if the question was painful. ''By being logical. I started thinking... If the body identified by forensics wasn't yours and the body matched the records, then obviously the records belonged to the dead man—but had your name on them. I checked the chain of evidence and it was secure. No one could have tampered with the records after they arrived in the hands of the authorities. So the person who *supplied* the records had to have made the substitution. I took a second look at the report and found the identification was done solely through dental and sinus X rays supplied by your stepfather, who also happened to be your dentist. Since he'd also done most of Bret's early dental work, he had records for both of you. All he had to do was switch the names.''

''But you can't prove it. You can't prove I'm James.''

''You're right. I can't. But I can prove you're *not* Bret. I had a cop friend compare your fingerprints to the ones on Bret's old arrest record, and they don't match.''

''You took my fingerprints?''

''No, but I had them on one of my computer disks. You picked it up that last day at the kitchen table while we were talking. The disk was new. I'd gotten it out of the box that morning to make a backup of a file. The only prints on it were yours and mine.''

''Hell.''

''Your stepfather could be in a great deal of trou-

ble, you know. Tampering with a police investigation is a serious offense.''

''You're not telling me anything I haven't thought about or agonized over for years.'' He sighed and forcefully pushed his hand through his hair. ''What else do you know?''

''That you had a history of masquerading as Bret at least two years before the crash. Almost anyone would think the deed to this place and Pine Acres look fine, but the signatures had to be forged, because there's no way the real Bret could have signed them, even though he was still alive.''

''How did you figure that out?'' He was getting more exasperated by the minute. He'd known all along that she was clever, that she was one of the few people who knew enough about him to figure out what he'd done. But, he had to admit grudgingly, she was even more clever than he'd imagined.

''I used dates from newspaper articles, Bret's employment records and other sources, and had the computer run a chronology. Bret was on an oil rig in the middle of the Gulf of Mexico at the time this property was purchased, and until he got fired from the rig six months later, he didn't come ashore. The person who signed the papers had to be you disguised as Bret. Besides, he never had that kind of money. What I figure happened is that you used Bret's name and bought this place as…I don't know, some kind of hideaway. When you got tired of dealing with your fans and the media, you tucked your hair under your hat, put on a pair of cowboy boots and *became* him. The family resemblance was so strong that you were able to get away with it, despite the five-year age

difference. The ruse worked because the people here had never seen the real Bret. Did he even know about this place?''

"No, I never told him. I couldn't risk him showing up and people suddenly seeing two of us."

"Who knew?"

"Only Mom and George. Malcolm knew I had a place, but he didn't know where. And I never told the guys in the band."

"So you had this different identity conveniently available when you needed it, and everything worked fine until that night after the concert when you and Bret had your fight. He took your seat on the plane for some reason and you came here to cool off. When the plane crashed, your family didn't call you because they thought, along with everyone else in the world, that it was *James* who'd been killed. The telephone wasn't really unplugged, was it?''

"No. They didn't call me because they thought I was dead."

He blew out a heavy breath, closed his eyes and rubbed the spot between them where a headache was beginning to throb. He was also feeling queasy, a reaction, he supposed, to the stress he'd been under the past couple of days.

She'd caught him. And it sickened him that when she told, he'd be forced right back into the hell he'd managed to escape.

She touched his arm, causing him to open his eyes. He looked into her concerned face. "Are you all right?" she asked. "You're white as a sheet."

"Yeah, I'm okay. A little sick to my stomach."

"I've been through that myself the last few days."

Taking the brush from his hand and putting it down, she guided him to where he'd stacked bales of hay. She forced him to sit on one and put his head between his knees, pushing aside a confused Sallie who was trying to lick his face. "Go lie down and let me take care of him now," she told the dog.

She stood in front of him and lightly rubbed the back of his bent head. Out of compassion? He prayed it was something deeper.

When he felt better, he lifted his head and leaned against the wall. She sat down next to him. "You haven't slept, have you?" she asked.

"Not in a couple of days."

"And you probably haven't eaten anything."

He told her he hadn't, finding it frightening that she knew him so well. No wonder he was in this mess.

"You're going to make yourself sick," she said. "You have to start taking better care of yourself."

"Under the circumstances I don't really think it matters very much, do you?"

"I can't see how it will help for you to have another breakdown." His question must have shown on his face because she added, "I assumed you had some sort of breakdown or a serious case of depression after your brother died. I can't imagine you not going to his funeral only out of fear that you'd be recognized. You loved him too much. You must have been physically unable to go."

The fact that she didn't think him a total monster, that she understood how devastated he'd been by Bret's death, gave him a glimmer of hope.

"I was sick for months. I loved him, Kate. If you

don't believe anything else I've told you, believe that. I didn't want him to die."

"I know. I never doubted that."

"It was supposed to be me."

She turned away, but before she did, he thought he saw something in her expression. Pain? If it was, then perhaps he hadn't crushed whatever feelings she'd once had for him.

"What are you going to do?" he asked.

She leaned back against the wall, tilted her head upward and studied the aging beams above them. "I honestly don't know."

Indecision. That was good. He'd expected her to know exactly what she was going to do, to threaten to burn his ass in print for the lies he'd told her. This had to be a huge story, one that every reporter in the world would be ecstatic to write.

"This story will probably earn you another Pulitzer."

"That's not important to me, and you know it."

"Then walk away from it. Forget you know who I am."

There *was* pain this time when she looked at him. It distorted her lovely face and he suddenly had a sense of how difficult this situation was for her. She was hurting. She'd uncovered the biggest story of her career. And it was obvious she didn't want to have to tell it.

"Please…walk away," he urged again.

"You don't understand what you're asking. I've spent my whole life standing up for one thing—the truth. That's not some intangible principle to me, but a very real and precious thing."

"I'm not asking you to lie. Just don't tell what you know. Don't finish this book."

"My silence would be the same thing. If I don't correct the lies, I'm validating them. Hiding the fact that you didn't die in the plane crash makes me as guilty of conspiracy as the rest of you. And I have to finish this book, James. If I don't, Marcus and my editor will become suspicious. They know I'd never abandon this project because I've been too passionate about it. And I have a contract."

"But if you finish it, you'll hurt Mom and Ellen and George. You'll hurt me."

"I know." Her voice was thick with anguish.

"I can't go back, Kate. I can't go back to what I was, who I was. That life came close to destroying me once. I couldn't survive it a second time."

"Did you hate it that much?"

"Yes. At least, toward the end I did. The music wasn't enough anymore. Too much overshadowed it. Lenny's breakdown, Lauren's suicide. Those fans getting killed. One tragedy followed another. Then, in those last few months, Bret started showing up unexpectedly, demanding large sums of money, saying I owed him for all the years he'd suffered for being my little brother. *Owed* him for being my brother. My God! Can you imagine how that made me feel? He started hanging out with people who didn't have anything better to do than party all night. When I caught him using drugs, that was it. I couldn't take any more. I quit."

"Quit?" She sat straight up. Her voice and her shocked look told him he'd finally said something she hadn't known.

"Yeah, Kate. Quit. I walked out without even packing a bag, intending never to go back. So you see, it wouldn't really be a lie if you said rock star James Hayes died that night. He really did. And before that airplane ever crashed."

THE CRITICS CALLED HIM a genius, but he was simply a kid who enjoyed music more than he enjoyed anything else. He couldn't understand why people paid to hear him play and sing when, to his own ears, he could never quite get the music he composed to sound right.

But they did come, night after night and by the thousands. And as long as they came, he played. He always considered the concerts an extension of the jamming sessions he and Lenny and some of the guys used to have on weekends in the basement of Lenny's grandmother's house. He played because it was fun—for a while.

Even now, with years to reflect on it, he wasn't sure when or how the golden life had started to lose its luster. Maybe it was because he'd been naive to think that charmed life would continue, that he could play how he wanted, when he wanted, with nothing to interfere. Stardom had been unexpected. And because he was too young to understood that stardom carried a price tag, he let himself be lured by it.

And everything happened so quickly. Within weeks of his first album's release, he couldn't go anywhere without being recognized. At first it was flattering. He was only a kid, after all, a thin kid with little sexual experience who suddenly found himself adored and desired by women he didn't even know. And for a

time he allowed himself to sample everything that was offered to him.

But he soon found himself a prisoner of the people he worked so hard to entertain. The fans literally tried to tear him apart if he let them get too close.

He endured it for years, until the slender threads that held him to his brother began to break, one by one. By the time of the concert in Rome, Georgia, he no longer knew the angry man he fought with in that hotel room. The good kid who'd wanted to follow in his footsteps had turned into a hate-filled man who blamed everyone but himself for his inability to find his place in life.

You owe me. The words Bret spat in anger at him that night still sliced James like a knife...

"YOU OWE ME, man. Do you have any idea what it's like being the little brother of the great James Hayes?"

The contempt in his brother's voice surprised James, and for a moment he was speechless. Their relationship had deteriorated over the past few months, but he hadn't realized how far until Bret had shown up tonight demanding more money.

"All I want is a measly five thousand dollars," Bret said.

"I gave you money two weeks ago. You couldn't have spent it already."

"You can afford it. You carry more than that in your wallet all the time. I've seen it."

"That's not the point."

"Then what is?" Bret moved back and forth across the bedroom with the nervous pace of a caged animal,

seeming more agitated by the moment. His eyes were wild; his body shook although the temperature in the suite was comfortable.

"You're on something," James said.

"No."

James wanted to believe him, but all the physical signs were there. He walked to him and grabbed him around the back of the neck, pulling his face close so he could look him in the eye. "Don't lie to me." Bret tried to pull away but couldn't. Growing up, even though Bret was younger, he was always bigger and stronger. James rarely wrestled him and won. But tonight James moved Bret around as easily as a rag doll. "I want to know what you're on."

"I told you, *nothing.*"

"I don't believe you."

"Who gives a shit what you believe?"

James let go of him and he fell back across one of the beds. "You'd better give a shit if you want my money. I'm not financing your drug habit."

Bret sat up and straightened his clothes. "It's not drugs."

"What, then?"

"I got in a little over my head on a deal." He nervously licked his lips. "I need to pay the people off."

"What kind of deal?"

He hesitated, then said, "A bet."

"Gambling?" James took his turn pacing now. "Who?"

"Better you don't know. Let's just say that if I don't come up with five thousand by midnight, I'll be permanently disabled."

"Why didn't you tell me this to begin with?"

"Because I was afraid you wouldn't help me."

"Haven't I always helped you when you needed me?" Bret didn't say anything. "Haven't I?"

Bret stood. "Yeah, big brother. Every time I get my sorry ass in trouble, you're right there to bail me out and remind me what a disappointment I am to you. Your *help* always comes with a lecture. So how about giving me the money and the lecture and letting me get the hell out of here?"

"When are you going to get your life together? You can't keep a job. You have no plans. No goals. Mom and George are going crazy wondering what to do about you." Bret didn't respond, just gave him a blank stare. "I don't understand why you're so unhappy. I'd give anything to be you, to be free to do anything I wanted."

"Free?" Bret asked angrily. "I'm not free. I'm James Hayes's little brother. Do you have any idea what that's like?"

"You keep throwing that in my face. Why don't you enlighten me?"

"Because it's not worth wasting my time." He turned and headed toward the door.

"Wait!" With a sadness that cut him to the bone, James opened his wallet, took out five thousand dollars and offered it to him. "That's it, Bret. I mean it. Settle your debt and don't come back asking for more because I won't give it to you. No more money. And no more lectures."

"AND WHAT DID HE DO?" Kate asked, bringing James back the present.

"He took the money and left without a word."

"But it wasn't the last time you saw him that night, was it?"

"No. Later, after the concert, we fought again like I told you. Physically."

"So everything you told me about that night was true?"

"Yes. I cut the last set short and went back to the hotel. He wasn't expecting us so soon. He was having a little party in my suite with four or five people I'd never even seen before. He'd lied to me, Kate. The story about the gambling was a cover."

"He admitted that?"

"Yeah. He used the money I gave him to buy drugs."

"I'm so sorry," she said, putting her hand over his. He turned his hand to thread his fingers through hers, finding comfort in touching her.

"When I walked in and found him putting that blotting paper in his mouth, I went crazy, started beating the hell out of him and had to be pulled off by some of the band members. When I calmed down, Bret begged me to help him get straightened out, but I thought it was another of his lies and I couldn't handle it. I'd had enough, so I told Malcolm and the guys I was leaving for few days to cool off. I didn't tell them I didn't intend to come back."

"Why was Bret on the plane?"

"I don't know. Christmas was coming up and the band had a break until after the holidays, so I'd like to think Bret decided to catch a ride home. But the truth is, he could've been so out of it, the guys stuck him on the plane and hoped Mom and George would

deal with him when they landed.'' He shook his head. ''Only...they never landed. Webb, Malcolm—all of them were gone in an instant. When I heard the body count and that *I* had been on the plane, I knew it was Bret.''

He thought the tears would come then, but they didn't. After so many years, so many tears shed, perhaps there were none left to fall.

''I can't help thinking,'' he continued, ''how ironic it is. I envied Bret the freedom he had. I wished more than once I could change places with him permanently and be able to go anywhere and do anything I wanted without people recognizing me. That night I got what I wanted. And in a sad way I think Bret got what he'd always wanted, too.''

''What was that?''

''To be me.''

CHAPTER FIFTEEN

"WHAT ARE YOU GOING to do?" he asked her again.

"Fix you something to eat."

"That's not what I meant."

"I know, but at the moment that's the only answer I have."

They walked to the house where Kate made him an omelet and prepared a pot of coffee. She sat quietly at the table while he ate, thinking about everything he'd told her and how difficult it had been for him to share it.

What *was* she going to do? She wished she had an answer. This was an impossible situation with no obvious solution. She saw no way to finish this book and maintain her integrity without exposing him. But to expose him, to subject him to the media circus that would follow... If he thought his life had been hell before the crash, it would be a hundred times worse if he suddenly showed up alive. And there was no guarantee, despite the advanced age of his mother and stepfather, that they wouldn't face criminal charges.

"I can see the wheels in your head turning," he said.

"I was thinking about your family. Did you tell them I know?"

"Hell, Kate, I never even told them I was giving

you an interview, much less about this. When you came here, I warned them you were digging around, but then I lied and said you'd given up and gone back to Chicago. What about you? Did you tell your brother? What about this cop? Does he know?''

"No one knows but me. My friend who looked at the prints won't think twice about them, and Marcus believes I'm down here tying up a few loose ends. He doesn't completely buy my cover story, though, and he suspects there's something funny going on, but he loves me enough not to press me at the moment. He and I have always been close.''

"I'm close to my family, too. I talk to them by phone a couple of times a week and we exchange letters once a month or more. Mom's always been there for me. George, too, after my dad died and he and Mom got married.''

"You should practice not calling him George.''

"Why?''

"Bret was only five when your real father died. George was the only father he knew, wasn't he?''

He nodded with understanding. "And Bret called him Dad, not George. I'd never even thought about that. I'm not very good at this intrigue stuff, am I?''

"You almost fooled me.''

"Yeah,'' he said, frowning. "Almost.'' He pushed a piece of egg around his plate with his fork as he glanced down at Sallie, no doubt wishing he'd fed *her* to the dog that first afternoon.

"Did you plan the cover-up?''

"No, I'd never have done that or even approved of it. I didn't even know about it until after Mom did it. That's no excuse for not rectifying things when I

found out, but emotionally I couldn't handle anything right then. When I could function normally again, the damage was done. Too much time had passed to keep Mom and George out of trouble.''

"I find it incredible that she conceived this scheme, much less got away with it.''

"She convinced herself it was the only way to save me from a life I hated. She'd already lost Bret. She didn't want to lose me, too.''

"But the whole world believes that drug-filled body in the wreckage was yours. Your reputation is ruined forever because of what she did.''

"It's a small price to pay for my freedom.''

"And what about the tarnished reputation you gained by becoming Bret? How do you live with that?''

"By trying constantly to improve it.''

The significance of what he said hit her full force.

"Memorials! My God, they're memorials to your brother! The plaques with your—I mean Bret's—name on them, Pine Acres, the other ranches, all the money you've given away, have been in *his* name. You told me you didn't want to profit from your brother's death, but as Bret, you *were* profiting indirectly by running all those millions through your foundation and not his. I couldn't reconcile that contradiction. But you did it because you wanted *Bret* credited for the gifts, and not you. All the donations will live on as memorials to him.''

"I guess you could call them memorials. I don't have the power to bring him back, but I can take this life he gave me and do something better with it, make

him somebody people look up to and remember. He didn't leave much of worth, but I can change that.''

"I couldn't understand why the information you gave me was so different from my research, but when I realized who you were, the discrepancies made sense. You were purposely trying to sabotage my book. You were afraid I'd make Bret look bad and you look too good.''

"I had to do it, Kate, but I *am* sorry.''

"Sorry won't help repair the damage you did to my work. And you told me so many lies I'm not even sure I know how to fix things.''

"I could help you.''

Her eyes narrowed with suspicion. "Help me? Two minutes ago you begged me not to publish it. Why would you want to help me?''

"To buy time to convince you not to publish it. I'll help you in exchange for time.''

She shook her head. "I'm not dealing with you anymore. I can't trust you to tell me the truth, and I'm already in danger of missing my deadline.''

"Please hear me out. I swear I'm not trying to coerce you or mislead you. I'm only asking for the chance to convince you not to print what you know. And in exchange for your time, I'll answer honestly anything you want to ask me.''

She took her cup to the sink and rinsed it out, needing a moment to think and to put some distance between them. It was difficult to be rational when he was within ten feet of her. She constantly battled the desire to put her arms around him, to express physically the feelings she'd always held for him.

He came up behind her, reached around and put his own cup in the sink. "Please?"

She turned to face him. "I can't tell you what I'm going to do, because I don't know yet. This is too big a decision for me to make without a great deal of soul-searching. But I *will* promise not to do anything for a couple of weeks."

"Thank you."

"And I won't insist you help me fix the book."

"That's an unexpected concession."

"I got myself into this mess and I'll get myself out—somehow." He was standing close, too close, and she fought back a choking emotion. "What am I supposed to call you now?"

"Continue to call me Bret. That's what my family does. That's who I've become. I think of myself as Bret now."

"But you aren't Bret. You're James. And a part of me has known that all along, I think, even with the disguise."

"I worried about that, especially when you dropped that bomb on me and said we'd met before. I got scared you might recognize me."

"Did you remember me from when we met at Columbia?"

"No," he said, breaking her heart. "Something about you seemed familiar and nagged at my memory, but I met so many people at interviews and concerts back then, and it was so long ago."

"Of course it was." She was crazy to think she might have made the same impression on him that he'd made on her.

"I went nuts that night at the motel, trying to come

up with the details of our meeting. I kept asking myself—did she interview me? Did I sleep with her? What? I thought about going back to your door, banging on it and asking, but I was afraid my curiosity might make you suspicious.''

"That's why you asked me to go riding, wasn't it."

"I needed an excuse to talk to you about it some more. I had to know what happened, whether or not I'd hurt you, and taking you to see the ranch gave me a way to do that. You have to understand that in my early days I was bad about getting drunk and waking up in bed with women I didn't know. I had to make sure you hadn't been one of them.''

"I wasn't.'' She told him the complete story, how he'd convinced her to stay in school and have faith in herself. "It was innocent, like I told you, until I stupidly offered myself to you. Thank God, you turned me down.''

"Must be one of the few times in my life I did the right thing.'' He put his hands against her face. "I won't turn you down again. I'm giving you fair warning about that.''

"Don't.''

"Don't what? Don't tell you that even now, when I know you're probably going to expose me, all I can think about is how much I want you? Don't tell you how much I need you in my life? I'm empty without you, Kate.''

"Please, Jamie, don't.'' She tried to move past him, but he held her tight and refused to let her go.

"Oh, no, you're not running away from me or from

what I have to say to you. I was miserable when you went home to Chicago. Losing you tore me in half.''

''Don't lie to me. Not about this. It's too important.'' She turned her head, but he forced her to look at him.

''I can't blame you for not trusting me. I've lied to you. I said awful things to you that night we fought. But it was because I'm in love with you, Kate, and I completely lost it when I found out I was competing with myself.''

She couldn't respond.

''I said I'm in love with you.''

She was barely able to find her voice. ''I heard you. But you're only saying this so I won't go through with the book.''

''No, I'm not. If you won't believe what I'm telling you, I'll have to show you.''

He took his time kissing her, engulfing her to the point that she couldn't protest, couldn't think, almost couldn't breathe. She clung to him because her body wouldn't let her do otherwise, and because she suddenly felt weightless, as if she might drift away without the anchor of his arms about her.

When at last he lifted his head, what she saw in his eyes extinguished her breath completely.

He was telling the truth.

THAT AFTERNOON James brought Henry back to the house for a visit, and the boy squealed when he saw Kate, holding out his arms to be held. Once numerous kisses were exchanged, Henry stuck out a tiny boot-covered foot and showed it to her.

''See, Mo?''

"Oh, what do we have here?" she asked. "Are those new boots?"

He nodded and pointed to James. "Bet bot me lik him boos."

Kate looked at James in desperation. "Can you translate that? I don't have a clue."

"He's trying to tell you I bought him boots like mine a couple of weeks ago."

"Oh!" She made a big show of examining Henry's boots and fussing over them. "I think those are the best-looking boots I've ever seen. You can use those to ride Patch, can't you?"

His dark head bobbed.

Watching them together filled James with such longing that he nearly couldn't speak when Kate asked him how the other kids at the ranch were doing.

"What's wrong?" she asked, becoming concerned at his odd behavior. "Are the kids okay?"

"Nothing's wrong," he said at last. "The kids are fine." He took Henry from Kate's arms. "Come on, partner. Let's get this jacket off you."

"Toons?" Henry asked. He pointed to the TV.

"Okay, but I bought you something that's going to be fun, and I want you to use it and not sit here watching cartoons all day." He put in a Bugs Bunny video, then took a drawing pad and crayons from a paper sack in the bookcase and gave them to the child.

The three of them settled on the couch and, to James's disappointment, Henry sat in the middle. But it wasn't long before the boy was sprawled on top of them both, his legs in James's lap and his head in

Kate's. She scratched lightly across his small back as he drew.

"What's the status of you-know-who's case?" she asked. Henry attention was glued to his artwork.

"It goes to court in three weeks."

"Anything new happening?"

"Nothing."

She gazed down at Henry, who was distracted by the colored circles he was drawing. "He loves you, you know. He thinks of you as his father."

James swallowed hard. "I know he does."

He'd thought about Henry a great deal in the past few days, what effect it might have on the boy if Kate published her book. And if she didn't. His sad conclusion was that he couldn't adopt the child either way. The risk was too great.

Besides, Henry needed a complete family, one with two parents and siblings. After what he'd been through, he deserved the best life could give him. James didn't know if he even possessed the qualities necessary for fatherhood. He'd failed so miserably at being a good brother. Chances were he'd probably fail at being a good father, too.

Henry giggled and pointed to the scribble on his sketch pad. "Mo."

"Oh," Kate said. "Let me see. You drew my picture?"

Henry nodded.

Kate looked at it and pretended amazement. "That's so good! I can't believe you drew that. I'm in a tornado? What are all these things around me?" She pointed to a series of spirals.

"Uh-oh," James said.

"Mo...debil," Henry said, then he gestured at the TV where the Tasmanian devil had whirled to a stop in front of an unconcerned Bugs Bunny.

"Who told you I was like that?"

Henry grinned at James. "Bet."

"You're in big trouble, Hayes."

"Hayes? Is that the name you've decided on?"

"It's the best I can do."

"I can think of some better ones."

"Like what?"

"Darling. Sweetheart. Lover."

She shook her head. "I think I'll stick with Hayes."

"But that's what you call me when you're irritated with me."

"I know, and I have a feeling that's going to be appropriate most of the time."

"Does that mean I won't ever get to see that pretty smile of yours again? I sure have missed it."

"Don't try to charm me. It won't work."

"I'm simply stating facts. I've missed a lot of things about you, the way you snort when you laugh too hard, and how you sing off-key when you cook. I've missed your smell in the house and seeing your shoes next to mine at the back door. I've actually missed those pencils sticking out of your hair like antennae."

She bit her lip. Patches of color appeared on her cheeks. "Ha, ha."

"I even miss your annoying chatter," he added.

"You're crazy if you've missed that."

"Crazy about you."

Henry sat up and thrust his pad at them. "Bet," he said, pointing to a swirl.

"I like that," James told him. "And this one? Is that you?"

Henry nodded.

James looked at the drawing and his mood plummeted. Kate. Him. Henry. *Together.* At least as scribbles on paper. What he wouldn't give to have that in real life.

SHE NEVER AGREED to let James help with the book, but he was an expert at slyly easing things into the conversation. By the end of the next week they'd settled into a comfortable routine of getting together after he finished his work each day to have supper either at his house or the grill and to talk.

He was so open in what he told her, so interesting as he related the tales of his boyhood and rise to fame, that she conveniently forgot she wasn't going to let him help her. She looked forward to their sessions, to simply seeing him, much like a child who knows she's going to Disneyland every night at six o'clock. Each time he walked through the door at the motel, fresh from the shower and smelling like heaven, her stomach fluttered.

This night he didn't make it until eight. He handed her a sweatshirt, a flannel shirt and a thick jacket and told her to put them on. "We're going to be outside," he said. "Wear heavy socks and your tennis shoes. And go change into your oldest pair of jeans. Nothing that can get messed up."

"Messed up? Now wait a minute, Hayes. You

know I'm a city girl and I don't like getting messed up. Where are you taking me?''

"It's a surprise."

"I don't like surprises."

"You'll like this one, city girl."

Quilts and pillows lay stacked in the jump seat of the truck. He'd also brought a full grocery sack and clothes hangers, which only increased Kate's curiosity. "If you get me dirty or bitten by something, I'll never forgive you," she told him. "I'm warning you, I go more than a little nuts over spiders. *And* lizards. *And* roaches. And don't even *say* the word *snake* to me. I mean it."

He chuckled. "Will you relax? This is an adventure. Enjoy it."

When they turned onto the dirt road leading to his house, Kate sighed in relief, certain he'd only been teasing her. But he drove past the house to the gate that marked the end of the yard and the beginning of the back pasture. Opening the gate and ordering Sallie to stay in the yard, he took the road that led away from the lighted barn.

"Hayes, I'm not sure about this," she said uneasily, seeing little except darkness beyond the headlights of the truck. He was taking her into the middle of nowhere, and nowhere wasn't a place she wanted to go.

A few minutes later he stopped the truck, put it in Reverse and backed up a few yards, stopped again, put it in Park and let the engine idle. "We're here," he announced, a playful tone to his voice.

"You're joking." Kate looked through the back window and saw nothing. No house, no barn, no food

to appease her growling stomach. Nope, this wasn't going to be the kind of adventure she enjoyed.

He adjusted the heater. ''Stay in the truck where it's warm until I get the fire going and the lanterns on.''

He disappeared out the door and for a time, she couldn't see or hear anything. Then she heard a popping sound, and a fire roared to life behind the truck. Two lanterns flickered on to chase away the darkness.

He opened the door, leaned in to shut off the engine and said, ''Come on out.''

Reluctantly she did. They were in a pasture, miles away from civilization.

''Grab those pillows,'' he said, pushing the seat forward to get the grocery bag and the quilts.

''Why do we need quilts and pillows?''

''For the show.''

''What show? I hate to point this out, but there's no theater here.''

''This is a different kind of show. But first I'm going to cook you dinner.''

''*You're* going to cook? The man whose idea of a hot meal is sticking his bowl of cereal in the microwave? Now I *know* this adventure isn't for me.'' She followed him anyway, as he walked around to the back of the truck to let the tailgate down and deposit everything on top of it.

''Trust me, Kate. This kind of cooking I can do.''

She looked in the sack and saw hot-dog wieners, buns and chips. ''And how do you intend to cook these things?'' He picked up the metal clothes hangers and rattled them; Kate shook her head. ''Hot dogs

cooked on a clothes hanger? That's your idea of dinner?"

She laughed, unable to help herself. When he'd called and said he wanted to take her out for a change, she'd imagined them driving out of town for an intimate dinner at a nice restaurant and maybe going to a late movie.

"Now I know why you were so secretive and why you laughed when I offered to pay for dinner."

"You'll like this. Now loosen up and spread those quilts in the bed of the truck while I get the hot dogs ready."

He left her no choice but to do what he said. She took care of the quilts while he burned the ends of the clothes hangers to sterilize them and prepared the hot dogs for cooking. When she'd finished, she joined him by the fire.

Obviously he'd planned this "dinner" in advance. The wood had already been stacked for the fire and he'd dragged a fat log near it that made a perfect place for sitting. He'd placed the lanterns several feet outside their small circle to give them light but draw the bugs away. Nearby was a small ice chest.

With the fire and the dark sky filled with millions of twinkling stars, she had to admit it was better than any dinner at a restaurant could have been. "You surprise me," she said, sitting next to him on the log. "This is nice."

He gave her that sexy smile of his and handed her a wiener with a wire pushed through it. She stuck it in the flames. "I was sure that once you got out here, you'd like it," he told her.

"When did you plan this?"

"The beginning of the week, but I didn't know until this afternoon whether it would be clear enough to see the show."

"And what show is that?"

"Look up and watch for a few minutes." She did. Before long a meteor streaked across the sky, then another. "The guy on the news said it's supposed to be pretty impressive. I thought you'd enjoying watching the meteor shower if you had a comfortable spot. After we've eaten, we can crawl under those quilts and have front-row seats."

Warmth suffused her, and she couldn't blame it on the blazing fire. His idea had been so simple, yet she found it incredibly romantic. He was offering her a sky full of stars.

He reached behind them and opened the ice chest. "How about something to drink? I've got a bunch of different stuff."

Kate leaned back and looked at the variety of soft drinks in the ice chest. "What, no wine to go with the hot dogs?" She picked up a grape soda and popped the top.

He laughed, but then he said seriously, "I don't drink anymore, Kate. When I was young I did a good bit of drinking and, well, running around with women, but both quickly lost their appeal."

"So what you told me before was true? You had a problem with alcohol?"

"No, not to the extent I led you to believe. Yeah, I drank a lot there for a while, more than I should have, but I gave it up easily and I've never missed it. My decision to stop wasn't based on fear that I was becoming an alcoholic, but on wanting to take back

control of my life. And despite what the tabloids said, I never used drugs. Never.''

"What about the women? Did you really screw your way across the country?" She asked the question in the same matter-of-fact way he'd thrown the comment at her during their argument weeks earlier. Asking it hurt, but she had to know the truth.

He took a sip of his Coke, considering his answer. "Boy, you dig right down to the bone, don't you? I forget that sometimes."

"You promised no more lies between us."

"I don't want there to be."

"Then tell me the truth about the women, about Lauren. You say you loved her, but still you saw other women. You slept with other women."

"Yes, I slept with a lot of women, but I never slept with another woman while Lauren and I were together. I would never do that to someone I cared for, and I swear that's the truth. If she'd felt the same, maybe Bret and I wouldn't have drifted so far apart."

"What are you telling me?"

"You know what I'm telling you. You already know he was in love with her. He was also sleeping with her—which helped widen the rift between us."

"I heard the rumors, but I wasn't sure it had gone that far."

"I blame her and not him. She only did it to hurt me, but Bret really did care for her."

"What did you do when you found out?"

"I was angry and hurt. She'd used him, used both of us, and I broke off the relationship. Bret blamed me for what had happened between them. He said if I'd paid more attention to her, she wouldn't have

needed to turn to him. Maybe he was right. I don't know.''

"Why did she want to hurt you? Because you were reluctant to help her solo career?''

"She didn't have the talent or maturity to go it alone, Kate. And emotionally she wasn't a very stable person. Sometimes it frightened me how despondent she could get and over the simplest things.''

"I'm surprised she stayed with the band after you broke it off.''

"Only because she thought she could finally talk me into helping her.'' He gave her a sheepish look. "I had a reputation for being a soft touch with the band and the road crew. Lauren thought she could eventually convince me.''

"And she did.''

Sighing, he said, "Against my better judgment, I let her do a couple of songs on that last album.''

"And when the fans and critics hated her, she couldn't handle it and she killed herself. Do you blame yourself for that, too?''

He turned away to stare into the fire. "Sometimes. I cared for her once and I wish I could've talked her into seeing a shrink, getting some help.'' He cleared his throat. "Uh, I think you've cremated that hot dog.''

Kate yanked it out of the fire, where it had slowly turned black as they talked. The meat resembled a lump of coal, and smoke rose from the end. "Oh, shoot.''

"And you claim *I'm* a bad cook.'' She punched him in the shoulder for that remark. "Here,'' he said,

handing her his. "Finish cooking this one while I fix some more."

He rose and stuck several more wieners on the wires. This time Kate was more successful, and it wasn't long before they were able to eat. "Not bad," she said, finishing her third one.

"Want another?"

She patted her full stomach under the layers of thick clothing. "No, I think that was plenty."

"Was it as good as going to a restaurant?"

"Ten times better."

That made him smile. "How about some music?"

"I'd love some."

He got up and walked to the truck, and Kate expected him to turn on the radio. When he pulled out a guitar from the jump seat, she held her breath. It must have been under the quilts, because she hadn't seen it.

Sitting down next to her again, he tested the strings to see if they were in tune. "I'm rusty at playing in front of anybody," he said. "Don't be too critical."

Critical? Was he kidding? She was a private audience for James Hayes and he was afraid she'd be critical?

His long fingers began to move over the strings and the sweet clear voice she knew so well filled the air. But this was a song she'd never heard before, although she knew—somehow—that he'd written it. The last note faded to silence and he stared at her. She couldn't speak.

"You're killing me, Kate. Say something."

"That was incredible. Why haven't I ever heard it before?"

"Because I only composed it a few months ago."

"It is very different from your earlier songs, but I love it. Do you compose often?"

"A good bit. For myself and Sallie."

"Will you play some of the songs for me?"

He played several more, all as beautiful as the first. Kate turned toward him on the log, crossing her arms over her knees. She put her head down to listen. Closing her eyes, she allowed herself to forget her problems and enjoy the moment.

"Hey," he said, bumping her. "You're not going to sleep on me, are you?"

"No, I was listening to you sing and play. Your voice is even more beautiful today than it was when you were performing. And I love these new songs. They're wonderful."

"Thanks. I think they're the best I've ever written."

"I still like your old ones, too."

"Do you have a favorite? Name it and I'll sing it for you."

Her heart squeezed painfully. He'd asked her the same thing the night he'd brought her up on stage. "'Coming Home to You,'" she said, her voice quaking.

He sang the ballad, the story of a man who achieves fortune and fame only to realize that everything of importance is waiting for him at home. As a teenager she'd fantasized that *she* was the wife of the man in the song, that *she* was the mother of the children he raced home to be with. And, of course, Jamie was the husband.

"Do you miss the life you had?" she asked when

he'd finished. "I know you were unhappy, but isn't there some part of it you enjoyed? I know I'd be devastated if for some reason I couldn't write."

"I still like composing and playing my guitar."

"But is it enough to do that only for yourself and not for an audience?"

"I don't know. I never really liked performing, but sometimes I wish..." He shook his head and she prodded him to continue. "Sometimes I wish people could hear the new songs I've composed. And my symphonies."

"Symphonies?"

"That's something I've tried in the last couple of years. I really love it, but I'm not sure I'm any good. I'm used to composing on a piano and I don't have one here, so I've had to do the composing for all the instruments in my head."

"James, I don't know much about composing, but that has to be an incredible accomplishment."

He shrugged. "Well, it's interesting, anyway. My only regret is I'll never hear the music actually played by an orchestra."

"I regret that, too. I'd love to hear it."

"But to answer your question, I'm happy living here and raising horses, being able to do small things like going out to the grill and having a leisurely breakfast without some fan trying to tear me apart."

"Or some nosy reporter stealing your bacon?"

"Yes," he said, chuckling. "This freedom's a wonderful thing after years of having to hide inside my house in Chattanooga. It makes up for not being able to sing and play publicly."

"Honestly?"

"Yes, but…I have to admit I didn't realize how lonely this life would be. In some ways I'm still a prisoner, because I'm shackled by the lies I've told. And any woman who shares my life would also have to share my lies and honor my decision not to have children. I know it's not fair to ask anyone to do that, to live with me knowing that at any time my secret could be discovered and our lives could change. She'd have to be pretty special. And she'd have to love who I am *now* and not the rock star."

His eyes told her he wanted her to be that woman.

"James, I don't know what you expect me to say."

"Yes, you do, but obviously you're not ready to say it. I can wait." He took her hand, lightly rubbing his thumb across her fingers. "Sorry, I didn't mean to spoil the night for you."

"You haven't. I've loved every minute of it."

"You'll love this next part even more. The meteors are really starting to pick up. Want to watch a country boy's idea of a show?"

"Country boy, I wouldn't miss it."

HE'D BROUGHT six quilts, enough for padding underneath them and cover to keep them warm. Until she was lying next to him in the makeshift bed, James hadn't considered how difficult it would be to keep his hands to himself. Within minutes he'd shed his jacket, the heat of his desire making him feel like one of those wieners roasting over the fire.

Bad analogy, he realized as he shifted to relieve the pain of his arousal.

Despite the cold, he could easily make love to her right here, and he sensed that it wouldn't take much

on his part to persuade her. He was, after all, an expert at talking women out of their clothes. But this wasn't just some woman he'd picked up to ease his need for sex. This was the woman he loved. He didn't want to hurt her. Before, when she thought he was Bret, they had moved too quickly toward a sexual relationship. When, or if, they had one now would depend on her.

"Are you uncomfortable?" Her voice broke the silence.

"No, why?"

"You're so restless."

Restless wasn't the word for it.

"I'm fine," he said. "Are you comfortable? Not too cold?"

"Too warm, actually. I think I'll take off this jacket."

Better leave it on if you know what's good for you.

"I'll help you."

She sat up and he pulled off the jacket, tossing it at their feet. Settling down under the quilts again, she sighed, "Much better."

A large glowing light raced across the sky. "Fireball!" they shouted in unison.

"I saw it first," Kate said.

"No way. You only yelled after I did."

"I did not! I saw it at least a second before you did. I can count more shooting stars than you any day of the week, Hayes."

"No way, Morgan. You're on." Two more shot through the sky and he called them out. She saw the next one first, but then he saw two more. "See, I'm already ahead," he teased. "When you lose, you have

to cook a special dinner for me. I want something Creole or Hawaiian with a fancy name I can't pronounce and lots of shrimp in it. And you have to wear a costume to serve it. A very tiny costume.''

She cackled about that. ''And if I win, what do you do for me, Hayes? And don't say cook. You used up the coat hangers, so you've exhausted your skills in that department.''

''Anything you want. Just name it.''

She was silent.

''Well, what's the matter, Morgan? Can't decide?''

''No,'' she said softly. And then she added something that made him certain he would never, ever love a woman the way he loved her. ''I can't think of anything you haven't already given me.''

CHAPTER SIXTEEN

SHE NEEDED to get some work done, but as she sat that next afternoon at the computer in her motel room, Kate's thoughts kept drifting to the night before.

James hadn't brought her back until the wee hours of the morning, and even then, it was much too soon to suit her. What a magical night. She could have stayed forever.

Deciding she wasn't going to do anything productive today, she shut off the computer. The clock on the bedside table said four-thirty, and already the winter sky was darkening. James expected her at the house by six.

She needed to call Marcus and check in, but that was a daily chore she'd come to dread. Lying to Marcus, pretending she was hard at work following up with additional questions for the book, was killing her.

With a heavy burden of guilt, she called and was relieved to find him already gone from the office and not yet home. "Tell him everything's fine and that I'll talk to him tomorrow," she told his wife, hanging up.

She took her bath and was about to get dressed when the telephone rang. She answered, expecting it to be Marcus calling her back.

"Miss Kate?" a voice said.

"Yes, this is Kate."

"This is Aubrey."

"Oh, Aubrey, hi. I didn't recognize the voice."

"Miss Kate, I'm sorry to bother you, but...well, somethin's happened and I didn't know what to do, who else to call."

Kate's heart nearly stopped beating. "What's wrong?"

"It's Bret, ma'am."

"Oh, no! Is he hurt?"

"No, ma'am, calm down. He's not hurt. Well, not the way you think. But I'm pretty sure he needs you to come out."

"Aubrey, tell me what's wrong."

"That Jane lady called, the one who runs the kids' ranch. Seems Henry's mama decided to 'fess up to what she done. She's signed papers sayin' she don't want to be Henry's mama no more."

"But, Aubrey, that's wonderful news!"

"Yes ma'am, I thought so, too. At first. Only that Miss Jane said they have a family to adopt Henry and they sent him off."

"Sent him off permanently?"

"Yes, ma'am. He's gone already. And poor Bret, they won't tell him nothin', not even where the boy's gone. He's takin' it real hard."

Kate sank to the bed. She'd feared this might happen, but she'd resisted telling James, not wanting to be the one to give him such news. With no claim on the boy, James had no legal right to know where Henry was going or who he'd be living with.

"Aubrey, where's Bret now?"

"I left him at the house. He asked me and Willie to go home early, said he had to be alone, but, ma'am, he's hurtin'. He's in a real bad way. I think maybe you're the only one who can help him right now. He loves you. You know that, don't you, ma'am?"

"Yes, Aubrey, I know that."

"If you have any kind of feelin's for him..."

"I'm on my way."

Darkness had fallen by the time she arrived, and no light came from the house. She'd scolded James frequently about never locking his doors, but tonight she was thankful he hadn't listened to her. She found him sitting in his bed, barely visible in the dark.

When she reached for the light switch by the door, he said, "Please, don't turn it on." His voice was flat and lifeless. "They took Henry away, Kate."

"I know. Aubrey called and told me." She walked to the bed and sat down. She couldn't see his features clearly, but she located his hands and held them.

"You shouldn't have come," he said.

"You shouldn't be alone."

"I am alone," he said in anguish. "Being alone is my hell for what I did to my brother."

She leaned forward and wrapped him in her arms, laying her head on his chest. His soul was tortured, not only over Henry, but over his brother's death, and he had a long way to go before he could deal with the grief and guilt. He'd never really faced it, despite what he might believe.

He held on to her, trembling. "You're not alone," she whispered. "You have your family. You have me."

"Don't pity me, Kate. I can't stand it."

"Pity? I feel so many things for you. Admiration.

Awe. I feel more passion and love for you than I could ever express. But pity? No. Never that.''

She felt his tears rather than heard them. They slid silently down his face and fell on her like drops of sweet gentle rain. ''You love the cult idol James Hayes,'' he said brokenly. ''You love an image. That's not who I am.''

''Yes. I love him. He stole my heart years ago and no man has been able to even come close to taking his place.'' She lifted her head and framed his face with her hands. ''Until now. Until I looked beyond the image and fell in love with the man. I love you, James. I love the tender side of you that finds so much pleasure in growing your little vegetable garden. I love the way you've given yourself to those kids at the ranch, and how you treat that ugly mutt like it has a mile-long pedigree. *You're* my hero. Not the man I once knew as James Hayes. The love I have for who you *were* pales beside the love I have for who you *are*.''

He didn't speak and she sensed his turmoil. He wanted to believe her, but he was afraid. So much had come between them. So much still threatened them.

''I guess,'' she said, throwing his own words back at him, ''I'll just have to show you.''

HER FINGERS WENT to his shirt to undo the buttons and lay it open. James lost his breath and his voice with the touch of her palms against his bare skin and the tender way she stroked him.

''Your body is so incredible,'' she told him. She ran her fingers across muscles formed by years of

digging fence post-holes and tossing seventy-pound bales of hay. "I want to touch and kiss every inch of skin. I want to feel your naked flesh move against my own, to know what it's like to have you explode deep inside me."

He could do nothing but wait in tormented anticipation as she bent and kissed his neck...his shoulder...his midriff. She kissed down the center of his chest, then moved lower to gently graze him with her teeth through his jeans.

He almost leaped off the bed.

She unfastened his belt, pulled it from his pants and tossed it aside, then lowered his zipper. "I fell in love with you even when I thought you were Bret," she said. "It drove me crazy not being unable to separate my feelings for you and him. When the man I thought was Bret kissed me, I saw the face of James from long ago. And when I thought of James, Bret would somehow force himself into his place. That day at the pond. That's why I called you by your real name. My heart knew who you were even when my eyes couldn't see it."

Raising her head, she teased his nipple with her tongue, and still he was so moved by her words of love, her desire for him, that he was unable to respond. Never had he wanted a woman more or felt so unsure of his ability to please her.

"Say you believe me, James. Say you believe that I love you. The real you."

She kissed him on the mouth, thrusting her hand through the open fly of his jeans to stroke him intimately at the same time.

Like a spark that ignites the flame, her touch ig-

nited something hot and raw that had been simmering below the surface since he'd met her. "Katie," he moaned, returning the kiss. He could no longer hold back. He brought her into his arms with an urgency born of passion too long denied.

Clothes quickly came off and were thrown aside until nothing but skin met skin and their bodies were free for each other to touch. He pulled her down beside him on the bed and caressed her breasts and the velvet-soft hair at the juncture of her thighs, his fingers serving as his eyes in the darkness. He wanted to memorize every part of her, to know by heart the shape of her legs, the curve of her hip. He already knew every freckle on her face. Were there freckles elsewhere? If so, he'd find every one. He'd kiss them, commit them to memory.

"God, how I've wanted this," he said, his voice cracking in his attempt to control the desire that threatened to overwhelm him. His mouth followed the trail his fingers had blazed, sucking hungrily at her breast before moving between her legs to open and taste her. His hands and mouth played her like an instrument. Her moans, her words of love and passion, were the music, rising in crescendo toward climax.

He wanted to feel her come while his mouth was on her, but she urged him onto his back. "No, James, you lie there and let me love you," she said. He protested, but then her mouth closed over him, and he could no longer speak.

Lord help him, it was an exquisite sensation to be treated so by someone you loved. He was an expert

at giving pleasure, but rarely had any woman put his pleasure above her own.

With one swift movement, he picked her up and set her on top of him, easing into her as he brought her down. She gasped as he made his entrance and he nearly spilled into her before he'd even thrust.

She began to move against him and he quickly stilled her. "Kate, wait, I…hell, I don't have any protection."

"Too late," she said with a small breathless laugh. "Now that I've finally got you, I'm not letting you go." She tightened her muscles around him to emphasize the point and began to rock her hips, slowly at first, then more feverishly. He met her passion stroke for stroke as the old bed squeaked its approval.

He turned on the lamp then, wanting the light, wanting to see her face in its soft glow as she moved above him with her long hair a waterfall across her bare skin. Like the rest of her, her breasts were small and beautifully formed. The hair between her legs was pale and he touched her there, finding the hidden bud of sensitivity and rubbing it with his thumb to the rhythm of her movement.

She held his gaze, letting him know without words how she felt about him, how she felt about what he was doing to her. The look on her face sent him to the edge, and he grabbed her hips and moved her faster. The control he'd carefully honed over the years had deserted him the moment he'd felt what it was like to have her close around him.

He tried to hold back, but the powerful orgasm that ripped through him was stronger than his will. His

release triggered her own, and she flung back her head and cried out his name.

She collapsed onto his chest and lay there motionless. He, too, was spent, unable to move.

"Do you believe me?" she said after several minutes, still unmoving.

"Yes," he said with genuine awe. "I believe."

He lifted his hand to stroke the back of her head. For the first time in years he felt almost happy. And it was because of this woman who'd fallen in love with him. Twice.

JAMES JERKED AWAKE. The bed was empty, but the sheets still held the heat of Kate's body where she'd lain against him, her feet tucked under his legs to keep them warm and her arm draped over his chest.

"Kate?" he called out in concern.

"I'm here."

He looked over his shoulder at the window. She was curled on the old padded love seat with a quilt wrapped around her. The night had no moon, but the curtains were open and the yard light filtered through the glass to surround her in a pale, almost unearthly glow.

"What are you doing?"

"Thinking. Worrying about Henry."

"Come back to bed where it's warm."

She held the quilt open in silent invitation for him to join her, and he got up and went over, squeezing his long body onto the love seat behind her. He pulled her back against his chest and adjusted the quilt. Her hair was sweet-smelling and soft and he buried his face in it.

They sat listening for a long time to the sounds of the old house and the beating of each other's hearts, knowing without saying it that these idyllic hours together were the calm before the storm and should therefore be savored.

She let out a sigh. "I wish we could stay like this forever. We could lie here in each other's arms and forget about the things that have hurt us, that will hurt us."

He put his face against hers. "You're not only talking about Henry, are you?"

"No, I was thinking about everything, about our families and what we're going to tell them about us. And this damn book... I have an obligation to my publisher, but I don't know how to fulfill it without exposing you, which I won't do."

Sorrow tinted her voice, a sorrow that cut him to the quick because he was responsible for it. The enormity of their problems had hit her and she was wondering, like him, how they were going to get past them.

He kissed her cheek. "I don't have answers, Kate. I hate asking you to lie for me, but James Hayes has to remain dead."

"I know he does, but it bothers me that people will never have the chance to hear those wonderful songs you've composed in the last few years. And they'll continue to think you were an addict. You've been branded a hypocrite for using drugs while preaching against them. That really galls me."

"I don't care."

"Well, I care. I don't want them to remember you like that. You'll spend the rest of your life making

sure the world remembers Bret with kindness and that he leaves the right legacy, but what about you? What about *your* legacy? You deserve to be remembered as the gifted, decent man you are, not as a rock star with a drug habit. I want people to know the love you have for your family, how you tried to help Bret with his problems and the compassion you showed Lauren, despite the fact that she betrayed you. But I don't see any way to tell those stories without revealing the source of the information.''

''You're getting yourself worked up and it's not going to help.''

''I know, but I hate the unfairness of it. I started this project to give you back the respect you've been denied, and unless I finish it and tell the truth, I can't do that.''

''I don't need what you're trying to give me, Kate.''

''But *I* need it, James. I need to give it to you. You were right when you accused me of being obsessed with this book. I *am* obsessed, because it represents my love for you. I want to clear your name.''

He understood, he supposed. If their positions were reversed and Kate's reputation had been unfairly tarnished, he'd want to do whatever he could to set the record straight. But he'd deserved some of the bad things the media had written about him, and he didn't care what people remembered.

''I'm sorry,'' she said. ''I shouldn't have brought this up now, when you're still so upset about Henry. I didn't get the chance to know him very well, but I know you love him. And I came to care for him very much.''

His arms tightened around her. "You've eased the pain by being here, by loving me."

"What did Jane Logan tell you about his new family?"

"Only that the father's a minister, and both he and his wife are young. Seems they want a big family and they plan on adopting other children and having some of their own." She didn't comment, but he knew she was thinking the same thing he was. "Sounds like the perfect situation for Henry, doesn't it?"

"Yes, but little consolation when your heart is breaking."

He pushed back the pain as a memory came into his head of that day a few weeks back when he'd taken Henry to buy shoes and the child had insisted on the boots they'd eventually ended up getting. He'd told James in his garbled baby talk that he wanted to be like "Bet." The boots were meant as a gift to Henry, but James felt he was the one who'd received the true gift that day.

"I'd give anything, Kate, to have adopted him, but a child deserves a stable home with a normal father and a normal life, not a father who lives in fear of having his life snatched away from him at any time."

"I'm not sure that's the real reason you're reluctant. I think your unwillingness to adopt a child is a way of punishing yourself for your failure to help Bret. You've picked the thing you want most and then denied yourself the ability to have it."

He frowned, wondering if she was right.

"I have to live by this decision," he told her. "No adopted children. No biological children." He thought again about their unprotected lovemaking.

"God, please tell me there's no chance I got you pregnant tonight."

"No, don't worry about that."

Her answer brought conflicting emotions of relief and disappointment.

"Kate, I..." This wasn't going to be easy to say. "I love you and I want us to be together, but I don't have anything to give you. I can't give you kids, except the ones from Pine Acres who will come and go from your life. You'll fall in love with them, think of them as your own, and then have to give them up—always. I can't even give you my real name. Can you possibly be happy under those circumstances?"

"I have to be. I have no other choice."

"But with another man you'd have a better life, a *normal* life."

"I've belonged to you in my heart since I was nineteen, and I don't want another man. So it doesn't matter what the circumstances are, because anything is better than losing you."

"Then you'll live with me?"

"Yes, I'll live with you."

"We have so many problems."

"And I wish I could say I have answers for them, but I don't. All I know is that as long as we're together, I don't care about anything else."

His throat tightened. "Maybe we should go to Chattanooga," he said quickly, before he lost his nerve.

She sat up and looked at him. "Seriously?"

"Yeah, seriously."

"Are you ready for that?"

"No, but I can't put off telling my family about

you much longer, and if we're going to have any chance at a future, I've got to deal with the past. If I can find the courage."

"Oh, Jamie." She brought her hand to his cheek. "You can. I know you can."

She held him and whispered words of love, and he took her there on the couch in an exquisite melding of body and spirit that was unlike anything he'd experienced before. Afterward they lay with arms and legs entwined, two pieces of a puzzle, a perfect fit.

Chattanooga. He hadn't been there since the crash. At first he hadn't gone because he'd feared recognition. Later he'd realized he couldn't go because of the memories and pain that awaited him there. He'd hidden away in this house, thinking one day the pain would ease and he'd be able to go home. But it never had.

Now the time had come to face it. He didn't know if he was strong enough.

CHAPTER SEVENTEEN

THEY LEFT IN JAMES'S TRUCK the next morning after securing a promise from Aubrey to take care of Sallie and the horses for several days. Although Kate urged James to call his mother and stepfather and reduce the shock of their arrival, he was adamant.

"Doing that will only cause them hours of grief while they wait for us," he said. "I'd rather explain to them when we get there."

They arrived in midafternoon, following a light rain that had dressed the air with mist broken by patches of returning sunlight. Kate had noticed James's rising panic the closer they got to the city, and now perspiration beaded his face.

"Are you okay?" she asked.

"Nervous." He pulled the truck into the parking lot of a convenience store, stopped and stared upward at his parents' house. "Well, there it is." The stone structure with its jutting turrets sat perched, like some horrendous bird, on the mountain ahead of them, at complete odds with the beauty around it. "I built it for my mother with the money I made off the first album. I was just a kid and I wanted her to live in a castle. What do you think of it?"

"Do they really need all that room for the two of them?"

"Probably not, but she loves the house."

"Mmm." She wondered how that was possible, given what she knew about the formidable Marianne Conner.

The narrow road up Lookout Mountain gave them a spectacular view of Chattanooga and the Tennessee River that wound through the city like a snake. A few minutes later they turned into the private drive leading to the Conner house and stopped at the security gate. A guard called the house and James talked briefly with the housekeeper. He got back in the car and for the first time in hours, smiled. "They're a little excited I'm here," he said.

"I guess so."

"Ready?"

She took a deep breath. "As I'll ever be."

James's mother didn't wait for him to get to the door but met him in the stone courtyard at the front of the house. She was already weeping, and she flung herself into his arms when he stepped out. Kate stayed in the car, not wishing to intrude on their reunion.

"I can't believe you're here," his mother said, drawing back to look at him. "I've prayed and prayed you'd come home someday. I have to call George at the club. And Ellen will want to see you."

"Mom, not yet." He faced the car where Kate sat unnoticed, steeling herself for the inevitable hurricane. He motioned for her to get out, and she came and stood beside him. He grabbed her hand and she clung to it in support. "I've brought someone I want you to meet. Mom, this is Kate. Kathryn Morgan. The lady who's writing the biography."

She watched his mother's surprise turn to recog-

nition, then disbelief, then horror. At that moment Kate knew what it felt like to be someone's worst nightmare.

His mother turned to James in panic. "Why have you brought this woman here?"

"Mom, I want her to talk to you."

"What have you done?"

"I...she knows, Mom. She figured out what we did."

"Oh, God, no! She'll ruin us all!"

MARIANNE LOOKED DOWN the dinner table at the sullen faces and wondered how they'd gotten through the meal. George was drinking and not even trying to hide it. Ellen, morose and sporting new bruises from the current bastard she lived with, hadn't said two words since she'd arrived. And James was furious at all of them; it was evident from the way he picked at his food.

Marianne cleared her throat to get their attention. "Well, I suppose Ms. Morgan and I should talk and get it over with. The rest of you go somewhere and entertain yourselves."

James loudly let it be known he wasn't going anywhere, but the Morgan woman put a restraining hand on his arm and whispered something that silenced him. Finally he stood, and with a look at Marianne that warned her he'd be back if things got out of hand, he followed his stepfather and sister out of the cavernous dining room.

"Ms. Morgan..." Marianne had been prepared to tell the woman off the moment they were alone, but recalling James's attentiveness to her all afternoon,

and his startling announcement that he was in love with the creature, Marianne decided it would be wise to ask a few questions first. "Would you like a glass of port?"

"Yes, thank you."

Marianne went to the sideboard and poured them each a glass. They strolled, glasses in hand, looking at the eighteenth-century tapestries that covered the walls, tapestries Marianne had gone to a great deal of trouble to find to make the house bearable.

"Your furnishings are exquisite," the woman said.

"And the house itself?" Marianne asked, curious at the answer she'd give.

"Awful. The ugliest house I've ever seen."

Marianne laughed. She couldn't help it. No one had dared say that to her face before, although they extracted great joy from saying it behind her back. "You're very straightforward, Ms. Morgan. Can we be straightforward about the things we have to discuss?"

"Yes, Mrs. Conner. I came prepared to do that."

"Good. Then let me start by admitting I'm very distressed that you've uncovered our little secret and equally distressed about this relationship you've undertaken with my son."

The woman smiled, rather than appearing offended. "I'd be surprised if you were happy. You must be greatly concerned about what I plan to do."

"Yes, I am."

The woman walked silently for a moment, then said, "I don't know. I'm in a very difficult situation, both professionally and personally. I don't want to

hurt James, yet I have a commitment to his biography that I need to resolve.''

''I see.''

''I won't reveal he's alive, though. Nor will I tell anyone what you and Mr. Conner did. That's not something you need ever worry about. For what it's worth to you, I give you my word on that.''

''That surprises me a great deal.''

''I don't believe you hurt anyone but yourselves by switching the records and concealing James's survival. No good will come of telling the truth now.''

''I must say I'm finding this all very hard to accept. I'm particularly overwhelmed to learn James was helping you with your book even *before* you discovered his identity. It's unlike him to lie to us.''

''Are you aware James discredited himself in those interviews?''

Marianne stopped, completely astonished. ''No.''

''I didn't think you were. As hard as you work to preserve his memory, I can't imagine you'd go along with something so ridiculous.''

''How did he try to discredit himself?''

''By telling me wild stories about James Hayes and his countless encounters with women and booze. He wanted me to present him to the world as a drug addict and a drunk who never possessed a creative thought and took credit for music Webb Anderson composed.''

''You're not serious?''

''Oh, yes, and I think you should know he went to great lengths to make sure I had a very favorable, almost saintly, image of Bret.''

Marianne sighed. That troubled her even more. "I can't believe he thought he had to do that."

"Can't you? Mrs. Conner, I don't want to hurt you, nor am I without compassion for Bret and what happened to him. I know that despite his problems he was your son and you must have loved him very much. But he was responsible for his own life, for the choices he made and for his own failures. So I can't understand why, even though he's dead, all of you are still making excuses for him and shouldering the blame that's rightfully his. From what I've seen here today, he's manipulating all your lives."

Marianne started to disagree, but stopped. The woman was right. Bret still had a hold on all of them because of the guilt they felt about what they'd done.

She'd loved Bret as much as she loved James and Ellen, but she couldn't deny there'd been a weakness in her younger son. In Bret's eyes, the blame for every unpleasant thing that happened to him belonged to someone else. *It's not my fault.* How many times during his childhood had she heard him say that when he did something wrong? And they'd all allowed him to get away with it.

Even as an adult, when he lost job after job because of his hostile attitude, he always claimed the boss hated him or else someone got him fired out of jealousy. Never did he take responsibility.

"Would you like grandchildren, Mrs. Conner?" the woman asked, startling her.

"Grandchildren?" Marianne could barely say the word.

"I want children. James's children. And perhaps even some adopted ones. But he doesn't believe he

deserves any. He started Pine Acres and the other ranches to perpetuate Bret's name in a good way. I also think the reason he chose those specific charities was so he could have personal contact with children.''

"I didn't...I never realized."

"After Bret's death, James gave up his dream of a house full of his *own* children and condemned himself to a solitary life on his little farm."

"I suppose I've allowed myself to believe he lives alone out of fear someone will recognize him."

"He's convinced himself of that, too, but I think it's more punishment than fear of discovery. Despite what he says, he wants children very badly, and it's a crime for him not to have any. He's so good with them.''

"Is he?"

"Oh, yes, he's wonderful."

"Like his father," Marianne said, unable to conceal her smile. That had been what attracted her to David, the easy way he had with children.

They came to the doors of the sun parlor. Marianne opened them and went through, needing the warmer brighter colors of the haven she'd created in this dark and depressing house. She crossed to the table by the window and sat down, motioning for the woman to take the chair across from her. The lights of the city punctuated the darkness below them. A barge moved slowly along the river.

"You've surprised me, Ms. Morgan, and I'm not easily surprised. You're telling me things about my son I didn't know, things that upset me very much."

"You can't blame yourself for not knowing. James

doesn't *want* you to know. He's not willing to tell you how badly he hurts."

"Why, then, are *you* telling me?"

"Because he loves you, and he needs you to know so he can begin to heal. He wants to put Bret's death behind him, but he's not sure how to go about it. I'm convinced that subconsciously he wanted me to find out who he is, and that's why he gave me so many subtle clues. He revealed his identity in a hundred different ways."

"But it doesn't make sense for him to want to expose the truth after so many years."

"It doesn't make sense to us, but in James's mind, it's a way to force something to happen. For years he's confined himself to this emotional prison he's created, and he hasn't let himself out of it. But now there's an external force—me—with the power to do the job. By allowing me to discover his secret, he handed me the key to his prison door."

"I'm beginning to understand."

"James knows he should have died instead of Bret, and that only a twist of fate put his brother on that plane. He also feels a tremendous amount of guilt for having assumed Bret's identity."

A tear formed at the corner of Marianne's eye, but she compelled it by sheer will not to fall. "I was only trying to save him, to give him a chance to start over."

"I know, and it took incredible love and strength to do what you did. I'm not sure I could have done it, had they been my sons."

"Once we'd switched the records, it was too late to go back."

"Did you know about Bret's drug use before then?"

"Lord, no. If I had, if I'd known they'd find drugs in his body when they did the autopsy, I never would have let the world believe it was James."

"I don't think James really cares about the drugs. He's dealing with too many other issues."

"Is he so unhappy?"

"Only because he can't get beyond what happened that night or his inability to help Bret. I'm hoping, once he realizes he did all he could for his brother, he'll find happiness. He enjoys his business and the freedom of his new identity. He doesn't miss the life he gave up."

"Then what I did wasn't all for nothing."

"No, I think you and your husband probably saved him, just as you intended."

Marianne took a calming sip of wine and stared out into the darkness. This woman truly seemed to care about James, to want him to be happy. But could they really trust her? So much depended on it.

"This book of yours," Marianne said. "You're required to finish it?"

"Yes, although I haven't come up with a way to be honest or complete in what I say and still protect James's identity. I need to figure that out."

"Could you not abandon it?"

"I wish I could, but I don't see how I can without making the people close to me suspicious. And to be truthful, I *want* to finish it. You, more than anyone, might understand my reasons." Her face softened. "I love him, Mrs. Conner, and I can't stand the idea of people thinking badly of him. This book can't right

all the wrongs that have been done to him, but it can remind the world how special he is. With all my heart, I believe that.''

There was such conviction in her voice that Marianne was inclined to believe it, as well.

WHEN BRET DIED, James had assumed that Bret's few belongings had been stored up in the attic. He was surprised now to find them displayed in the bedroom he'd used while he was still living at home, as if Bret was away and expected back anytime.

Sports trophies and school pictures decorated the bookcase and the walls. A scrapbook lay on the desk, opened to a yellowed newspaper clipping of the third-grade district spelling contest, in which Bret had been a finalist.

This room held many memories. Good memories. And James smiled as he sat on one of the twin beds and slowly turned the pages of the photograph album he'd found. He came upon a shot of him and Bret with their arms around each other's shoulders, standing in front of one of the band's buses. He remembered this one, taken the summer after Bret graduated from high school; he'd joined James on tour. They'd been close then, not only brothers but friends. Why, he wondered, couldn't things have stayed like that?

''I still have difficulty believing he's not coming home,'' his mother said from the doorway. She crossed the room and sat on the bed next to him. The open album made her smile, and she pointed to a photograph on the opposite page—one of him and Bret riding double on an old mule at what had been

their grandfather's house outside Shelbyville. "What was it your grandfather called that mule? Bessie?"

"Beulah. Bessie was the goat that used to pull us around in a little green wagon."

"Oh, that's right. You learned to ride on that old mule, didn't you?"

He nodded, smiling at the memory. "She had to be thirty years old, but gentle as a lamb. That's what started me wanting a horse of my own, visiting Pop and Granny Mag in the summer and helping take care of the animals." He studied his mother's tired face and red-rimmed eyes. "This has been hard on you. I'm sorry."

"I'm fine. Don't worry about me."

"We shouldn't have come."

"No, I'm glad to see you. You know that."

"But not Kate."

"I can't say I'm happy she knows what she does, but she seems to care for you very deeply. I can only pray this will somehow resolve itself without hurting anyone." She smiled tenderly and patted his hand. "I hoped one day you'd come home, Jamie. And finally here you are. George and I aren't as young as we used to be. Visiting you is getting harder and harder."

"I know, and I'm sorry I haven't come before. I finally realized I couldn't keep avoiding this trip forever." He glanced at the doorway, wondering why Kate hadn't sought him out after her talk with his mother. "Where is Kate? You didn't dissect her and feed her to that cat of yours, did you?"

"Darling, you make me sound absolutely predatory. The young woman can hold her own, as I'm sure you've already discovered. I left her in the parlor

in one piece. She wanted to call her family and let them know where she is."

"She's probably calling her brother Marcus. She's been pretty upset about having to lie to him, and it tears me apart because I know it's my fault."

"You've come to love her very much, haven't you?"

"Yes, but she's loved me even longer." He related the story of how the two of them had met years ago and how she'd spent most of her life preparing to write this book. "And now the book is the very thing between us."

"Have faith that things will work themselves out."

"I don't see how. I'm beginning to think we'd all be better off if I confessed everything and got it over with. At least, that would solve Kate's problems."

"Please, don't even think that. You would never be happy going back to your old life. You'd only risk your health again."

"But Kate's running out of time. I've got to find some way to help her."

"You're frustrated. Wait a few days. I'm sure if we all put our heads together, we can come up with a solution."

She was right. He *was* frustrated, frustrated by his inability to provide Kate with an answer to her dilemma. She was giving up her chance at a normal life and a family to be with him. He wanted to give her something back. But what? How?

"Do you ever regret what we did when Bret died?" he asked his mother. He'd wanted to ask her that question for a very long time, but had never had the courage.

She sighed and gave him a sad smile. "My only regret is that you haven't been able to come to terms with it, to forget what happened and go on with your life. Until today, when I talked with Kathryn, I didn't realize how difficult things have been for you."

"I've been okay."

"Have you really?"

He shrugged and said yes, but he glanced away so she couldn't see into his eyes and know he was lying.

"Jamie, look at me." Reluctantly he did. "You can't continue to grieve. You did everything you could to help your brother, and you have no reason to feel guilty. You always spent time with him and took an interest in whatever he was doing, even when you were on the road. He loved you."

"I know he did," James said, but a part of him wondered if it was true.

She gave him a hug and stood. "I guess I'd better go find your stepfather. He's likely to embalm himself with Kentucky bourbon if I don't keep an eye on him."

"I'm sorry we caused such an uproar. Kate fussed at me—said I should call and warn you she was coming."

"I think we'll survive."

"Ellen doesn't look good. Did that guy she's living with put those bruises on her arms?"

"I suspect he did, but she claims she fell."

James shook his head and swore. He wished he could get five minutes alone with the jerk. He'd make sure he never touched his sister again.

Ellen was the gentlest person he'd ever known. He owed her his life, and he hated to see her abused.

She'd come to Alabama and taken care of him after Bret's death, when he'd mired himself in depression. She'd helped him find his way out of the blackness.

"Why does she let him do that? I don't understand it."

"Everyone handles their guilt differently, Jamie. Ellen gets involved in unhealthy relationships, George drinks too much, and you wrestle your demons in your own way."

"What about you? How do you deal with your guilt?"

"One day, darling, perhaps I'll tell you all about it. But not tonight. Let's not spoil your homecoming."

When she left, he went downstairs to see if Kate wanted to go for a ride and maybe see where he'd grown up. The house was a museum now and he didn't want to go inside, but he'd like to drive by and take a look. Or maybe he'd show her where he'd lived at the time of the crash, or his high school.

The door to the sun parlor was ajar. He started to push it open and go in, but Kate's distressed voice as she talked on the telephone stopped him.

"...not crazy. Things aren't going like they should, and I think I should abandon the book before I waste any more time on it." She paused to listen, then said, "I realize that. Yes, I know what'll happen if I don't fulfill this contract." She sighed and he could hear her heels tap the floor as she paced. "Marcus, calm— No, he didn't influence my— Marcus, I don't care about that! Will you shut up!"

James stood there for several minutes and listened with growing concern. It wasn't hard to figure out

what was going on. Her brother was trying to talk her out of dropping the book, pointing out the serious consequences if she did. A reputation she'd spent a lifetime building might be ruined.

Because of him. He'd done this to her. She was giving up her work, risking everything, because she refused to hurt him or reveal his secret. Somehow he had to find a way to fix that.

KATE ROSE LATER the next morning than she'd planned, the strain of meeting James's family and fighting with Marcus in the same day having wrung her out emotionally.

She hadn't slept well, anyway. She'd insisted she and James stay in separate rooms while under his mother's roof and that, too, had made it difficult to rest. Expecting him to ignore her edict and slip into her bedroom in the middle of the night, she'd slept lightly. But he hadn't come. Not last night. Not this morning. She'd wrestled with her problems—alone.

She poured herself a cup of coffee from the carafe on the sideboard in the dining room and sat at the table where Mrs. Conner was reading the newspaper. "We have sausages, eggs and muffins," the woman said without looking up.

"Coffee's fine. Have you seen your son this morning?"

Mrs. Conner peered at Kate over the top of her reading glasses. "Your door was closed, so I assumed he was with you."

Kate reddened at the implication in the statement. "No, I haven't seen him since last night."

"Then he must have gone somewhere with George.

He was up and out of the house early this morning, as well. What are you planning for today?''

''I have no idea. I guess whatever he feels comfortable doing.''

Mrs. Conner folded the paper, laying it on the table beside her plate. ''Have you given any more thought to your problem with the book?''

''As a matter of fact, I have. I'm throwing it in the trash.''

Mrs. Conner's face reflected her shock. ''Are you certain?''

''I don't see any way around it.'' Kate glanced at the door. ''Are we alone? Can we talk freely about this?''

''Yes, but keep your voice down. Agnes is in the kitchen.''

''If I turn in the story I originally had,'' Kate said softly, ''it won't be complete, and I'd never forgive myself for that or for the dishonesty of it. I could add material James has given me and tell an *almost* complete story, but I'd need written documentation for it, which I don't have. And obviously I can't use him as a source.''

''But he could give the information as Bret, couldn't he?''

''Too dangerous. He'd come under scrutiny from the media.''

''Perhaps I could be your source. Or pretend to be.''

Kate shook her head. ''Thank you for the offer, but no. You live with enough deception as it is, and I'm not going to add to it. I'd rather face the consequences of breaking my contract.''

"I'm speechless. This book means so much to you."

"Some things mean more."

"And the suspicion your actions will arouse?"

"I see no way to avoid it entirely. But it's the lesser of two evils."

Mrs. Conner appeared thoughtful. She sat back in her chair and stared at Kate, those intense blue eyes unreadable.

"Having my son home has been wonderful," she said finally. "I love those long lovely letters he sends me, but they're not the same as having him here in person."

"He told me you two correspond often."

"Quite often. He's always been very good about letter-writing. Granny Mag—my mother—forced him to do it when he was younger, and surprisingly, he's kept it up all these years. I'm thankful because they're beautifully written and so descriptive they made me feel as if I was with him. "

"Have you kept many?"

"Oh, every one. Tirades from summers at camp about the awful food. Pleas from his grandparents' house to get a horse when he got home from his visit. Chronicles from every tour he made with the band. Up until the last few years, he was very open about his feelings. His letters, I suppose, have always been an outlet to express what was too personal to put in his songs. Many of them are more similar to journal entries than letters."

"A journal?" Kate trembled as she put down her cup.

"Let's look at them and you'll see what I mean."

Kate followed James's mother to her study. The letters were in a beautiful old trunk in the corner. They pulled them out and placed them on the desk, hundreds of them, tied with blue grosgrain ribbons. She picked up one bundle of letters and looked at the dates. This group went back twenty-five years.

"I often get these out and read through them again. I think there's one letter you might be particularly interested in," Mrs. Conner said. "What was the date you met James?"

"March 10, 1987."

She went through the stacks, scanning several letters, until she found the one she was looking for. "Ah," she said, smiling. "I remembered this last night when Jamie told me how you and he first met."

She handed Kate the letter. The first few paragraphs were about inconsequential things. Then came something totally unexpected.

...Some students from Columbia spent time with us last weekend while we were playing in Manhattan. One of them's kind of a whiz kid. I was afraid she'd be a pest, but she wasn't at all. I guess because she knows what it's like to be different. We talked for a long time. When she left, I felt—I don't know—strange, like I'd lost something important. I'm not sure I believe in kindred spirits, and it's more likely that the connection I felt to her was loneliness rather than anything mystical, but I haven't been able to get her off my mind. She was a tiny little thing, probably didn't weigh more than 100 pounds or so, and she had the biggest green eyes I ever saw

and a funny mouth. Pretty, though. She reminded
me of those dolls you give Ellen every year for
her birthday that are nice to look at but too special to touch. I had a hard time making her laugh
at first, but I showed her a picture of Bret with
that big catfish and told her what a daredevil he
is. She got tickled when I told her about that time
he fell out of the tree playing Tarzan and broke
his arm. She said one of her brothers did the
exact same thing when he was ten. Her name
was Katie. I wish I'd thought to get her last name
and address, but I didn't, and Malcolm's reluctant now to tell me how I can get in touch with
her. I only wanted to write and say how much I
liked meeting her. He wants me to let it go,
though, so I guess I will. Do you think a time
will ever come when I can stop worrying about
bad press, paternity suits filed by women I've
never met and pleasing other people? I hope so.
I'd like to have a little farm and raise horses and
tomatoes, maybe even find a girl like Katie and
raise a ton of kids....

Tears streamed in rivers down Kate's face. James *had*
thought her special, at least at the time.

"Open and read some of these others," Mrs. Conner said.

Over the next hour they went through all the stacks,
picking letters at random and reading them out loud
to each other. Some were amusing, with amazingly
well-drawn caricatures of people he'd met. Some
were sad, expressing his feelings of helplessness at

tragic events like Lenny's illness and Lauren's suicide.

"His whole life is here," Kate said. "And in his
own words."

"The letters are yours, Kathryn, for your book. Use
them to remind the world how special he is."

Stunned, Kate couldn't speak at first. In her mind
she saw the book in a new form, her narrative combined with his letters and drawings, and she wanted
to squeal with joy. Nothing could be more perfect!
But would James go for it? The decision had to be
his.

"How," she said, finding her voice, "can I ever
repay you, Mrs. Conner? This is an incredible gift."

"First, by calling me Marianne. And two, by remembering I'm partial to boys."

"Boys?"

"Boys. Grandsons. Although a little girl would be
nice, too."

Kate laughed through her tears. "Convincing
James might be difficult, but I promise I'll do my
best."

"We'll work on him together."

A knock on the study door made them both quickly
wipe their eyes. "Yes? Come in," Marianne said.

Her husband opened the door, looked at their tear-
streaked faces and frowned in confusion. "What on
earth is going on in here?"

"We're having a party," she said. She walked over
and hugged him tightly, confusing him even more.
"Kathryn and I have hatched a plan, but we need
everyone here to talk about it. Where's my darling
son?"

"I have no idea. Isn't he here?"

"We thought he was with you," Marianne told her husband.

"No, I had to run to the club. I haven't seen him."

Marianne looked at Kate. Panic showed in her eyes, putting a knot in Kate's stomach. "I don't like this. Last night he was talking strangely. I'm afraid he's thinking of doing something foolish."

"What did he say?"

Kate never got an answer. The housekeeper came up then, alerting them that there was a reporter on the telephone wanting to speak with Mrs. Conner. "He wants to know if he can get a comment from the family before the press conference at ten," the woman told her.

Marianne clutched her throat and screamed, "Merciful heavens," but Kate didn't hear. She was too busy listening to the anguishing sound of her dreams shattering into a million pieces.

CHAPTER EIGHTEEN

"HURRY, HURRY!" Marianne shouted, but Kate was driving George Conner's antique Cadillac as fast as she dared, considering she had no idea where she was going. She was a robot following directions. Turn left. Turn right. She swerved to avoid a car slowing to make the same turn, and she didn't even look before she veered into the other lane.

The hotel where the reporter said he'd been told to be at ten wasn't that far away, according to Marianne, but they were quickly running out of time. So much depended on getting there before James said anything.

What had he been thinking? If only he'd told her…

Marianne was on the verge of tears. "We're not going to make it!"

"We'll make it," Kate said. But God help them all, she didn't think they would. She squealed to a stop under the glass canopy of the Marriott, then jumped out and raced toward the door. Marianne surprised her by keeping up.

"Press conference?" she asked the valet.

"Meeting room C, upstairs." He pointed at the escalator to the right of the lobby.

She handed him the keys to the Caddy and a twenty-dollar bill with instructions to park it. Both women took off at a jog.

"There," Marianne said. When they reached the top of the escalator, they could see people with television cameras spilling out of a room into the hall. James's voice came over the microphone.

"I appreciate your coming today on such short notice, but what I have to tell you is of extreme importance."

Kate ran faster, leaving Marianne behind.

No, James! Don't do it!

"There's no good way to ease into this, so I'm just going to say it. James Hayes...is alive."

Kate made the doorway just as the words left his mouth, and it was like hitting a brick wall. She stopped, unbelieving. She'd been too late. Too late!

Marianne came up beside her and clutched her hand for moral support. They waited, as did James, but the expected reaction didn't materialize. No gasps. No shrieks of surprise. What they heard, instead, was a tinkling of laughter, starting in the back row and quickly spreading through the room.

"Good one," somebody said.

A woman nearby leaned over and said to the man next to her, "The guy's got a weird sense of humor."

Kate and Marianne looked at each other, and a silent message of thanks and hope passed between them. The reporters thought James was simply breaking the ice before the real announcement. Kate quickly stepped in before James had a chance to do any more damage.

"I'm sorry I'm late," she said. She picked her way through the crowd to the front. "For those of you who don't know me, my name is Kathryn Morgan and I'm

a biographer. I'm one of the people who asked you here today.''

James grabbed her arm. ''Hold on a minute.''

''Oh, you're right. I'm sorry. I forgot to introduce Bret's mother. Mrs. Conner, will you come up here, please?'' Heads turned and gazes went to the back of the room.

''Kate...'' James said again as his mother hurried forward.

Kate pulled him away from the podium and used the time while the reporters were distracted to tell him about the letters and his mother's idea. ''That means you don't have to do this if you don't want to.''

He drew back and looked at her in astonishment—and what she felt sure was relief.

''But the decision is yours,'' she added. ''You, more than any of the rest of us, will have to live with whatever action you take today. I can't tell you what to do.''

''You'll support me, whatever I say?''

''Whatever you say. Whatever you do. Nothing that happens here today can ever change what I feel for you.''

''Remind me when we get home to show you how much I love you.''

''Oh, I definitely will. You can count on it.''

Without hesitation he returned to the podium and told the reporters, ''I'm going to step aside and let my mother and Ms. Morgan explain why you're here today, since they're overseeing this project.''

Marianne, under a barrage of flashes, took his place. James moved to the side of the room beyond the range of the cameras.

Kate leaned forward to the microphone again. "Thank you for coming. The Hayes family and I have a major announcement about my forthcoming book on James Hayes and his band, Mystic Waters. We wanted to share this with the media in the family's hometown and give you the opportunity to have the story first. You'll be scooping everyone. Isn't that delicious?"

That brought chuckles.

"Through the generosity of the family, certain letters have been placed at my disposal. These are letters written by James Hayes to his mother from the time he was a child up until his death. Not only are the letters insightful and very personal, they contain original poems and drawings." Inspiration hit her. "And they include songs never before published."

"Songs?" someone blurted out. A ripple of excitement went through the room.

Kate glanced at Marianne who, despite her surprise at Kate's wild announcement about the songs, had the good sense to smile and act as if she knew exactly what was going on.

"Yes, songs no one's ever seen or heard."

A lady raised her hand. "How many songs?"

"I haven't counted them, but I would estimate several hundred. And you'll be particularly delighted to know he composed several complete symphonies during his lifetime, as well."

The excited reporters scrambled to ask questions. Kate let them for a while and then silenced them with her hand.

"I know you're all interested in the songs, but until the family decides if they'll be recorded, they've

asked me not to release them in written form.'' A collective groan of disappointment echoed through the room. "However, I did bring one of the early letters. James wrote it when he was only nineteen and on his first road tour. He was wonderfully naive and impressionable. Would you like to hear it?''

She received an overwhelming response. Taking the letter from her pocket, she unfolded it and handed it to Marianne.

"Would you mind, since it was addressed to you?''

Marianne slipped on her glasses, cleared her throat and began. '' 'Dear Mom. A short note this time. We're on the bus, somewhere in Virginia—I think— and headed to Indiana. The land here is a lot like Tennessee, with hills reaching right up into the clouds and miles and miles of nothing but trees.

'' 'It's not all pretty, though. Lots of people live in houses that a good wind might blow away, and I don't know how they stay warm. Makes me feel sad and kind of guilty, too. I'm spending all that money on the castle and these people have so little. But you've been poor, too, and you deserve something nice, so don't mind my crazy talk. I remember what it was like after Dad died and you had to give up the place on Tennessee Avenue. I don't want you to ever feel that bad again.

'' 'When you get a chance, let me know how the house is coming along, okay? Or take some pictures if you think of it.

'' 'Did you see anything about the Richmond concert on the news? You wouldn't believe how the fans treated us! Like we were royalty or something, although they got a little crazy and wouldn't stay be-

hind the barriers. Malcolm thinks I shouldn't stop and talk to them anymore because it causes security problems, but I hate not to do it. That's the only reason I'm here—the fans. I want them to know how much I appreciate them listening to my music.

"'I feel bad about missing Bret's birthday, but I'm glad he liked the electric guitar. He wants to join me on tour for a few days during spring break, but he's afraid you won't allow it. Will you please say yes? I swear I won't let anything happen to him. Malcolm will be watching him, too, and you know what a good guy he is. I'll ask Malcolm to call you soon, so think about it. I'd really like Bret to come. I don't know when I'll get home again and I miss him. I miss all of you so much.

"'It's lonely on the road. The guys are great, but being together all the time is rough. We fight about stupid things. Webb wrote a couple of songs and I don't think they're good enough to use, and neither do Billy and Tyler. So now Webb's mad at all of us. Lenny's acting weird, too. He doesn't seem to ever sleep. But don't say anything to his grandmother, because I don't want her to worry about him. We'll all be okay after a break.

"'Well, I'd better go. Tell George and Ellen I love them and hope to see them soon. I love you, too, Mom. I don't know when I'll get the chance to call, but maybe I can find a minute on the bus to write again. I promise I'll try hard. Love, Jamie.'"

When Marianne finished, Kate stepped back up to the microphone.

"That's a small sampling of what you'll see in the book, words straight from the heart by a man who

cared deeply about his fans, missed his family and had to deal with the guilt of success at a very young age. He wasn't perfect, just very human like the rest of us. He made mistakes, and he paid for them in a very tragic way. But I want to remind everyone in this room—James Hayes was a genius. He was truly one of the greatest musical talents we'll ever see, and I think that's much more important than any problems he might have had in the last few years of his life. I thank all of you for coming today. I hope to see you again when the book is released next year. If you have further questions, I'll stay and answer them individually.''

That ended the press conference. Mrs. Conner took her husband's car back to the house so she could give him the good news in person, but Kate stayed and gave one-on-one interviews to anyone who asked, hoping the photographers would use photos and video of her, rather than James, in their reports.

After forty-five minutes, the reporters packed up their gear and left Kate and James alone in the room. Kate closed the doors so they couldn't be overhead by the hotel staff.

"That seemed to go okay," she told him, coming to stand in front of him. He remained in the spot where he'd listened to the remainder of the press conference. He leaned with his back against the wall, his hands in his pockets. "I've got to admit I'm a bit put out with you, though. Why didn't you tell me what you planned to do?"

"I was worried about what would happen to you if you didn't go through with the book. I overheard you talking on the phone with Marcus last night."

Kate sighed. "Is that what brought this on? My argument with my stupid brother?"

"Partly." He straightened and ran a hand through his hair. "Boy, I can't believe the scene in here today. I guess I'm lucky this whole thing didn't blow up in my face."

"We're all lucky. This could have been a disaster. But I think everything's going to work out fine. I can weave my background material between the letters and produce a book that's almost autobiographical. It won't be exactly the one I set out to write, but it'll be an honest portrayal of your life, and that's all I ever wanted to do."

"I had no idea Mom kept my letters."

"We had a great time going through them this morning."

"What will your publisher and editor say about this switch?"

"They'll be thrilled to have exclusive rights to print the material, and since it comes from your mother, its authenticity is above question. The book'll sell like wildfire."

"And you'll make a fortune."

"No, I want to give what I make to your foundation. Maybe we can use it to build another ranch for the children."

"You don't have to do that."

"I know, but I want to. With the royalties from the book and your songs, we can support *both* foundations. Think of all the wonderful things we can do."

"That sounds great." His forehead furrowed. "But I'm confused about the songs. I don't remember send-

ing any, and even if I did, it sure wouldn't have been several hundred.''

"You didn't. I lied about that part.''

He cocked his head. "Are you suggesting what I think you're suggesting? Those are new songs, not old ones.''

"Does it really matter when they were written? They're still *your* songs. You said you wished people could hear the ones you've composed in the last several years. Well, here's a way. You can continue to compose songs for as long as you want, and we can even find someone to record them for you. We can see about having someone produce your symphonies, too, if that's okay. Is that okay?''

She laughed at the slow grin that spread across his face as he realized the implications of what she was saying.

"I thought it might be. Think how perfect this is. You get to compose and have your songs recorded, but you don't have to *live* as James Hayes. It really is the perfect solution.''

"It sounds wonderful but—'' the grin vanished and was replaced with a worried look "—you lied for me today. You implicated yourself by getting up there and not telling the truth. And you'll have to continue to lie to your brother, won't you? Or do you plan to tell him?''

"No, I don't plan to tell him or anybody. When I weigh the public's right to know against your right to live normally, I'm sure I'm doing the morally correct thing. You and your family are the only victims of your masquerade, James.''

"But if somebody uncovers it one day—''

"Even if they do, which I don't think is ever going to happen, it won't matter. Nobody can hurt us now."

"How can you say that?"

"Because you told me something fourteen years ago that changed my life, and I believe it as strongly today as I did then."

"What did I say?"

"You said…people can't hurt you unless you give them the power to hurt you. And you're right. We have to refuse to give anybody the power to hurt us. We're together. And we're going to stay together forever, no matter what happens. Let them take their best shot at us if they want to, but it won't do any good."

He put his arms around her waist and pulled her against him. "I like that 'together' part a whole lot."

"Me, too." She kissed him, then leaned her head on his chest. "We'll go forward and not look back."

"I want that, Kate, but there's one thing I still have to do. I can't live with a shadow hanging over my life."

"I know."

"Will you come, too?"

"If you need me."

He hugged her more tightly. "I'll always need you."

THESE OLDER CEMETERIES had always seemed like special places to him, with their ornate headstones and words meant to comfort the living. Forest Hills was a work of art, fragrant and colorful during the warm months, but beautiful even on a cold winter day like today.

He parked the truck along one of the narrow drives

where hundred-year-old oaks stood guard, remembering the many times he'd come here as a child. Most
often it had been with his grandmother Hayes, who'd
appointed him her "weed puller" and had dragged
him here at least once a month.

Granny would make a gallon of lemonade and
they'd spend Sunday afternoon tending the graves of
her husband and her babies who'd been born dead.
Later, another of her sons had died and been buried
here—James's father—giving them even more reason
to visit.

Growing up, James had accepted those visits as
part of his duty. But he'd honestly enjoyed coming
because Granny would sing while they pulled weeds,
and she'd had a wonderful voice. Often she talked to
him about his father. He'd only been ten when his
father died, but through Granny Hayes's stories he'd
come to know his father well.

Granny Hayes had since died herself and rested in
the graveyard with Granny Mag and Pop, his maternal
grandparents. And Bret was here now, although it was
more difficult to accept that.

In the spring the dogwood trees and azalea bushes
would bloom to make this place look more like a
garden than a cemetery, but today it was cold and
cloudy, and James shivered despite the warm air
blowing from the car heater.

He'd called the cemetery office ahead of time and
requested the mausoleum be closed to the public for
a couple of hours. The staff had placed a sign on the
front gate, and that had dispersed the crowd. Only a
few fans hung around waiting for the reopening.

"I've decided I need to go in there alone," James told Kate.

She understood why without his having to explain it, as she understood so much about him. She gave him that soft crooked smile he'd come to love. "I'll wait here," she said.

"I won't be long."

He hesitated, fiddling with the keys in the ignition. Now that it was time to get out and walk inside, he wasn't sure he could. She didn't say anything. She offered no words of encouragement. He knew Kate believed that he'd somehow find the strength within himself, and no prompting was necessary.

With his insides in a jumble, he got out of the truck and slowly walked up the cement path to the white-marble mausoleum that stood like a light amid the graying stones and hand-carved statues of the older graves. Arrows and messages marred some of the gravestones. Fans had marked the path to the mausoleum, just as they'd marked the path to the grave before that.

Appeals from the family hadn't stopped the desecration. The media said it was a way for the hundreds of thousands who visited every year to express their feelings about his death.

The guard at one of the doors checked his identification. "Me and Eddie will be down near the drive so you can have some privacy, Mr. Hayes," he said. "You take as much time as you need."

"Thank you."

The rectangular building allowed visitors to enter one door, walk past the vaults in the wall and exit through a second door. Practicality had been a pri-

mary consideration in the design, yet his mother had insisted it also be beautiful. Somehow the architect had fulfilled both needs. The structure could handle crowds without problem, but was also a fitting tribute to the people James loved.

The cemetery sat at the base of the mountain, and he could see his mother's house above, an ugly thing, he realized suddenly. For the first time he also understood why his mother had selected this site. Every time she looked down from the window seat in the parlor where she liked to sit, she had to look at the tomb of a dead son she couldn't acknowledge.

Demons. Guilt. Self-punishment. This was what she was talking about last night.

He went inside the mausoleum and shut the door behind him. For a moment he stood there, letting the quiet surround him and his eyes adjust to the dim light. The place was peaceful, though dark. On sunny days the stained-glass windows at the roofline likely let in the light and chased away the gloom, but sunlight today had been nonexistent.

He walked down the corridor to the first of the vaults. Engraved on the stones were the names Margaret Taylor Bridges and Mason Bret Bridges— Granny Mag and Pop, his mother's parents. Next to them lay Eleanor Jefferson Hayes and Wilson James Hayes, his father's parents. Beyond them, he found his father, David James Hayes.

He remembered his father as a gentle man with a good sense of humor, who found fulfillment in having a family. His mother often told him that much of his father lived in him, and he supposed that was true, although he'd never thought so, growing up.

He glanced to the end of the corridor. He didn't have to read the name to know who rested there. Ropes kept fans from touching the stone in the wall, but they'd covered the floor in front of it with flowers, photographs and candles. Slowly he made his way to the vault.

"Hello, Bret."

Only his mind whispered a reply.

Seeing his own name etched in the stone gave him a strange feeling. One day he'd probably lie here like Bret, behind a stone with the wrong name on it.

"I've been meaning to come…" He swallowed the lump in his throat. "Finding the courage has been hard, considering the things we said to each other that night."

He unclipped the rope and moved the flowers aside so that he could stand at the stone and touch it. He ran his fingers over the letters.

"I thought for a long time that the reason I couldn't come here and face you was that I was afraid you wouldn't forgive me for what I did after the crash— pretending to be you. But that wasn't the problem. I don't think you care about that, do you? You're probably pretty happy to have all these girls come by every day to leave you gifts. You always did like to be the center of attention."

He smiled sadly.

"Guilt has kept me away, Bret, guilt over not being able to help you with your problems while you were alive. I've felt, too, that I somehow caused your death. I know you weren't happy in life, but I'm not sure why. I've agonized about it for years, what I could have done, what I *should* have done."

Tears formed. This was harder than he'd ever imagined, and yet he had an almost compulsive need to get it out, to rid himself of all the hurt inside him.

"I wish I could have fixed things for you. I'd have done anything, given you whatever you wanted, if it would have made a difference. But I don't know what I could have done to make you happy. That was something only you had the power to do. I love you. I'll always love you, and I'll always be proud you were my brother, despite the arguments we had. But it's time to go on with my life and forget about the past. I have to do this. I need a chance at happiness."

He could barely speak now. The pain was unbearable.

"I hope," he said in a whisper, "that you can hear me, and that you care enough to listen. Please...brother...you know what I'm asking, what I need."

He broke down. He put his face against the cool stone and sobbed. But for the first time since his brother died, these tears he shed in happiness. For in his heart, he knew that Bret had heard his plea.

And forgiven him.

EPILOGUE

JAMES AND KATE waited six months after the press conference, and when no one came forward to claim they'd seen him on television, they married. Alone one night with no one but a flop-eared ugly dog as a witness, they stood by a campfire in the middle of a horse pasture and pledged their hearts to one another for eternity.

Kate seemed content with that, but James wanted more. He married her a second time—as Bret—in a quiet ceremony in Chicago, attended by their families. Having made peace with his brother and no longer crippled by guilt, he found he couldn't deny himself what he wanted most in the world next to Kate. Children.

So Tom came to live with them.

Then Melissa.

Then the twins, Keith and Adam.

Then Kevin.

Then Shondra.

Then LaKeisha.

The following year Kate's publisher released her book, and it immediately shot to the top of the bestseller lists, introducing James to a new generation of fans. The first album of his songs, sung by ten different artists, coincided with the book's release. The

album debuted at the top of both the pop and country charts.

But number one in the Hayes household was the newest addition: James Bret Henry Hayes, age two months.

"We've got to have a bigger house," Kate said, rubbing her hand across the baby's dark head as he nursed, "or this family's got to stop growing. We have no place to put this child when he gets too big for the bassinet."

James, always fascinated by the intimate giving of life from mother to son, lay down on the bed in front of her and watched. He gave her a disarming grin, the one he knew she couldn't resist, the same grin he'd used to talk her into filing for the adoption of seven children.

"We'll build a bigger house," he said.

"I was afraid you'd choose that option."

"I've already been thinking about it." He reached over, took a piece of paper from the drawer in the bedside table and unfolded it. "A new house, but one that looks old and has a big front porch with room for rocking chairs. We can sit and rock and grow old together."

"I like that. How many bedrooms are you planning?"

"Twelve. Maybe thirteen."

Kate's eyes widened in horror. "Sweetheart, that's not a house, that's a hotel. Think of the cost, the electric bill, the cleaning, the—"

"I know it's big, but don't you hate it that Tom has to sleep on the couch when he comes home?"

"Yes, of course I do."

"And the kids will get married one day, and we'll have a house full of grandchildren."

"All right, Hayes, don't push your luck. I'm still getting used to the idea of being a mother. Don't turn me into somebody's grandmother."

"But you'll be such a cute little grandma. The kids can all call you Granny Kate, and you can teach them how to make peach cobbler."

She chuckled. "That might be kind of fun."

"Are we in agreement about the house?"

"I suppose so. Where are you planning to build this monstrosity?"

"I know an old homestead that smells of pine and rosemary."

"Your ancestors' land adjacent to Pine Acres?"

"Yes."

"I think that's a lovely idea."

"We should be able to get enough from the sale of this place to build the other house and expand my business. Maybe we could also build you a detached office. I know it must be hard writing and talking back and forth to Marcus when you've got screaming kids in the background."

"You don't have to convince me," Kate said. "Whatever you want to do is fine. I have one request, though."

"What's that?"

"No turrets."

His lips twitched. "No turrets. I promise. I still can't believe my mother lived in that house all those years and wouldn't tell me how much she hated it."

"Don't fret about it. Your mom and George love their new house, and the old one's perfect for the next

children's shelter. Those kids will love living in a castle.''

"I hope so."

"I know so. And Ellen is so excited about heading up this project. I think it's going to be what she needs to get her life back together."

He nodded in agreement. "I haven't seen her this happy since she kicked that jerk out."

Little Jamie's loud sucking sounds drew their attention, and James leaned closer to have a look.

"He's perfect, isn't he?" Kate asked.

"Like his mother." He kissed her and rolled off the bed to his feet. "I'm going to lock up and check the kids. Be right back."

Tom, home for the weekend from Auburn University, was in the kitchen studying for his final exams. James stuck his head around the door. "How's it coming?"

"Almost finished." Tom rubbed his hands across weary eyes. "I want to read this section one more time, make sure I know it."

"Okay, but don't stay up too late. You've got a long drive to school tomorrow. Night, son."

"Night, Dad."

Dad. The first time one of the children had called him that, he'd felt light-headed from the pleasure. Even now, though he heard himself called *Dad* a hundred times a day, it still moved him.

In the girls' room, he checked to make sure Melissa wasn't sleeping with her head under the pillow again. He rescued Shondra's bear from the floor and tucked it back under her arm. He covered LaKeisha against the chilly air.

Across the hall, where the boys shared a room, he found Adam already curled up in the bed with his twin, Keith. This child was having more trouble adjusting than the others, and only time and love would cure what ailed him.

In the bottom bunk on the other side of the room, Kevin also had a sleeping partner—Sallie—who had "adopted" him as her own the day he arrived. She slept at the foot of his bed every night.

James's thoughts drifted, as always during this ritual, to another child who should be sleeping in this room. Even though he'd been unable to provide a home for Henry, he would always carry him in his heart.

He scratched Sallie's head. "Night, old girl."

Kate was nearly asleep when he got back to their bedroom. He took the sleeping baby from her and put him in the bassinet by the bed, then made her get under the covers.

He turned out the light, stripped to his shorts and climbed into bed. She immediately moved over and wrapped her arms around him, resting her head on his shoulder. "Did you finish the book today?" she asked groggily.

He'd tried repeatedly to read the final manuscript before the book came out, but the letters about Bret had been too difficult for him. Only now, after months of healing, had he been able to manage it.

"I finished while you and the baby were taking your nap this afternoon."

"And?"

"It's wonderful, Kate. Reading the early letters, remembering the old days when Bret and I were close,

helped me feel better about things.'' He kissed the top of her head. ''Thank you.''

''I'm sorry there was no way to be truthful about the drugs, but I think the rest of it helped a great deal to repair your reputation, don't you?''

He knew how important it was for her to feel she'd redeemed him in the eyes of the world. ''Yes, Katie. The book is everything you promised—and much more.''

She sighed with contentment and nuzzled closer to him. ''I'm glad, Jamie,'' she mumbled. ''I love you so much.'' Within moments she drifted back to sleep.

For a long time he lay quietly and held her. He wondered if any man had ever felt this loved or been this lucky. Thanks to Kate and her determination to write this book, James Hayes would be remembered for his music and his talent. A wonderful legacy for a man to have.

Then he thought about the children sleeping down the hall, and the little one in the bassinet nearby. All of them would soon carry the Hayes name. Through them, and the children they produced, Bret Hayes would be remembered, too, as a good father and grandfather.

He smiled in the darkness, realizing he had two legacies—the book for the man he used to be; the children for the man he'd become.

CELEBRATE VALENTINE'S DAY WITH HARLEQUIN®'S LATEST TITLE— *Stolen Memories*

Available in trade-size format, this collector's edition contains three full-length novels by *New York Times* bestselling authors Jayne Ann Krentz and Tess Gerritsen, along with national bestselling author Stella Cameron.

TEST OF TIME by **Jayne Ann Krentz**—
He married for the best reason.... She married for the only reason.... Did they stand a chance at making the only reason the real reason to share a lifetime?

THIEF OF HEARTS by **Tess Gerritsen**—
Their distrust of each other was only as strong as their desire. And Jordan began to fear that Diana was more than just a thief of hearts.

MOONTIDE by **Stella Cameron**—
For Andrew, Greer's return is a miracle. It had broken his heart to let her go. Now fate has brought them back together. And he won't lose her again...

Make this Valentine's Day one to remember!

Look for this exciting collector's edition
on sale January 2001 at your favorite retail outlet.

HARLEQUIN®
Makes any time special ™

Visit us at www.eHarlequin.com

PHSM

#1 *New York Times* bestselling author

NORA ROBERTS

brings you more of the loyal and loving,
tempestuous and tantalizing Stanislaski family.

Coming in February 2001

The Stanislaski Sisters

Natasha and Rachel

Though raised in the Old World traditions of their
family, fiery Natasha Stanislaski and cool, classy
Rachel Stanislaski are ready for a *new* world of love....

*And also available in February 2001 from
Silhouette Special Edition, the newest book in the
heartwarming Stanislaski saga*

CONSIDERING KATE

Natasha and Spencer Kimball's daughter Kate turns her
back on old dreams and returns to her hometown, where
she finds the *man* of her dreams.

Available at your favorite retail outlet.

Where love comes alive™

Harlequin proudly brings you

STELLA CAMERON
Bobby Hutchinson
Sandra Marton

in

MARRIED
IN SPRING

*a brand-new anthology in which three couples
find that when spring arrives, romance soon
follows…along with an unexpected
walk down the aisle!*

February 2001

Available wherever Harlequin books are sold.

HARLEQUIN®
Makes any time special ™

Visit us at www.eHarlequin.com   PHMARRIED

If you enjoyed what you just read,
then we've got an offer you can't resist!

Take 2 bestselling love stories FREE!

Plus get a FREE surprise gift!